The Long Dead

The Long Dead

A DCI JOHN BLIZZARD MYSTERY

John Dean

ROBERT HALE · LONDON

© John Dean 2006
First published in Great Britain 2006

ISBN-10: 0-7090-8183-9
ISBN-13: 978-0-7090-8183-8

Robert Hale Limited
Clerkenwell House
Clerkenwell Green
London EC1R 0HT

2 4 6 8 10 9 7 5 3 1

Typeset in 10/13pt New Century Schoolbook
Printed in Great Britain by St Edmundsbury Press
Bury St Edmunds, Suffolk
Bound by Woolnough Bookbinding Limited

For Alf

·· CHAPTER one ····

'THERE'S SOMETHING VERY badly wrong here,' said John Blizzard.

Brow furrowed, he looked up from his intense study of the ground and stared through the murk of the late afternoon mist at the bare winter fields stretching away into the distance. The grey shroud that had enveloped the countryside around the city of Hafton for days was thickening rapidly once more as dusk approached and the fog was rolling noiselessly in over copse and hedgerow. As he watched the fields disappear, the detective chief inspector was suddenly struck by how alone he and Detective Sergeant David Colley were as they stood on the edge of the makeshift grave.

Then something strange happened, something that caught him off guard. As Blizzard stared into the swirling fog, he felt for a moment, just a fleeting moment, an overwhelming sense of a past long gone. He could feel, almost as if it were physical, the acute pain of loss, the pain of those left to grieve for loved ones long departed. And he saw through the mist the indistinct image of a man's face; the dark hair cropped short, the smile crooked and knowing, the expression open and carefree, the eyes glinting with the merest hint of mischief, an image locked in memory and frozen in time on a tattered black-and-white photograph.

For a moment, the man's expression changed and Blizzard was transported to a wild place, the man's place, and heard the roar and the clatter, felt the panic as the man fought for his life, heard the death rattle of his final breath; saw in his face the pain, a different pain, the pain that comes with fear and defeat. The defeat of a man who knew he could never go home, would never see his loved ones again, would never feel the warmth of the evening summer sun on his back or the trusting embrace of a child. A man alone and unheard yet not unmourned. No, not unmourned. And not forgotten. At the going down of the sun, we will remember them. Remember them all. And in that moment, John Blizzard remembered the man. And mourned him.

Then the face was gone, receding into the mist, and with a start, John Blizzard was back in the icy chill of a November afternoon, standing on the fringes of a bare earth field and staring into a grave. Startled at what he had seen, or thought he had seen, the chief inspector shook his head to banish the images from whence they came, and noticed Colley looking at him oddly.

'This damned fog,' said Blizzard gruffly, his voice seeming, at least to him, strangely loud and echoing as he broke the oppressive silence.

A questioning look from the sergeant.

'Plays tricks,' said the chief inspector, embarrassed at having let his guard down.

'Tricks?'

'Nothing. It's just,' and Blizzard shrugged. 'I don't know, it's difficult to put into words....'

'Try,' said Colley.

'Like I said, it's just something's wrong. Something here. I feel it so strongly, David,' said Blizzard, surprising himself with the vehemence of his words.

'Not sure I understand, guv.'

'Neither do I but this place is speaking to me.'

Colley nodded; the chief inspector's instincts were famed throughout the force. For all his adherence to the hard rules of criminal detection, John Blizzard also greatly prized intuition and it was not the first time Colley had witnessed the chief inspector's instincts at work. That Blizzard should come out with these words now did not surprise the sergeant; what he said next sure as hell did.

'It's quite, I don't know,' and Blizzard shrugged unhappily. 'Unnerving.'

'Unnerved? You?' said Colley, looking at his colleague in amazement.

Over the years, he and Blizzard had stood and stared down at many a body – too many for their liking – and the sergeant had never heard the chief inspector talk like this, never seen such a strange expression on his face, never. As Blizzard had said many times, with a wry smile, the living might sometimes scare him but the dead sure as hell did not. They could not harm anyone now so why worry about them? It was one of his favourite sayings and Colley had lost count of the number of times he had heard it. But that was then and this was now – and now the dead had affected Blizzard and made him uneasy. And if John Blizzard was uneasy, that meant David Colley was uneasy as well.

What was more confusing for the sergeant was that when, shortly after three that afternoon, they had arrived at Green Meadow Farm, deep into the rural flatlands five miles to the west of the city, he had not felt that way at all. There had been no bunching in the gut, no unpleasant taste at the back of the throat as he had experienced so many times on the way to a death. No, this one was as straightforward as they come. All those bodies and none of them his problem, the sergeant had thought cheerfully as he struggled out of the car and into his blue windcheater before following Blizzard, who was already striding up the farm track. No arduous paperwork, no grieving relatives, no agitated top brass demanding updates on the inquiry; nothing to worry about, the sergeant had told himself as he fell into step with the chief inspector, their feet crunching on the frozen ruts.

Indeed, thought the sergeant as they turned through a gate and walked without speaking across the meadow, it was looking good for an early Friday night finish and a pleasant night out with his girlfriend, Jay. Maybe a curry, something hot, a vindaloo he had mused, something to warm his frozen ears on a day in which temperatures had barely struggled above zero. As they went through another gate into the next field and walked in easy silence through the wet grass, the sergeant chuckled out loud at the ludicrous thought that had just popped into his mind, an image of his ears turning bright red and emitting smoke as he sat in the restaurant. His laughter had caused the chief inspector to slacken his pace and glance at his sergeant, survey him for a moment, give a shake of the head in mock exasperation then quicken his step again, followed by the grinning Colley.

Now, fifteen minutes later, the sergeant was wondering if he had somehow missed something. He looked down again and pondered upon the skeletons laid out before them. They were in a long line, placed neatly side by side in a large hole in the ground; to call it a grave would be granting it too much dignity, thought the sergeant. Running parallel with the raggedy hedge and without a headstone to identify the location halfway along the field, the hole had been discovered by a workman doing drainage excavation. The bodies, which had been placed on their backs, looked as if they were many years old, the flesh long since rotted off bones to which clung obstinate tatters of grubby material. Around their necks were metal tags bearing their names. German names.

Colley looked thoughtfully at the laughing skulls staring up into the gloom of a fading winter's day. There were sixteen bodies in all. Colley knew that, he had counted them three times. Didn't normally need to do that with deaths but this case was different. He had not examined them particularly closely. They were long dead, he thought, and no concern of the police. Part of history. Part of military history, indeed. The name tags had confirmed their identities; these were men who rested in cold silence a long way from home, having given their lives for their country. Proud men who, more than fifty years before, had left wives and children, mothers and fathers, and headed to war with such optimism, only to perish on the edge of a bleak northern English city, the rousing patriotic songs of their departures long since choked in throats clogged by soil.

Sad, sure, but for Colley, who had never been fascinated by war, it meant little in the mid-1990s. To him, it was history and nothing more. Maybe, he mused, reflecting on the chief inspector's reaction a few seconds before, it was Blizzard's keen interest in history that imbued the scene with extra significance for him. Thought of Blizzard brought forth a little involuntary shake of the head from the sergeant. No, he could not see it. This was not evil; this was a routine job and the detectives were simply there to make sure all the rules were followed and that the paperwork could be filled in. A quirky case for the N.F.A file. Something to tell the lads over a pint then move on. Nothing more. No, definitely nothing more.

Musing completed to his satisfaction, brief uneasiness of a few moments before banished, the sergeant looked up and morosely surveyed the skeletal hedgerow, the damp and wispy grassy field margins, the black claw-fingered trees and the bare earth with its barren ridges and furrows stretching away into the mist. He shivered, suddenly acutely conscious of how cold he had become in the damp late afternoon chill. Oh, what he would give for a warming cuppa, and he glanced enviously across the fields to the distant farmhouse with its welcoming lights glowing ever brighter in the deepening gloom.

'Are we done?' asked the sergeant hopefully, looking at the chief inspector, who was still staring into the grave.

'No.' The reply was curt, then, as the chief inspector remembered himself, repeated in softer tones. 'No, David, I do not think we are.'

'But it's straightforward, guv,' protested Colley.

'Don't think so.'

'Yeah, but....'

'I mean it, David,' said Blizzard, wrenching his gaze away from the bodies, that intensity in his voice again as he stared hard at the sergeant. 'Something wicked happened here.'

'Not according to the archaeologists, guv.'

Colley knew the archaeologists were sitting in the farmer's kitchen and he could almost feel, behind the steamed-up windows, the heat rising from their mugs of tea and hear their laughter and chatter. He glanced at the distant farmhouse wistfully while Blizzard pondered the comment. It was the archaeologists who had called the police in, the moment the bodies had been unearthed by a workman's digger two days previously. The team, seconded from a Midlands university by English Heritage, had been working several hundred yards away from the graves for almost four months, painstakingly exploring the faded green wooden huts arranged in three neat rows that were once Hafton Prisoner-of-War Camp.

Home at any one time during the 1940s to as many as 600 captured German soldiers, the twenty-four huts had fallen into disrepair following the camp's closure when peace returned to Europe. They had stood largely unnoticed for the following fifty years, used by successive farmers to house tractors and store animal feed, and increasingly obscured from sight by the alder trees and scrubby bushes that had grown up around them. Their existence was brought to public attention again when it was revealed four years previously that the landowner, a farmer called Henderson Ramage, was seeking to sell part of his land for a housing development, fifty-five plush mock-Georgian detached houses biting deep into the green belt around the nearby village of Hawkwith.

The revelation provoked fury among local people and a protest committee was quickly assembled, villagers voicing their anger at noisy public meetings in Hawkwith and outside city hall whenever planning councillors debated the issue, as they did many times because it became a long drawn-out saga. Within a month of Ramage's plans becoming public, a housebuilder expressed an interest in the site, planning applications were submitted, rejected and re-submitted and in the end, after a final refusal by the council and the breakdown of protracted negotiations, the decision was referred by the city council to a planning inquiry. That took time to organize and after a two-week hearing and six months to write his final report, the government inspector finally recommended approval. By then, the dispute had rumbled on for four years.

It was during this process that a young council officer on a routine visit to the site stumbled across the huts. A keen amateur historian, he stood and gazed at them for a moment or two, not quite able to believe what he was seeing. Most people, apart from older locals, had forgotten the camp was there and it certainly did not feature on any of the council's more recent maps. Checking back through the records and realizing the importance of the eight-acre site, the officer informed English Heritage, whose experts announced they were keen to see the camp preserved and were alarmed that the edge of the proposed housing development came perilously close to the huts. Loath to submit themselves to further delays, Henderson Ramage and the housebuilder initially refused to co-operate with the historians but eventually, faced with a mixture of cajoling and legal threats, they reluctantly relented, permitting the university team six months to examine the site while everyone waited for the decision of the planning inspector. What would happen when permission was granted was unclear but the historical experts were confident that they could come to some kind of deal to preserve at least some of the huts. It was not a view with which Henderson Ramage concurred.

The six-strong university team, including four students, restricted themselves to the camp itself so it was one of the digger drivers excavating a drainage ditch for the new houses who stumbled across its secret. To his horror, he unearthed the bodies when he plunged his scoop into the crusty soil to reveal a bony hand clawing the air for the first time in half a century. With a cry of alarm, he abandoned his machine and ran to raise the alarm. Suspecting a POW grave, the archaeologists informed the coroner and, with his blessing, spent the following two days scraping and digging under the bored eyes of a succession of uniform constables from Western Division, sent to ensure that all went smoothly. Now that the bodies were fully revealed, the coroner had called in Blizzard to survey the scene before darkness fell and had sent the last relieved constable scuttling off to the farmhouse for a warming cuppa. How Colley envied him.

'So what do we do now?' asked the sergeant, rubbing his hands briskly in a way which he hoped would persuade the chief inspector to lead them to the farmhouse.

'I think....' began Blizzard but stopped on hearing a footfall.

They turned to see a figure walking across the field, identity obscured by his anorak hood. As he approached, they could see he was the lead archaeologist, Dr Richard Hamer, a tall, thin and sallow man with a nose that was long and hooked, sunken cheeks, eyes which were dark and strangely lifeless and teeth that were prominent and jutting out.

'Marvellous,' sighed Colley, 'here comes Dracula.'

'Respect,' said Blizzard. 'That's Mr Dracula to the likes of you.'

'Probably only comes out at night,' chuckled Colley, glancing up at the darkening sky as the archaeologist neared.

'So, can we have them back?' asked Hamer, nodding at the grave and wearing an expression that suggested he assumed it was a formality.

'I am afraid not,' said Blizzard.

'Why?' The friendly tone had been replaced by an edge to the archaeologist's voice.

'I want our forensic team to have a look.'

'Why on earth would you want to do that?'

This time the voice was more uncertain than confrontational, Hamer having been thrown off-guard by the unexpected direction in which the conversation was going.

'I'm not satisfied,' said Blizzard.

'Oh, come on,' protested Hamer, 'this is routine, we all know that.'

'You may jump to conclusions in your profession but we do not,' said Blizzard sharply.

'Uncalled for,' replied Hamer, wounded by the comment. 'We pride ourselves on our thoroughness but let us be sensible about this, Chief Inspector. This is a 50-year-old burial site. There can be no doubt about it. Our research has confirmed that in the winter of 1944/45, there was an influenza epidemic that killed a number of the POWs.'

'Then why were they buried here?' asked Blizzard, nodding to the grave, 'and not in a local churchyard?'

'Maybe the churches did not want to take them for fear of spreading the virus.'

'And why well outside the camp?' said Blizzard, flapping a

hand to the huts looming out of the mist a couple of hundred metres away.

'Probably the same reason,' shrugged Hamer. 'Anyway, it is not really important.'

'I think it is,' said Blizzard calmly.

'Surely,' said Hamer slyly, desperate to regain some sense of dignity, 'the local constabulary has got better things to do than investigate 50-year-old deaths from natural causes. I mean, isn't there some poor motorist you should be out hassling?'

Colley watched the chief inspector with anticipation; Blizzard had reduced men to tears for less. This time, however, the reaction was not explosive. The chief inspector considered the comment for a moment then smiled at the archaeologist; behind his smile was iciness. Colley knew the smile well. For some reason, it always reminded him of a lion just before it ate its prey.

'You know, Mr Hamer—' began Blizzard.

'Doctor Hamer,' corrected the archaeologist. 'It's *Doctor* Hamer.'

'Well whatever you call yourself,' said Blizzard abruptly, starting to walk away across the field, the conversation clearly at an end. 'Until I am happy about this, these bodies are mine, and I'll thank you to remember that.'

Hamer looked as if he was about to say something but before he could utter the words, Blizzard stopped and turned back to look at him with an expression that dared the archaeologist to disagree.

'And I am sure as hell not happy at the moment,' he said, then headed off through the gate and into the next field.

Gloomily, Hamer watched him go then glanced at the sergeant with a questioning look on his face.

'When the man ain't happy,' said Colley with a shrug of the shoulders, 'the man ain't happy.'

'Is he ever?'

'Oh, yes, back in 1986 I think it was. Christmas-time,' nodded the sergeant, then his face clouded over. 'Oh, no, hang on, that can't be right, the guvn'r hates Christmas.'

And Colley walked off to organize an all-night guard for the grave, leaving the bemused Doctor Hamer standing alone in the field with only his thoughts and the ghosts of sixteen dead men for company.

·· CHAPTER two ····

'OK,' SAID JOHN Blizzard, leaning forward and resting his elbows on the desk. 'Tell me there is nothing wrong with that burial site; tell me I have lost control of my senses.'

It was the following Monday morning and none of the five people in his office at Abbey Road Police Station was about to start the week by doing something that ill-advised. Even the archaeologists, annoyed that their excavations had been disturbed for what they saw as no good reason, kept their doubts to themselves. It had not taken them long to glean that John Blizzard's fearsome reputation was well earned.

Dr Hamer, perhaps sensing safety in numbers, had brought his colleague, 28-year-old military archaeologist and historian Elspeth Roberts, to the meeting. A mousy woman, with long, lank brown hair, neat, slightly nervous features, and dressed in brown cord trousers and a chunky green pullover, she sat with her hands on her lap, constantly removing and replacing her wedding ring as she uneasily surveyed the chief inspector. Leaning against the wall by the office door, Colley had tried desperately to stifle a low chuckle when she entered the room, recalling Blizzard's earlier words. Glancing out of his window, the chief inspector had given a snort when he saw her walking across the misty car park with Hamer, informing the grinning sergeant, 'Lock up your lentils, the chunky sweater brigade has arrived.'

For their part, unused to the ways of the police as they were, the archaeologists had no idea what to make of the chief inspector, who had summoned them to the meeting in an early-morning phone call. Hamer's suggestion that they could make some time late on the Thursday afternoon was greeted with a sharp riposte to be there at 10am that day, the doctor's protestations cut short when the line went dead as the receiver was replaced at the other end. Now Hamer and Elspeth Roberts sat eyeing Blizzard uncertainly; this was not the way people acted in the academic circles in which they usually moved. They were used to a slower pace of life with more niceties. Blizzard, who did not do niceties, surveyed them with devilment in his expression, thoroughly enjoying the confusion his demeanor had caused.

Broad-chested and slightly heavier than a man of five foot ten inches should be, the chief inspector was in his mid-forties with brown tousled hair and clear blue eyes. He was dressed in his customary dark suit and red tie dangling loosely at half-mast. The chief inspector had taken his jacket off a few minutes before the meeting, the police station's unpredictable central heating having produced a dry and airless atmosphere in his office, and now sat with shirt-sleeves rolled up. Uncomfortable under his steady gaze, and not sure whether or not he was putting on an act, the archaeologists' uncertainty about John Blizzard was entirely understandable; not many people could work him out.

Having gone into the police straight from college, Blizzard's quick mind had rapidly gained him a reputation for intuitive policing that earmarked him for a career as a detective. But with the intuition came an attitude that had made him plenty of enemies, not, it had to be said, among officers in the rank-and-file, rather among officialdom. Described by some as 'old school', Blizzard was known for blunt speaking and straightforward views and the officers on the ground liked that, liked knowing where they stood. John Blizzard believed that fighting crime was a war and that the police had to treat it as such and win it, whatever the cost to bruised egos. His language often, and deliberately, evoked the imagery of conflict and if that view rubbed a few politically-correct senior officers up the wrong way then John Blizzard was prepared to live with the consequences.

Besides, if his reputation caused him problems in the corridors of power, it was a potent weapon outside them, where in the chief inspector's mind it really mattered: on the street. Apart from the odd secondment elsewhere, Blizzard had always worked in Hafton, mostly in the Western Division, and that meant he was known by every villain in his area and respected among colleagues for his ability to strike fear into even the worst wrongdoer with a few well-chosen words or a stern look. A couple of well-intentioned, but naïve, university archaeologists stood no chance.

David Colley was one of the few officers who could truly call himself a friend of the chief inspector and one of the even smaller number who knew how to handle him. A decade younger than Blizzard, tall and lean, the sergeant was, as always, smartly turned out. His black hair was neatly combed, his round, almost boyish, face clean-shaven and his black trousers and dark blue shirt perfectly ironed by Jay. His black shoes shone as usual. The sergeant leaned against a wall now and, as the chief inspector prepared to speak, took a couple of moments to peruse the two other men completing the gathering crammed into the small office.

Both men were, in their own ways, enjoying the impact Blizzard's brusque style had on the archaeologists, and the fact that, this time, it was not directed at them. As Colley looked first at Peter Reynolds, the ghost of a smile played on the sergeant's lips, one of anticipation; the presence of the Home Office pathologist always guaranteed good sport. Reynolds, a balding middle-aged little man with piggy eyes gleaming out of a chubby face, and dressed in a shabby, ill-fitting black suit, had more reason than most to be resentful of the chief inspector. He knew that Blizzard had never liked him, which meant their meetings were usually more akin to jousts, Reynolds' sardonic wit pitted against Blizzard's short temper. This morning, Reynolds, annoyed at being summoned to the police station when they normally met at the hospital, was sorely tempted to take up the chief inspector's challenge to question his senses, but declined the offer. No, this morning, the pathologist had a bombshell to deliver and, eyes gleaming, he wanted to savour the moment without any distractions.

Sitting next to him, his excitement also hardly suppressed, was Detective Inspector Graham Ross, divisional head of forensics at Abbey Road Police Station, dressed as immaculately as ever in a pressed grey suit with red silk tie, black shoes shining and with his brown wavy hair beautifully groomed as usual. His eyes shone: over the weekend, Ross and his team had carried out an examination of the graves as Reynolds worked on the skeletons back at the hospital mortuary. Initial scepticism at the chief inspector's instincts had gradually turned to amazement and Ross and Reynolds had spent several hours running over their findings. Indeed, it was only that morning that they felt confident enough to reveal what they knew to the unsuspecting detective.

'Well?' asked Blizzard, irritated by the smug expressions on the faces of Reynolds and Ross. 'Have I taken leave of my senses?'

'I hate to say it,' said Peter Reynolds in his strangely nasal voice, 'but you have not, and I speak as someone who would happily have signed the papers to have you sectioned many years ago.'

Colley smiled slightly. Game on, he thought.

'Thank you for the sentiment,' murmured Blizzard, letting the comment go. 'So what have you found?'

'There is indeed something very wrong with the grave,' said Reynolds.

'He's right, guv,' said Graham Ross, unable to contain himself any longer. 'We're looking at a murder!'

'That is a preposterous statement!' exclaimed Hamer. 'And even if—'

'There will be plenty of time for your comments later,' said the chief inspector sharply. 'Perhaps. But for the moment, Reynolds here has something of import to tell us. So, who's murder are we looking at?'

'I am coming to that,' said the pathologist, bridling at the use of his surname, as he always did with Blizzard. 'Having spent my weekend examining the skeletons – missing out on a good game of golf, might I say....'

'No you may not,' grunted Blizzard, whose own weekend

had been frustrated by the slow pace of the pathologist's examinations.

'You are such a delightful man,' scowled Reynolds. 'Anyway, Mr Hamer here—'

'Actually, it's *Doctor* Hamer,' said the archaeologist.

'Yes, well whatever he is,' said Reynolds dismissively, fishing out some papers from his battered briefcase, 'he gave me names of the POWs from the camp.'

'And?' asked the chief inspector impatiently.

'I have to say first that proving the identity beyond all doubt will be extremely difficult after all these years,' said the pathologist, 'but the name tags on the skeletons do match the recorded names of POWs who died of influenza in the winter of 1944/45. Examination of the skeletons confirms that they date from around that time. It's the same with all fifteen of them.'

'Fifteen?' queried Blizzard. 'I thought there were sixteen?'

'Indeed there are,' said Reynolds. 'Although it is difficult to be absolutely precise, I would say number sixteen died about four years ago.'

Reynolds sat back in his chair and, with a smug look on his face, waited for the reaction. It came within the blink of an eye.

'Bloody hell's bells!' exclaimed Blizzard.

'Indeed,' said Reynolds.

'So are you saying he was never a POW at the camp?' asked Colley, equally taken aback.

'That's the weird thing,' said Reynolds, holding up a brown file. 'According to the camp records, Horst Knoefler *was* an inmate and was released sometime in early 1946, not long before the camp closed. And he seems to have been alive and well when he walked out of the front gate.'

'And he was the murdered one, was he?' asked Blizzard.

'Indeed he was,' said Reynolds. 'And there can be no doubt that not only did our Herr Knoefler somehow clamber into that grave fifty years after his comrades-at-arms, but it seems that someone gave him a helping hand.'

The atmosphere in the office was electric and Reynolds and

Ross revelled in the astonished look on Blizzard's face as he tried to digest their revelations. It took a lot to surprise the chief inspector so such moments were to be enjoyed with relish; it might be a long time before one came again. Blizzard glanced at his sergeant.

'So I was right, David,' he said. 'Something was wrong.'

'So it would seem, guv,' nodded Colley, turning to Hamer. 'Can I ask where the records of the POWs came from, Doctor? I mean, are we sure they are genuine?'

'We believe so,' said Hamer, trying to recover his own composure. 'Two of our researchers found them among papers in the local history section of the city library. They had been there for many years, gathering dust without anyone taking much notice of them.'

'That's archaeologists for you,' said Blizzard.

'I meant the papers had been there for years,' replied Hamer tartly.

'Of course you did,' said Blizzard, whose distaste for anyone with an 'ist' in their job title was legendary.

'So, how was he murdered, Mr Reynolds?' asked Colley.

'See that?' said Reynolds, shooting a sly look at Blizzard. 'He called me Mister then. Such politeness. Most refreshing in the young. Maybe it's a generation thing, Chief Inspector.'

'Just tell us the sodding cause of death,' grunted Blizzard.

'A blow to the back of the head. The skull shows signs of significant trauma and there is an unmistakeable sign of a fracture.'

'Can you tell us anything else about the blow?' asked Blizzard.

'It must have smarted,' said Reynolds, deadpan.

'Any idea what he was struck with?' sighed Blizzard.

'Like I always say,' shrugged Reynolds, 'that's your department.'

'Care to hazard a guess?'

'Could be anything, a block of wood, a shovel, a sledgehammer, a piece of rock. Whatever it was, it was wielded with enough force to kill him pretty much instantly, I would say.'

'Graham,' said Blizzard, glancing at the forensics chief, 'I take it our Mr Reynolds has not embarked on a flight of fancy?'

'Not sure he does flights of fancy,' said Ross. 'But, yeah, there's not much doubt about it.'

'But how do we know?' insisted Colley. 'I mean, couldn't this Knoefler fellow have been murdered in 1945 and dumped in there with the others? It could be a 50-year-old murder for all we know.'

'Exactly,' said Hamer fervently, recognizing a way of getting his people back on to the site.

'We thought of that,' nodded Ross. 'We examined the rotted material on the bones. It took a while as it was in a real mess but we are sure the fifteen were wearing camp uniforms whereas Knoefler was wearing modern clothes, possibly a dark pullover of some kind and slacks. And his shoes were modern. Very nice actually, very stylish. Wouldn't have minded wearing them myself.'

'Thank you, Captain Gucci,' grunted Blizzard, who always found himself intimidated by the smart appearance of younger officers. 'But how do we know who he is? Surely he was not still wearing his name tag after all these years?'

'No, he wasn't,' said Ross, 'but he was wearing a watch that had his name engraved on the back.'

'A name, yes,' observed Blizzard, 'but that does not necessarily mean that it is *his* name.'

'Good point,' said Colley, grinning at Ross. 'I thought he was called Herr Swatch.'

'You and Reynolds should be on the bloody stage,' grunted Blizzard. 'But the watch proves nothing. Is it possible that he is not Horst Knoefler?'

'Yes, of course it is,' nodded Ross, 'but for the moment it's all we have go on so I, for one, am going to call him Horst Knoefler.'

There were a few moments of silence as everyone digested what they had heard.

'So what do you reckon?' asked Colley at length, looking at the thoughtful chief inspector.

'It is certainly intriguing,' mused Blizzard, leaning back in his chair with a look of satisfaction on his face and a gleam in his eye, delighted that his instincts had once again been vindicated.

'Sure is,' nodded Colley.

'And,' said the chief inspector, glancing at the large pile of documents on his desk, 'it beats all the paperwork I'm supposed to be doing.'

'I assume that means we cannot examine the graves any further?' asked Hamer gloomily.

'Or the camp. It is now all a potential murder scene,' said Blizzard cheerfully. 'And it's all mine until I tell you different. DI Ross here will want to spend more time out there, I suspect, and the last thing he wants is you flobbing about with your clipboards.'

'I must protest,' exclaimed Hamer, half standing up. 'There is important historical research that we need to do there before the—'

'Protest all you like,' snapped Blizzard. 'But when it comes to murder, my needs take precedence over a bunch of archae-ologists.'

And he suddenly looked at Elspeth Roberts, who had sat through the meeting with an expression resembling a star-tled rabbit captured in car headlights as she listened to the encounter with ever-widening eyes.

'You have been very quiet, Mrs Roberts,' said the chief inspector, and nodded at Hamer. 'Your colleague here insisted you be present at this meeting because of your expert know-ledge. Do you have anything to say which might throw some light on to this somewhat strange occurrence?'

She looked at him, an anxious expression on her face. For a moment, it seemed that the words had choked in her throat but somehow she managed to regain what little composure remained and opened her mouth.

'Well,' she said, voice tremulous with nerves, hand anxiously twisting and untwisting her wedding ring. 'It does rather make you wonder.'

'Wonder what?' asked Blizzard, fixing her with one of his stern looks but giving Colley the merest of winks.

'Well,' and she was now well and truly flustered, 'wonder what happened, I suppose.'

She looked around the room unhappily.

'I mean,' she said. 'Doesn't it?'

Her voice tailed off and she flushed red as she noticed everyone in the room staring at her, apart from an embarrassed Hamer, who looked downwards, seemingly suddenly fascinated with his shoes. Colley glanced at the chief inspector, whose mischievous expression suggested he was enjoying her discomfort.

'Such wise words in one so young,' said Blizzard, with a faint twitch of the lips as he stood up and walked over to the window.

'Still,' he said brightly, turning back into the room, 'it's always good to have an expert in on these little shindigs, isn't it, boys?'

And he beamed. Colley tried to stifle his laugh. But failed.

·· CHAPTER three ····

'THIS GETS STRANGER and stranger,' said Colley, walking into Detective Chief Superintendent Arthur Ronald's office without knocking, and tossing a brown file on to the desk.

'You sound like something out of Alice in Wonderland,' grunted Blizzard, his mood not improved by lack of progress on the inquiry. 'I expect the sodding white rabbit to come running past any minute.'

'You'd only arrest him,' said Colley.

It was 3.30 that afternoon and the chief inspector and Ronald, his direct superior at Abbey Road, had been taking a break from the intense pressures brought about by the establishment of a murder inquiry. Sitting at Ronald's desk, cradling mugs of tea, they were reflecting on the press conference they had staged at the station a few minutes earlier. Normally, they would have not taken such an action when so few of the facts were known, but a freelance photographer had stumbled across the police vehicles at the farm on the way back from a job and the local evening newspaper was going to run the story that night.

Their hands forced, the officers staged the hurriedly organized event in the police station canteen. Although the detectives declined to name the victim until his relatives had been informed, the reporters had lapped up every word; the story had everything they could have wanted: mystery, crime and the chance to use some atmospheric black-and-white wartime pictures. Blizzard, who disliked reporters intensely, realized that they could sometimes be useful and, with very little information about Horst Knoefler having emerged, he readily acknowledged that the wider circulation the story obtained the better.

'How could it possibly get stranger?' asked Ronald, looking up at the sergeant as he slumped in a chair in the corner of the room.

'It's all down to man's best friend,' said Colley, as if that explained everything.

Noticing their bemused expressions he grinned.

'Wuff-wuff,' he said enigmatically, putting his hands together in front of his face and making panting sounds.

'Have you the faintest idea what he is talking about?' asked Ronald, glancing at Blizzard.

'Not usually,' said the chief inspector, and his face broke into a rare smile as he saw the superintendent's bemused expression.

Ronald had always struggled with Colley's sense of humour whereas the chief inspector appreciated its importance in lightening the mood in difficult moments. And being confronted by a murder with absolutely no clues at all was as difficult as it could get. Besides, Blizzard knew, as did Ronald, that behind the sergeant's cheery façade was a detective as sharp as they came and that made it worth putting up with his little games from time to time. It was also why Blizzard always asked for Colley when something big broke. He knew that the closeness of their relationship irritated some other equally ambitious officers but the chief inspector did not worry about their opinions. When it came to solving crimes, David Colley was the man to have.

For their part, Blizzard and Ronald went back more than twenty years, having first worked together as rookie uniform officers, then in CID, before their careers took different paths. Blizzard remained a detective but Ronald went back into uniform, his diplomatic abilities, competence and consummate people skills ensuring that he rose rapidly through the ranks, including a spell as divisional commander at Burniston, one of the constabulary's northern towns. The men had been reunited at Abbey Road when Ronald returned to his roots to assume command of CID in the constabulary's southern half four years previously, and immediately demanded Blizzard be moved from the drugs squad and promoted as his new detective chief inspector in charge of Western CID.

Not everyone in the corridors of power welcomed the idea. Indeed, some resisted it fiercely because Blizzard's brusque style had never endeared him to many of the top brass at headquarters. Ronald, however, viewed it as one of those things which had to be borne if you wanted the best. It was a simple deal, he had told the gloomy chief constable at a prickly meeting shortly after his appointment to CID chief; if they wanted Arthur Ronald, they had to take John Blizzard. Although Ronald looked calm on the outside, his heart was pounding when he said it because he realized he was putting himself on the line, that his coveted new posting could so easily be lost even before it had started. But the gamble paid off and the chief constable relented, albeit extremely reluctantly, because he knew the chief inspector's low opinion of him. Because Blizzard once told him.

Ronald was relieved. With crime spiralling in Western Division, Blizzard was just the man to start bringing it down. Ronald had an ulterior motive, though, because John Blizzard could be extremely useful in other ways. Sometimes, the chief inspector made the kind of outspoken comments that the diplomatic Ronald himself would rather not be associated with directly, but that he wished to be aired nevertheless. Secretly, Ronald quite enjoyed the expressions on his colleagues' faces when they angrily recounted conversations with the chief inspector. Ronald's mouth might have said the right things in response to their complaints but his eyes never did. The complainants knew that and Ronald knew they knew. More importantly, Blizzard did not mind how his friend played the game because he had the superintendent's support; there was no going out on a limb where Arthur Ronald was concerned. It was CID against the world. And in four years, Western CID had increased detection rates by nineteen per cent and played a key role in helping cut crime by more than a fifth. And where the number-crunchers at headquarters were concerned, that was the factor that really counted. It was also the factor that kept John Blizzard in a job.

The men were very different personalities. University-educated Ronald, married with two teenaged children, was a slightly pudgy, balding man with ruddy cheeks and eyes with bags which sagged darkly. Given to constant worrying about mortgages and university fees, and a little prone, in Blizzard's view, to taking too much notice about what other people thought about him, he was not yet fifty but looked older. A smart dresser with shoes that always shined, a sharply pressed suit and a tie constantly done up, he was a charming man with an easy manner. But behind the avuncular appearance lurked a hard-headed detective who, like Blizzard, believed in locking villains up. It was what bonded the two men together.

There were plenty of villains to lock up in Western Division. The patch began on the edge of the city centre in an area of neglected Victorian terraces. Former family homes, most of the properties were now owned by seedy landlords who had turned them into a bedsit-land populated with drug addicts, alcoholics and drop-outs. Next to bedsit-land, fanning out away from the city centre and towards the suburbs, was a huge semi-circular swathe of housing estates comprising 1970s blocks of flats whose brightly painted colours had long since faded, whose concrete was crumbling and where weeds poked their way up between the cracks in quadrangle floors littered with broken bottles, fast food cartons and syringes. These were places where every other window was boarded up, most doors were gashed and the landings were stalked by heroin dealers, places long since abandoned by most of the respectable people and where even police officers went in pairs. But where they went nevertheless, the likes of Blizzard and Ronald insisting that nowhere in the Western Division was a no-go area.

Four miles out of the city centre, and at the heart of the division, was Abbey Road Police Station. Constructed as a temporary measure in the 1960s, the single-storey station was still there three decades later, the green paint on its prefabs peeling and the roof leaking. The station was situated amid a pleasant middle-class residential area sandwiched between the River Haft, a short distance to its south, and to the north, mile upon mile of more run-down sixties council estates with shuttered corner shops, burnt-out cars, abandoned pushchairs and abandoned hope.

But as the division stretched towards the western fringes of the city, the neighbourhoods changed dramatically, the housing estates giving way to wide tree-lined roads with mock-Georgian mansions hidden behind high walls and hedges and approached through ornate gates that opened out on to winding gravel drives. The houses, many ivy-covered and several of which had outdoor swimming pools, were owned by executives from the aviation plant in the city, self-made entrepreneurs, highly paid council officers and the occasional villain, his outward respectability hiding dark secrets. And then it was out into the farming flatlands beyond the city boundaries, the area where Blizzard lived in a detached house on a new development in one of the villages, and the area around Hawkwith village, where could be found Green Meadow Farm and its POW camp. And it was Green Meadow Farm that now occupied their thoughts.

'Perhaps you would like to explain the dog impression,' said Blizzard, picking up the file from the desk and glancing at the front cover. 'I seem to recall the name Willy Ramage – I assume he is related to Henderson?'

'Yeah, his father. He was shot dead by his dog.'

'He was indeed,' said Ronald with a nod of the head. 'Four years ago, if I remember correctly. It was bizarre. Everyone thought he had been murdered….'

'But they decided his dog shot him accidentally,' finished Colley.

'Yeah, I remember the case now,' said Blizzard. 'Just couldn't place the name. But it was not one of ours, surely? I thought it happened over towards Burniston. You were still commander there, weren't you, Arthur?'

'I was indeed. You were still in drugs squad at the time. The case was handled by our CID. DI Wheatley, if I am not mistaken.'

'It was,' nodded Colley. 'In fact, I have just come off the phone from him.'

'How is Danny?' asked Ronald. 'He's still in traffic isn't he?'

'Yeah.'

'Such a waste,' sighed Blizzard, earning himself a disapproving look from the superintendent, who had at one point been in charge of the southern traffic section.

'You had better watch what you say about him,' warned Ronald. 'They reckon Danny Wheatley will be a chief superintendent within five years. He's the chief constable's blue-eyed boy, remember.'

'And there was me thinking I was,' said Blizzard innocently. 'It would explain why I didn't get a Christmas card from him last year. Mind, I'm not surprised Danny's done well, he was always very good at shuffling paper clips as I recall.'

Ronald let the comment go.

'Anyway,' said Colley, 'it was Danny who told me all about Willy Ramage and the link with Green Meadow Farm.'

It had been a sensational story at the time. Willy Ramage was a typical north country farmer. A man of few words and even fewer airs and graces, he had grown arable crops and kept a dairy herd at Green Meadow for nearly forty years, like his father and grandfather before him. Over time, Ramage had developed his business until he was able to purchase a second farm at Burniston, ten miles to the north of Green Meadow. He moved his family there because the farmhouse was much bigger; his son Henderson, daughter-in-law and their two children lived with the Ramages and the house had become too cramped. Willy Ramage left Green Meadow to be run by a tenant farmer.

One spring morning, Willy went out on his customary early morning walk around his lands at Burniston, with his constant companion Ben, a black retriever, trotting by his side. They were after crows and Ramage had his shotgun with him as usual. By lunchtime, he still had not returned and

Henderson and one of the farmhands went looking for him. They found Willy Ramage sprawled in a copse, trusty dog by his side, guarding the body. At first, Ben seemed loath to let them approach, crouching low and growling, but eventually relented. However, it was already too late for the farmer.

The police were called and quickly confirmed that Ramage had sustained a massive shotgun injury to the leg and bled to death. There were signs that, although gravely injured, he had tried desperately to drag himself along the ground in the direction of the farmhouse a mile away. As he lay still and life-less on the damp spring grass, the officers were struck by the fact that, if he had been able to lift his head one last time, he would just have been able to glimpse the farmhouse through the trees; so near and yet so far. Perhaps he did see it as his sight faded that final time. It was a poignant thought for the investigating officers.

Initially, DI Danny Wheatley and his team treated it as a murder-style inquiry and questioned all the farmhands as well as 38-year-old Henderson. There was nothing to link anyone to the killing and, gradually, the detectives developed a theory which seemed bizarre but was the only one which fitted the facts. Forensic studies of the angle of the shotgun blast and markings on the ground led them to conclude that Willy had shot himself, the cartridge perhaps ricocheting off the hard ground and tearing into his leg. Given that there was nothing in his life to suggest that he would want to kill himself – he seemed happy, doted on his grandchildren and had no money worries – they came to the conclusion that he stumbled while walking through the copse and that the gun went off, ripping apart his leg.

Finding nothing else to explain such a stumble, they formulated the theory that in some way the dog impeded him, perhaps running across his path or jumping up. Maybe it had been after a rabbit or was spooked by a pheasant suddenly flying out of the trees in front of them, the detectives reasoned. Grizzled old local farmers sucked on their pipes and scoffed at the suggestion, muttering darkly about 'bloody townies', but that was the theory the police put to the inquest and the coroner, who said no one would ever truly know what happened, duly recorded a verdict of death by misadventure. The story made headlines the world over. *Dog shoots man.* The newspaper headline-writers loved it.

'And it all happened about the same time our Mr Knoefler was dumped in the grave on Ramage's land,' said Colley pointedly.

'Like you say,' said Blizzard, eyes gleaming, 'it gets stranger and stranger. And you know, I am sure I recognize the name Henderson Ramage from somewhere else as well.'

'You probably do,' nodded Colley. 'He's not exactly a good little mummy's boy. Got form for handling stolen goods and a couple of nasty assaults. He glassed a bloke in one of them. Bloke ended up being given seven pints of blood.'

'Sounds a nice chap,' grunted Blizzard.

'He's a nasty bit of work is Henderson Ramage,' said Ronald. 'When I was at Burniston, Danny Wheatley had him in on several occasions.'

'Yeah,' nodded Colley. 'Most of it happened in Burniston's patch. Danny gave me the low-down. Besides, I've had dealings with Henderson Ramage myself over here.'

'Hey,' said Blizzard, looking sharply at his sergeant and slapping his forehead. 'I knew I recognized the name. Wasn't Henderson Ramage the one that...?'

'Wondered when you'd clock it,' nodded the sergeant.

'God, I'm slow today,' said the chief inspector.

Colley said nothing but inwardly noted the fact that it was just one of a number of occasions since the events at the graveside in which Blizzard had seemed distracted.

'Would someone please care to explain?' asked the bewildered superintendent.

'The kids on Quarry Street,' explained Blizzard. 'Happened just before you got the job here.'

'Was that him?' asked Ronald, in surprise. 'I thought—'

'Na, Ramage was involved as well, I'm sure of it, guv,' said Colley vehemently.

'And I'm sure one of our lot investigated Henderson Ramage when I was on the drugs squad as well,' added Blizzard.

'Probably did,' nodded Colley. 'He's got form for a bit of heroin dealing. Nothing big-time though.'

'Did any of the offences take place at Green Meadow Farm?' asked Ronald.

'No,' nodded Colley, 'but one happened at the Burniston farm eight years ago. CID found him storing stolen tractor parts and discovered a couple of half-inched quad bikes in one of the sheds. Ramage claimed he did not know how they got there.'

'It's those blessed fairies again,' murmured Blizzard.

'Must have been, guv. They've got a lot to answer for. Anyway, he coughed to it.'

'And what did he get for that?' asked the chief inspector.

'Three months. Got out in five weeks apparently. Good behaviour.'

'Marvellous,' snorted Blizzard; his views on what he saw as an inefficient and unduly lenient justice system were well known.

'Actually, it was not that bad.' said Colley. 'One of the quad bikes was lifted from a neighbouring farm – the words "shit" and "nest" spring readily to mind. When he got out, the farm lads went round to hold a lively discussion on the rights and wrongs of property ownership with our Henderson. Gave him such a howking his skull thought it was a bagatelle machine.'

And he chuckled.

'Ker-ching ker-ching!'

'I take it he means a criminal assault upon Mr Ramage's person took place?' asked Roland sardonically.

'I believe so,' nodded Blizzard. 'Although Colley-speak can be a difficult language to translate into English. I'm thinking of running a course on it for beginners. You might want to enrol, Arthur.'

The sergeant grinned at Ronald's perplexed expression; he loved winding the superintendent up and the senior officer, for his part, knew it was the price he paid for having a damned good detective on the team. Besides, had Ronald tried to change the sergeant, the first complaint would have come from John Blizzard and the superintendent knew it. In an age in which Blizzard complained vociferously about what he liked to call 'cloned' police officers, David Colley represented a sense of individuality. It was why the chief inspector insisted he assist him on major inquiries.

'I take it Henderson still owns Green Meadow Farm?' asked Blizzard.

'Yeah, most of it,' nodded Colley. 'Apart, of course, from the bit he offered to the housebuilders. And that caused a bit of a fuss as well. Henderson Ramage was not exactly Mr Popular when news of that leaked out. I've sent Freddy Furnell to do some door-to-door in Hawkwith to see if he can turn anything juicy up from the locals.'

'Good stuff,' said Blizzard, nodding approvingly. 'And how are we doing with our Herr Knoefler?'

'Not so well. I put a call into the German Embassy in London this morning but they have not been able to turn anything up yet. They seemed to think they would, given a little time. She was a very nice girl, I talked to, mind, guv. Sounded busty.'

'I'm sure she did,' said Blizzard with a smile.

'Anyhow,' said Colley, with a gleam in his eyes. 'Forget Knoefler for the moment, I'm not finished about Green Meadow Farm. See, I got to thinking about Henderson Ramage.'

'I can see why,' said Ronald, turning to the chief inspector. 'He's got to be worth a pull, hasn't he, John?'

Blizzard nodded.

'Then what are we waiting for?' asked Ronald. 'Let's bring him in.'

'In which case, sir,' said Colley, with a mischievous look on his face, 'you might like to know that among Henderson's little mates is none other than one of the chief inspector's oldest and much-valued friends. In fact, it'll be a truly touching reunion.'

Blizzard raised a questioning eyebrow.

'Go on,' said Ronald cautiously, suspecting a sting in the tail to the comment.

It was duly delivered.

'Eddie Gayle,' grinned Colley.

'Marvellous,' sighed Ronald, raising his eyes to the ceiling. 'That's all we need.'

Blizzard beamed.

·· CHAPTER four ····

FAT, SHORT AND perspiring, Eddie Gayle somehow reminded Colley of a little round pig as he sat in the cramped interview room at Abbey Road Police Station late that afternoon. What was it with him and animal metaphors lately? thought the sergeant idly as he waited for the interview to begin. Then he remembered; a few days before, Jay had been telling him over dinner about a project that her young class were doing. Twenty-eight 9-year-olds producing drawings and writing stories on the theme of animals. And Jay said he never listened! The sergeant chuckled. Sitting next to him at the desk, and glancing quizzically at him when he heard the low laugh, was John Blizzard, the chief inspector's eyes bright as he relished the opportunity to confront an old adversary.

For his part, Gayle, aged in his mid-forties, thinning black hair covered by a poorly fitting wig and dressed as ever in a sharp dark suit which would have looked good on anyone else, glared back at the officers. He mopped his brow in the oppressive heat of the small room, the police station central heating system having continued to malfunction throughout the day. Cold as an ice box when the day shift reported for duty, the prefabs were now broiling. Colley, himself feeling uncomfortable in the heat beneath his sharply dressed exterior, noticed the flecks of dandruff on Gayle's jacket, the sweat rings round its armpits and the ugly red food stain on the pale blue tie. All in all, Eddie Gayle did not present an appetizing sight and the sight of him perspiring gave the sergeant grim satisfaction. Blizzard's first rule of interviewing, he thought: make them sweat. Indeed, on more than one occasion, the chief inspector had been known to turn the radiator up in the interview room.

Gayle was well known to the police. He was a low-life, a man who stalked the gutters of the city, spreading his own brand of fear and hatred. And yet he had proved, so far at least, an 'untouchable' for the police even though Blizzard and his detectives had been after him for years. Gayle's ability to twist and turn out of the very tightest of spots had long been a source of growing infuriation for Blizzard and Colley. Gayle's 'legitimate' business, the outwardly respectable façade behind which he sheltered, was property. Preferring to present himself to the public as a man of great standing within the community, he was the owner of many of the city's beautiful Victorian houses and liked to claim that he was helping to ease Hafton's acute accommodation crisis.

But successful entrepreneur was only the face that Eddie Gayle presented to the world. His real business was much darker; it was about making money whatever the cost to other people. Behind what little respectability his flash motors and cheap suits afforded him, Gayle was a selfish and nasty man, as well as being a crook and a thug. He spent little money on his houses and, despite the extortionate rents he charged for the rooms, most of them were pits of squalor with damp walls, curling wallpaper, tatty carpets and rickety furniture. And they were freezing in winter, Gayle having refused to invest in central heating systems for his tenants, who were a mix of DSS clients, drop-outs and impecunious students.

But woe betide those who complained. His reputation for intimidating council officials who tried from time to time to persuade him to raise his standards and tenants brave enough to speak out against him was well known, and detectives had investigated Gayle several times in connection with the violent actions of his bull-headed enforcers. But Gayle's most powerful tool of trade was fear and each time the police closed in, his henchmen would knock on doors at all times of day and night, and terrified victims and witnesses seemed to melt away, some refusing to sign statements, others leaving the city at dead of night. Dead was the word. Several had disappeared altogether and all police efforts to trace them had failed. Murder, no murder? No one knew. In addition to the protection offered by fear, Gayle was also shielded by the fierce loyalty of his henchmen, men who were well paid for their work and for their silence.

Eddie Gayle needed that loyalty because he was swimming in much deeper waters than beating up a few troublesome tenants. There were persistent rumours linking him to drug smuggling, illegal cigarette-trafficking and even, according to some reports, the importation of firearms for use by the city's criminal gangs. For all the persistent rumours, pinning him down had proved virtually impossible and every time he walked free, Eddie Gayle's confidence grew, the mocking smile became wider and his bravado more pronounced. He had also become increasingly adept at playing the game, often lodging official complaints against the police, John Blizzard in particular, so much so that officers felt more like the hunted and not the hunters. And with John Blizzard, such tactics meant that it had become deeply personal between the two men.

So delicate had the situation become that a few months previously Arthur Ronald had been summoned to see the chief constable after yet another complaint from Gayle. The superintendent had been ordered to instruct his officers, Blizzard among them, to go easy on Eddie Gayle, something Ronald did with great reluctance and not without registering his distaste at the suggestion. It was yet another incident in the deteriorating relationship between the chief constable and his detective chief superintendent. For his part, John Blizzard hated the chief constable for the ruling but, mindful of the politically tricky situation and its consequences for his friend if things went wrong, he had tried hard to adopt a more circumspect tack in his dealings with Gayle. However, loyalty to Arthur Ronald only went so far, which is why Blizzard had grabbed at the chance to interview Gayle again. Surely, he reasoned, something had to give one day.

There in the interview room that afternoon to ensure the chief inspector showed due respect was Paul D'Arcy, himself no stranger to police attentions. A local lawyer who had become immensely, and mysteriously, rich, he was a thin-faced man in his late thirties, dressed immaculately in a dark pinstripe suit with a white handkerchief poking out of its breast pocket. A man who had helped Eddie Gayle wheedle his way out of more than a few tight spots over the years, D'Arcy interested the police greatly. Alerted to the lawyer's wealth by his large house on the western side of the city, and the expensive cars parked on its gravelled drive, detectives had long suspected him of laundering dirty money for organized crime in the city.

But, as with his client, proof was difficult to come by so the slippery D'Arcy remained at large, determined to grasp every opportunity to increase the pressure on the police and ensure that the detectives did not pry too deeply into his own affairs. Despite his hostile expression now, the solicitor actually welcomed the latest police decision to bring Gayle in for questioning. The lawyer found his client a particularly useful tool; if the police were looking at Gayle, they weren't looking at his solicitor. Gayle little realized he was being used; for the landlord, the world revolved around him and only him.

'I would like to place on record,' began the lawyer icily, 'that as an upstanding citizen, my client objects most strongly to the way he has been brought to this police station on yet another flimsy pretext.'

'But I thought he liked our little chats,' said Blizzard innocently, glancing at the whirring tape machine; the words would sound OK but the recorder would not pick up the thinness of his smile. 'I know I look forward to them immensely and the lovely letters Eddie writes to the chief constable afterwards, complimenting me on my work.'

'Is my client under arrest?' asked D'Arcy icily.

'Under arrest? Eddie?' said Blizzard, again feigning innocence. 'Oh, no, no, the very thought of it. No, in his capacity as an upstanding citizen he is here to help us with some inquiries. You are an upstanding citizen, aren't you, Eddie?'

Gayle glared at him but said nothing.

'So why exactly is he here?' asked D'Arcy impatiently, tiring of the games and bridling at the chief inspector's tone of voice, dripping as it was with sarcasm. 'My client is a very busy man....'

'Yes, well once we get this sorted out, he can go back to beating up people.'

'I resent that!' snarled Gayle, leaping to his feet.

'Sit down,' snapped Blizzard.

The landlord hesitated then looked deep into the ice-blue of the chief inspector's eyes and slumped back on to his chair, where he sat eyeing the detective balefully.

'So what *is* this about?' asked D'Arcy, angry at the ease with which Blizzard had provoked his client into losing his temper. 'Another pointless fishing expedition, I assume?'

'We are making some preliminary inquiries into the discovery of the body at the old POW camp,' said Blizzard.

'So it is another fishing expedition,' said the lawyer.

'Yeah, I ain't got nothing to do with that!' exclaimed Gayle.

'I am sure you haven't,' said Blizzard, 'but he was found on land owned by one of your associates, one Henderson Ramage, a farming gentleman of this parish.'

'Is that why we are here?' asked the lawyer incredulously, picking up his shiny black briefcase and pointedly snapping it shut. 'Because of Henderson Ramage? Well, this has nothing whatsoever to do with my client. It sounds like you are desperate, Chief Inspector. As per usual.'

'At this stage, I am just trying to get a picture of what happened on the land,' said Blizzard coolly.

'Then talk to Mr Ramage and don't pester my client with these fatuous questions.'

'Mr Ramage is out of town on business,' said Blizzard, 'whatever that business may be. So I am talking to your client first. And I am interested, Mr D'Arcy, because it seems to me that the name means something to you and your client. Would you care to explain that?'

'We have no comment to make,' said the solicitor.

'Yeah, and I ain't saying nuffin,' said Gayle bullishly, sitting back in the chair, crossing his arms and staring defiantly at the detectives. 'I hardly know him.'

'Fair enough,' nodded Blizzard.

The chief inspector looked down and started to flick idly through the brown file on the table. Watched uncomfortably by the landlord as he turned the pages over, Blizzard finally settled on one of them and leaned forward to look closer, seemingly entranced by the contents. The seconds lengthened. The silence was oppressive. Gayle and D'Arcy eyed the file uneasily.

'What is that?' asked the lawyer, unable to contain his curiosity any longer.

'What's what?' replied Blizzard innocently.

'That.' And now the solicitor's voice was more than a little concerned as he nodded at the document.

'That?' said Blizzard, looking down as if he had only just noticed its presence. 'Oh, that is a file, Mr D'Arcy. Surely you have seen one before? Your office must be full of them. I believe they are usually made out of some form of card.'

Colley allowed himself a smile.

'Don't mess with me,' said D'Arcy, irritated at the sergeant's response. 'What does it contain?'

'It is the file on your client's associate Garry Horton.'

'I ain't never 'eard of him,' blustered Gayle, running a hand round his grubby shirt collar as he started to sweat even more.

'Oh, come on,' said Colley, his voice hard-edged as he stared at the little landlord. 'Horton works for you. We all know that.'

Eddie Gayle thought for a moment. Next to him, D'Arcy looked uncertain for the first time in the interview, not quite sure about the detectives' tactics and desperate to find out what his client knew about Horton's most recent movements before he responded to any questions. D'Arcy and Eddie Gayle did indeed know about Garry Horton; it was probably the closest the gangster had come to seeing the inside of a prison cell. D'Arcy had worked hard to earn his money that day and the lawyer was acutely conscious that the investigating officer had been David Colley – and that the sergeant had never forgotten it.

Horton, a 17-stone bruiser now in his early forties, was an

ex-bodybuilder with a long record of violence stretching back to his late teens and who had worked for many years as one of Gayle's enforcers. His reign of fear came to an end when he was jailed for a savage attack carried out four years previously in one of Eddie Gayle's bedsits. Two tenants, a couple in their late teens, had complained about the state of their room and threatened to go to the city council when Gayle refused to do anything about it.

Late one night, they received a visit from Horton and another heavy, who was never identified; honour among villains and all that. Although he was never able to prove it, Colley had always privately believed the second attacker that night was Henderson Ramage; the farmer knew Horton from school and they were known to associate with each other still. Whoever it was launched the attack, they smashed down the door and carried out a ferocious assault on the couple, beating the young man to within an inch of his life with wooden staves and knocking the girl unconscious by smashing her head against the wall. Both spent weeks in hospital, the girl recovering from a fractured skull and the man from broken legs, a broken arm and a shattered jaw. He required five operations in what was one of the most horrifying assaults the city had ever seen.

Despite an ugly atmosphere of intimidation, including veiled threats against himself, one of the reasons Colley shared Blizzard's distaste for Gayle, the sergeant eventually managed to persuade the terrified couple to give evidence after several weeks of delicate negotiations at their hospital bedsides. When it came to crown court, Horton indicated he was going to plead not guilty but, faced with the weight of evidence, changed his plea on the eve of the trial and was jailed for seven years. However, even when facing a stretch behind bars, he refused to take Eddie Gayle or Henderson Ramage with him and neither was ever charged in connection with the incident. Colley was commended for his persistence and courage by the judge, and by his chief constable, but the sergeant had remained frustrated at what he saw as an inadequate sentence and his inability to put anyone else in the dock alongside Garry Horton. Those feelings had risen to the surface once more when the name of Henderson Ramage entered the inquiry into the death of Horst Knoefler.

'And what is so interesting, of course,' said Blizzard calmly, flicking through the file then glancing at his sergeant, 'was the victims' nationality. German, were they not, David?'

'They were,' nodded the sergeant. 'Exchange students over from Hamburg.'

'Hey, I've just realized, our victim in the grave was German, too,' said Blizzard with fake surprise, fixing Gayle with a steely glare as he dropped his pretence. 'So you can see why we are so interested in you. After all, Garry Horton is your heavy, is he not?'

'He don't work for me,' blustered Gayle, realizing what Blizzard had been driving at and becoming alarmed.

'But surely all this is irrelevant, Chief Inspector,' said D'Arcy, recovering his composure despite his concern at the direction the questioning had taken. 'Even if my client did know this Mr Horton, and we deny that to be the case, the events of which you spoke happened some time ago. Mr Horton has been in jail for four years and could not possibly have killed the man you found at the farm.'

'It is a point to consider,' nodded Blizzard, as if the thought had only just struck him.

'Somewhat of an oversight on your part, I can't help feeling,' added D'Arcy.

He smiled triumphantly at the chief inspector, but it was not a convincing smile, more of an act; nagging away at the back of the lawyer's mind was the realization that long experience had taught him Blizzard did not make those kind of mistakes. Colley sat back, enjoying the verbal jousting match and waiting for Blizzard's next move. The chief inspector's features were inscrutable. He would have made a fine poker player, thought Colley, as he did so often in these kinds of situations.

'You are absolutely right, Mr D'Arcy, it would indeed be an oversight,' said Blizzard calmly, adding casually, almost as if it were of no import, 'Were it not for the fact that Garry Horton got out two weeks ago. Indeed, my officers have been looking for him but he seems to have vanished off the face of the earth. Your client would not happen to know anything about that, would he?'

D'Arcy looked at him in silence but the detectives could see the thoughts racing behind his eyes. One of the thoughts was the lawyer's fury that he was unaware of Horton's release, another an acute irritation that he had been outflanked by the chief inspector. A further concern was that Blizzard knew more than he was letting on. He'd fallen into too many of Blizzard's traps to think any other way. Had the lawyer known that his first instinct was correct – that the chief inspector was indeed fishing – he would have felt considerably happier. But he didn't and Blizzard was not about to enlighten him.

'My client knows nothing about this,' said the solicitor, glancing at Gayle wondering if the statement was even remotely true. 'And even if he did, none of this proves anything. My client has not seen Mr Horton since he got out.'

'No, maybe not,' admitted Blizzard, 'except our victim was actually murdered four years ago – at just about the time friend Garry was stomping around the city beating up innocent Germans, oddly enough. At your client's behest, might I add. Strange coincidence, is it not?'

The landlord went pale and his solicitor bit his lip. It was always like this representing Eddie Gayle, he reflected gloomily; you were never quite sure of exactly what he was guilty, you just knew it was something. Adding to D'Arcy's unease was the fact that he knew Horton did indeed work for Gayle. Everyone in the room knew it. Knowing it was part of the game.

'But surely,' said the solicitor slowly, 'the radio said you only found the body at the farm a few days ago. It did not mention anything about four years ago.'

'It must have slipped my mind,' said Blizzard, deadpan. 'But that's when he was killed before being buried on land owned by one of Eddie's associates. You know, now I say it like that, the coincidence really does strike you. What do you think, Sergeant?'

'It certainly makes you think,' nodded Colley.

Gayle and D'Arcy sat there in silence for a few moments, digesting the information. The landlord, perspiring even more now, glanced hopefully at his lawyer, who was thinking quickly for a way to regain the initiative. Everyone knew that once you let John Blizzard gain the upper hand in interviews, life could become extremely difficult indeed.

'Whatever the truth or otherwise of those statements,' said D'Arcy at last, choosing his words carefully, 'none of this has anything to do with my client.'

He knew it was a weak response but it was all he could think of for the moment and he needed to buy some time. Gayle did it for him.

'Yeah, I ain't got nuffin' to do with some dead square-head!' exclaimed the landlord angrily.

'Such a wonderful respect for multi-culturalism in this city,' murmured Blizzard. 'No wonder people regard you as such an upstanding citizen, Eddie.'

'Please, Eddie,' hissed the lawyer, noticing Colley's smile, 'let me handle this.'

'Na, he ain't getting away with saying I attacked them Krauts!' said Gayle angrily. 'He can't prove that!'

'Perhaps I don't need to,' murmured Blizzard.

'Chief Inspector,' said D'Arcy firmly. 'I do not appreciate your little games and I fail to see where this is leading us. As I recall, your sergeant here tried cynically to implicate my client in the terrible attack on those two poor exchange students at the time Mr Horton was arrested, and patently failed to do so.'

'Yeah, funny that,' said Colley sardonically. 'Even though it happened in your house, no one living there seemed to know who you were, Eddie. And you such a pillar of the community, too.'

'I like to keep a low profile,' said Gayle uncomfortably.

'Rather like your witnesses,' said Blizzard.

'I have had enough of this,' said the lawyer angrily,

suddenly standing up with a scrape of his chair. 'And since nothing seems to have changed, and since my client is not under arrest, and since you are clearly on a fishing expedition, we are going to take our leave of you. What's more, I will be writing to your chief constable to protest about the way my client has yet again been harassed.'

'I'm sure you will,' murmured Blizzard, leaning back in his chair, wafting a hand at Colley and watching the sergeant escort them out of the room.

As he went, Eddie Gayle leered and made a writing movement in the air at the chief inspector.

'Make sure your lawyer does the letter, Eddie,' said Blizzard sardonically. 'Your spelling is atrocious.'

Gayle glared at him and disappeared into the corridor. The chief inspector walked slowly back to his office and closed the door. He was still there two hours later, contemplating whether or not it was time to go home as the office clock edged towards seven. Blizzard stared moodily out of the window into the inky blackness of a winter evening, scowling as the rain started to fleck against the glass. With a sigh, he glanced back down on to the desk, where Garry Horton's file had lain open for the past thirty minutes. The chief inspector's reverie was disturbed by Colley, who entered clutching a piece of paper.

'Penny for your thoughts?' said the sergeant, perching on the edge of the desk and noticing the far-away expression on Blizzard's face.

'Not sure I have any at this stage.'

'Do you really think Knoefler is a racist murder?'

'No, not really,' sighed Blizzard. 'And let's hope it isn't, we'd have every civil rights campaigner in Hafton besieging the station if it was. Not to mention that silly woman from the diversity relations department or whatever they call it. Agatha Fish-tank or something.'

'Agnetha Flitcroft,' grinned Colley. 'She's Swedish.'

'Whatever,' grunted Blizzard. 'You know the one I mean, the bimbo with the blonde hair and the three-feet heels.'

'You've always been so politically correct,' grinned Colley, adding mischievously, 'I bet Danny Wheatley would never say something like that.'

'He'd be too busy counting bollards,' grunted Blizzard, and suddenly recalling once again, as he had many times in recent days, his strange experience at the graveside. 'Besides, this goes beyond Eddie Gayle and his hired thugs, I am sure of it. There is something much deeper to this, David, and the answer lies at Green Meadow Farm.'

'This place has really got to you, hasn't it?' said Colley.

Blizzard did not comment and there was silence for a moment, broken only by the increasingly insistent drumming of the rain on the office window. Colley eyed his friend for a moment.

'What?' asked Blizzard, noticing the look.

'Are you finally going to tell me what spooked you at the graveside?'

'No.'

'I've never seen you like that.'

'You live and learn,' said Blizzard.

The tone of his reply suggested it was a closed matter.

'OK, OK, I get the message,' nodded Colley. He knew Blizzard would open up to him in time.

The chief inspector looked at the piece of paper in the sergeant's hand.

'What's that?' he asked.

'It's a fax from the German Embassy,' said Colley, handing it over. 'I told you they'd come through. *Vorsprung durch Technik* and all that.'

'I didn't know you could speak German,' said Blizzard in surprise.

'I had an Audi once.'

'Do they know much about Knoefler?' asked the chief inspector, pointedly ignoring the comment.

'Na, they just make cars,' said Colley, trying not to laugh.

'I mean,' sighed Blizzard, 'the embassy?'

'A bit, not much, mind.'

'Well, whatever it is,' said Blizzard, who never wasted an opportunity to press the case for better computerized systems at Abbey Road, 'it's bound to be a damned sight more than our records department would ever dredge up. If it was down to them, it would take us another four years to even find out where bloody Germany is. Now, if we had that new system like they've got over at....'

His voice tailed off as he watched Colley, who had heard it all before from the chief inspector, walk round the room, occasionally stopping to peer intently at the floor.

'What on earth are you doing?' asked Blizzard.

'I just wondered if I could see any hobby-horse shit,' said the sergeant, straightening up and sitting down in the chair at the other side of the desk.

Blizzard gave him a withering look and scanned the fax. According to the embassy, Knoefler had indeed been a prisoner-of-war at Hafton Camp, one of the last POWs to be released just before the complex closed in the middle of 1946; it had stayed open for almost a year after the end of the war. He married an English woman from Hafton a year or so later and they moved to Wales, where Knoefler concentrated all his energies on building up a successful agricultural supplies company which, as the years passed, went into land ownership as well, snapping up considerable acreage in Wales and south-west England from farmers and selling it to housebuilders wishing to expand.

It all made Horst Knoefler a wealthy man and, the couple having not had children to inherit the business, he sold the company in the mid-eighties in a multi-million pound deal and he and his wife settled into comfortable retirement in a large house in a remote village in the Welsh countryside. According to the embassy, the last they heard of Knoefler was five years previously when he told them that his wife had died of a heart attack. Grief-stricken, the retired businessman sold their house and promised to inform embassy officials of his new address. He failed to do so and attempts to track him down over the subsequent years had drawn a blank until his body was found in the grave. According to the embassy's calculations, Knoefler would have been into his late seventies at the time of his death.

'So where did he go after selling the house?' asked Blizzard, putting the piece of paper down on his desk. 'David, have you still got that Taffy mate?'

'Sure have, although how Agatha Fish-tank would react if she heard you calling him that is open to debate.'

'Oh, dear, what a pity,' said Blizzard. 'Anyway, get on to him will you, see if he can tear himself away from chewing on a leek and find out anything about our Herr Knoefler.'

'Ahead of you on that one, guv. Just come off the phone from Jonathan. He contacted a friend of his in the village where Knoefler lived. It's a tiny place, only ten or 20 houses. Turns out the guy just disappeared one day. Never even said his goodbyes, which was unlike him, apparently.'

'Yeah?'

'Yeah, the locals reckoned he was a polite and courteous guy. Always stopped to say good morning to people on his way to the shop to buy a newspaper, that sort of thing. Everyone liked him.'

'Good work,' nodded Blizzard approvingly. 'You know, Ronald may be right, you might just make a detective one day.'

'You're too kind.'

'So, Knoefler just upped sticks and left, eh?'

'Yeah, the villagers never saw hide nor hair of him again. And a few weeks after he disappeared, his house went on the market. A young couple live there now.'

'No police investigation?'

'There didn't seem a need and no one reported him missing.'

'We need to find out who he was running from.'

'If he was running, guv,' cautioned the sergeant. 'Lots of people sell their homes after their partner dies. Can't live with the memories. My nan did that. Saw grandad everywhere. Got too much for her in the end – he was getting in her way, she said – so she sold up.'

'No, Knoefler was running scared. A bloke who always let the embassy know where he was suddenly disappearing off the face of the earth without so much as a by-your-leave? No, that would have offended his sense of German efficiency.'

'Maybe.'

'Definitely, David,' insisted the chief inspector. 'I am telling you, it was not his style. Besides, look what happens next, he turns up dead. That's too much of a coincidence. The events have got to be linked.'

'OK,' nodded Colley, 'but if they are, where does it leave dearest Eddie Gayle and Henderson Ramage?'

'Not sure,' shrugged Blizzard. 'Maybe it leaves them nowhere but, involved or not, it's nice to remind Eddie and his scumbag lawyer that we are watching him, is it not? I don't like the idea that Eddie can run around the city doing whatever the bloody hell he likes. It's gone on for far too long and I don't care what the chief constable says, it has got to end.'

'Agreed,' nodded Colley, his sense of injustice over the Horton case as strong as ever. 'But his lawyer is going to kick up a fuss again; you know what a reptile D'Arcy is, guv. And the super's not going to like that.'

'Not like what?' asked Ronald, walking into the office and fixing the sergeant with a hawkish expression.

'Whoops,' grinned Colley, 'me and my big mouth again.'

Blizzard gave him a pained look.

'I know,' said Ronald, turning on his heel and walking out of the office, his voice floating back down the corridor. 'If I pretend I didn't hear anything, perhaps it will go away and I won't have my flabby ass hauled into the chief's office tomorrow morning to explain why we are harassing Eddie Gayle again. Goodnight, gentlemen....'

'Goodnight, Arthur,' shouted Blizzard, with a gentle smile and a wink at his grinning sergeant. 'Sweet dreams.'

All they heard was a grunt.

· · CHAPTER five · · · ·

'YOU DO KNOW how to show a girl a good time,' said Fee Ellis.

'I do my best,' said Blizzard, smiling cheerfully at the woman who had transformed his life over the past year.

'It's a bit of mess, though.'

'No, it isn't,' said Blizzard, as he scrabbled over the pieces of metal piled along the edge of the dimly lit corrugated iron shed. 'It's lovely.'

'Whatever,' said Fee, shivering with cold and pulling her thin black leather jacket around her.

As she watched him battling his away across the shed, she marvelled at the hold that its contents had exerted over Blizzard for years. She knew that the shed had been the chief inspector's secret place for years, his bolt-hole at times of stress, the place to which he ran when he needed to clear his thoughts. Even though she had been there a number of times, Fee still felt somehow out of place, as though she did not belong, as if this was his place and she was intruding.

Fee – real name Fiona – had been the chief inspector's girl-friend for a year. Colley used to say that the only way Blizzard could ever hope to hook up with a woman was if he arrested her. He was nearly right; twenty-eight years old, Fee had been a police officer for six years. Having graduated from university, she initially served as a uniformed constable for five years, over on the eastern side of the city, showing such promise in the field of investigation that she had been seconded to Western Division CID to gain experience as a detective. She was still based at Abbey Road Police Station more than twelve months later.

The daughter of a retired detective sergeant, with whom Blizzard and Ronald had worked briefly in their early days, Fee had impressed the chief inspector the moment she had walked into the squad room, and not just for her professionalism. Five foot eight and slim, she had short, slightly waved, blonde hair and a face with soft lines, a face that presented a striking contrast, sometimes suggesting someone cool, collected and unapproachable, at other times a person who was warm and animated. Also, on rare unguarded occasions, it suggested the air of vulnerability felt by any woman trying to survive in the man's world that was Hafton CID. She was also a woman who appreciated, right from her initial attraction to the chief inspector, the difficulties of going out with a man like John Blizzard. Avowedly single and set in his ways, and as hardened a detective as they came, he was a man wedded, colleagues said, to his job and striking up a relationship had meant many changes in both of their lives.

Not that Blizzard had been blind to the challenges, or his personal flaws. Once their relationship had started to develop, surprising the chief inspector after more than a decade alone following his acrimonious divorce, both of them had tried to resist the inevitable. Blizzard resisted because he was acutely conscious of their age difference and the way some office gossips would insinuate that Fee was receiving favourable attention because of her relationship with him. For Fee, such considerations were to be viewed as just that, considerations and nothing more. Fully realizing the difficulties which might lie ahead, she also recognized very early on that more powerful forces were at work.

The thing about the inevitable is that it always happens and, after a short while, the forces won and the couple gave in to temptation, seeing each other secretly at first then more openly. After the initial gossiping, everyone at Abbey Road seemed to accept the situation; and even if they did not, the couple decided very early on that they did not care what people thought.

Dressed tonight in jeans and a purple sweater underneath her jacket, Fee was standing in the presence of John

Blizzard's other great love. Or perhaps his only great love since she found that fathoming out his views about her was not always easy. Assessing his views about the contents of the engine shed was much simpler. All officers had their releases from the pressure of the job; Colley was a keen rugby player; Chris Ramsey, one of Western CID's two detective inspectors, loved martial arts; Fee was a keen cyclist and for Blizzard, the escape was provided by the Old Lady, a steam locomotive. His fascination with steam stretched back to a grandfather who was a shedmaster in industrial Yorkshire in the pre-war years and a father who worked for a while as a train driver. Before his father's job took them, reluctantly, north from rural Lincolnshire to grimy urban Hafton, the young Blizzard used to enjoy standing at the bottom of the garden of their cottage watching the steam engines thunder past the village and listening for the spine-tingling long whistle. It was, he always thought, one of the most evocative sounds in the world – that and the distant noise of a freight train passing through the darkness. As a man who did not sleep well, the midnight freight train heading for Hafton docks was a sound with which Blizzard was well acquainted and which he had, over the years, come to regard as a friend as he lay awake in bed, a reassurance that all was well in his world.

The Old Lady, housed in the shed on wasteland on the edge of the city centre, was more correctly known as the Silver Flyer. Childhood passion reaching deep into adulthood, more than fifteen years previously Blizzard had helped form the Hafton Railway Appreciation Society, a small group of enthusiastic volunteers who restored steam locomotives. Most of them were retired railmen and the Silver Flyer was their prize possession. For many years, she had hauled carriages between the city of Hafton and the Midlands, until taken out of commission in the 1960s as the dying embers of the golden age of steam finally spluttered and were extinguished. For a long time, no one seemed to know where she was, even though she had sat neglected and cold in the shed behind the central railway station all that time.

Blizzard had stumbled across the building while investigating a serious assault some years before, standing in amazement as he scraped off the rust to reveal the locomotive's nameplate. It did not take him long to persuade society members to raise the cash to buy and renovate her. A society delegation, led by Blizzard, had also held several recent meetings with the city council to discuss ways of renovating the derelict Tenby Street railway station close to the city centre, with a view to turning it into a railway museum in which the Silver Flyer could be displayed when the work was finished.

They were meetings that tested Blizzard's patience to the utmost, the council officers appearing to him to throw obstacle after obstacle in front of the society members, citing regulation after regulation, health and safety this, health and safety that, when in his view all that was needed was a bit of common sense and imagination. Common sense and imagination, he had concluded many years ago and had voiced on a number of occasions, that were not in great abundance among the people with whom he dealt at city hall. Nevertheless, progress was being made and for Blizzard, it was a project that promised to take up more and more of his time, something which he and Fee had discussed on several occasions, she concerned that she might find herself edged out of his life by railways and the relentless demands of the job, he trying to reassure her that a balance was still possible.

This night, though, it was a brief visit to the shed, Blizzard simply checking that the building was secure because none of the society members had visited for several days; the month before, one of them had unlocked the shed one morning to discover a break-in in which tools were stolen. Blizzard was furious but anger was replaced by delight when one of his CID officers caught the offender and recovered the tools.

'So what *do* you see in her?' asked Fee, shaking her head as he clambered over a pile of engine parts, edged past the main frame of the locomotive and reached up to check the grimy window at the far side of the building.

'She's beautiful,' said Blizzard, giving a satisfied grunt as, having found the window secure, he began the tortuous journey back, patting the engine affectionately then cursing as he barked his shin on the edge of a workbench.

'But she's just a chunk of metal,' said Fee, winding him up as she watched him grimace, rub his leg then swear as he discovered a rip in the knee of his black trousers.

'That people can say such things about something so beautiful,' replied Blizzard, straightening up and trying to appear offended, 'will forever be a sadness to me. And when we get Tenby Street turned into a museum, it will be brilliant.'

'But she's a rust-bucket,' said Fee, pointing to the locomotive.

'You sound like Colley. He always says that.'

'You can't blame us,' said Fee, gently mocking him. 'After all, aren't you a touch old to be playing with train sets, Mr Blizzard?'

'Colley says that as well,' replied the chief inspector, adding with a sly look, 'and he also says that having a love affair with one old boiler should be enough for me.'

'Wait till I get to see that sergeant of yours,' said Fee, noting through the humour that it was the first time Blizzard had used the word love in her presence. 'Talking of which, is that Saturday OK for dinner at their place?'

'Sure is,' said Blizzard, clambering over the last of the pieces of metal and taking her arm. 'I talked to Colley today. He's playing rugby in the afternoon but says he should be out of casualty by eight. Now come on, I seem to recall promising you a drink, young lady.'

'You did,' she said, pushing open the creaking door and walking into the sharp chill of a winter night. 'Old man. And you can tell me all about Eddie Gayle.'

'Why ruin a nice evening?' grunted Blizzard.

He snapped shut the padlock on the door and followed her across the wasteland towards the car, broken glass crunching beneath their feet and the lights of the city centre twinkling in front of them. For Blizzard, who had grown used to making the journey on his own over the years, it was still a source of wonder that he could do so with Fee Ellis. And he, too, was struck by the thought that he had used the word love for the first time. The chief inspector was glad it was dark and she could not see him grinning like a schoolboy.

An hour later, as the couple settled down in a cosy nook by the roaring fire in Blizzard's village pub, cradling their drinks, he a pint of real ale, she a white wine spritzer, the uniform constable deputed to guard the murder scene at Green Meadow Farm a few miles away was having a much less enjoyable time. Graveyard shift good and proper, he thought morosely. Stamping his feet to keep warm and glancing longingly at the bright lights of the farmhouse a couple of fields away, he occasionally shone his torch into the darkness, watching uneasily as the beam pierced the night and the shadows danced before his eyes.

Nearby, the grave lay still, silent and empty. The forensics team that had spent most of the day sifting through the cloying soil in the hope of unearthing further evidence had departed as dusk fell, leaving a single officer to stand guard. Now, the constable, who had taken over the watch from his colleague an hour previously, sat down on a small chair at the edge of the grave, greatcoat pulled tightly around him, cup of coffee from his flask warming his hands, and cursed his luck. Periodically, he glanced down at the luminous hands of his watch, praying for midnight to come around quickly so he could be relieved and flee to the relative warmth of Abbey Road Police Station; even though the heating system had broken down again late that afternoon it would still be more pleasant than the field.

The constable's unease had not been helped by the stories circulating round the station, spread by other officers who had done the duty and reported how eerie the whole experience had proved. This was the constable's first time at the farm and he was not sure if they were being genuine or had been winding him up, knowing it would soon be his turn. A light breeze blew up and the nearby copse rustled and sighed, and as the officer peered into the darkness, he could have sworn he saw a figure move among the shadowy trees. But just for a moment. Then it was gone. If it were ever there. The constable shook his head and tried to ignore the prickling down his spine; it would be a long enough night without spooking himself with fanciful thoughts of spooks, he rebuked himself as he took another sip of coffee.

And yet as he sat, the ghosts of the sixteen dead men seemed to bear down heavily upon him and he felt as if he were being watched. The same sensation John Blizzard had felt. There was indeed something strange about this place, the constable reflected nervously. He was not sure where the words came from but they reverberated in his head. At the going down of the sun, we will remember them, he thought. And in that moment, the constable did just that.

.

· · CHAPTER six · · · ·

HENDERSON RAMAGE WAS a man of few words – and even fewer than that as he sat in the interview room at Abbey Road Police Station. At thirty-eight years old, he was a burly man, the face fleshy and jowly, the nose slightly bent after one drunken altercation too many and the teeth yellowing and crooked. His hair, black and lank, did not look as if it had been washed for a while and he had not shaved, his chin covered in black stubble. Dressed in a tattered green jumper, brown cords covered in mud-flecks and workmen's boots caked in dried soil, he sat glowering across the table at the detectives.

An exasperated Blizzard surveyed him for a moment. Like Eddie Gayle, Henderson Ramage was a thug, but locking him up for a long stretch had proved beyond the many frustrated police officers who had investigated him down the years. Colley now sat eyeing the farmer with ill-disguised contempt. Normally an easygoing man, Colley was as resolute as the next officer when it came to bearing grudges. If proving Ramage's guilt was difficult, establishing a link with Eddie Gayle had proved much easier; police knew they both drank in the Red Lion, a seedy pub on one of the estates in the Western Division and a well-known haunt for Hafton villainy. Surveillance over the years had confirmed that Ramage, Gayle and Garry Horton spent a lot of time in the Red Lion, which had been raided many times by officers, including as part of regular investigations into the city-wide racket in stolen goods. Colley had once quipped that all the pub needed was a sign bearing the words 'Discount Store' because it was possible to obtain everything from cheap knock-off video machines to fake Rolex watches over the bar.

It was one such police raid that had led officers to the stolen equipment stored at Ramage's Burniston farm, which eventually saw him serve his only prison sentence, if briefly. However, subsequent police attempts to prove that Ramage was anything more than a small-time crook, like so many others frequenting The Red Lion, had foundered against a wall of silence. One thing was clear: Henderson Ramage was no farmer and he was well used to fronting out detectives in interviews and this afternoon there was a bullish confidence about his demeanour. Sitting next to him was Edward Elsden, his lawyer, a thin well-dressed man whose smart dark suit, blue silk tie and beautifully coiffured, if greying, hair were in sharp contrast to his scruffy client. The lawyer shuffled slightly in his seat, seemingly a trifle embarrassed at Ramage's unkempt appearance.

'So, Henderson,' said a shirt-sleeved Blizzard wearily, 'let's go through it again, shall we?'

'My client has nothing further to add,' said the lawyer.

'I'm getting sick of this,' sighed the chief inspector and glowered at them both.

It was approaching 2 p.m. and they had been in the interview room for just over an hour. It had been a thoroughly dispiriting experience for Blizzard and Colley. Ramage had been picked up by Detective Inspector Graham Ross who, as he was leaving Green Meadow Farm that morning, noted a battered white pick-up edging its way along the track. Ramage looked for a moment as if he would turn and flee but thought better of it and surrendered himself to police custody without a struggle, telling Ross that he had been away on what he called a business trip but one about which he was unwilling to divulge any details. For the detectives, his shifty reticence only served to heighten their suspicions.

It also continued a frustrating day. Before the two detectives went into the interview, Ross reported that his forensics team had found little of practical use at the graveside.

Adding to Blizzard's irritation was the news from Colley that all attempts to track down a relative of Horst Knoefler had also proved fruitless. He remained a mystery. Further increasing his gloom was Colley's conversation that morning with the tenant farmer at Green Meadow, a fresh-faced pleasant young man called Robin Harvey. Not long out of university when he took over and keen to try out some of his new ideas on agricultural practice, Harvey lived at the farmhouse with his wife and two small children. It was the third time he and the sergeant had spoken in recent days and, although Harvey had been the new tenant at the time Horst Knoefler's body was dumped, Colley's instincts told him ever more strongly that he was not involved. The farmer's shock at what had happened appeared genuine and he seemed truly bewildered, and a little unnerved, by the situation in which he found himself.

Having heard the sergeant announce over a lunchtime sandwich, snatched in Blizzard's office before the interview with Ramage, that Harvey was an innocent bystander, the chief inspector had morosely nodded his agreement. Adding to his frustrations was that intensive inquiries marshalled by Detective Sergeant Dave Tulley, assisted by Fee Ellis, had found nothing to link Eddie Gayle to events at the farm, other than his relationship with Henderson Ramage. And Ramage, a veteran of interviews with various police officers down the years, was not about to provide anything to change that. Nor was his lawyer, to whom Ramage had left most of the talking.

'Frankly, I really cannot see why we need to go over old ground,' said Elsden firmly. 'My client has already stated that this matter does not concern him, Chief Inspector. He is a simple farmer.'

'Simple farmer, my foot!' snorted Blizzard. 'Your client is as bent as they come and we all know it, Mr Elsden. I very much doubt if he spends much time milking cows.'

'That may be so,' nodded Elsden. 'He freely admits to less interest in the profession than his father exhibited. Nevertheless, he does acknowledge his responsibilities in the area and assiduously oversees the running of his farm at Burniston by his manager....'

'Oversees the storage of stolen goods, more like,' said Blizzard, flicking idly through Ramage's file on the desk.

'That was many years ago,' replied the lawyer.

'Maybe. Pray, why was your client visiting Green Meadow Farm when he was apprehended by my officers this morning?'

'My client also takes a keen interest in the running of Green Meadow Farm and visits periodically to check that all is well with Mr Harvey and his family.'

'I'll bet he does,' murmured Blizzard. 'So where has he been over the past few days?'

'As I have already informed you,' said the lawyer smoothly. 'Mr Ramage was out of the area on a business trip.'

'Yes, but he won't sodding well tell us what kind of business will he?' said Blizzard angrily.

'It was legitimate farm business,' said the lawyer evasively. 'Is that not right, Mr Ramage?'

'Yeah,' nodded the farmer. 'It were.'

'So what was it?' asked Blizzard. 'Because I am damned sure he was not out buying cabbage seed.'

'My client does not feel that he wishes to enlighten you as to its nature.'

'Well, I think he was up to no good,' said Blizzard. 'And I think it is too much of a coincidence that he does his vanishing act just as the JCB turfs up the skeletons on his farm.'

'You can be assured that my client's movements are nothing to do with the matters on which we have been speaking.'

'How can I be assured of anything if he won't tell me where he was or what he was doing?' snapped Blizzard.

'Whatever he was doing, my client does not, as far as he can recall, make a habit of dropping dead Germans into holes in his fields, Chief Inspector,' said Elsden with the wisp of a smile. 'It does so scare the livestock and my client cannot see why you are interested in him in relation to the events at Green Meadow Farm.'

'Because he sodding well owns it!' exclaimed Blizzard.

'Anybody could have trespassed on his lands to deposit the unfortunate Mr Knoefler in the grave.'

'Yeah,' said Ramage, nodding his head then flicking back a lock of lank hair that had flopped into his eyes. 'There's some real weirdos around.'

'I'll bear that in mind,' grunted Blizzard.

There was a knock on the door. The chief inspector nodded at Colley and the sergeant walked out into the corridor to find an excited Ross. After a hurried conversation, Colley nodded and returned to the room. Ramage watched him sit down but could read nothing into his non-committal expression. Even the lawyer seemed a touch concerned at his demeanour and Blizzard raised a quizzical eyebrow.

'May I?' asked Colley, nodding at Ramage.

'Be my guest,' said Blizzard, gesturing with his hand.

'Henderson,' said Colley with an affable smile. 'Tell me about the little get-togethers in Hut 23.'

Ramage started slightly and his lawyer looked at his client with a questioning look. Ramage's confusion was but momentary, and within seconds his face had regained its surly expression, but it was enough for the sergeant. His job was to spot chinks in armour.

'I am waiting,' said Colley, an edge to his voice.

'I don't know what you are talking about,' said Ramage evasively, the first time he had looked uncomfortable. 'Honest I don't, Mr Colley.'

'I think perhaps you had better start enlightening us,' said Blizzard, glancing at Colley, uncomfortably aware that he did not know what his sergeant was talking about either. 'All of us.'

'I think there has been more going on at Green Meadow Farm than our Mr Ramage has been letting on,' said the sergeant mysteriously.

'I ain't got nothing to say,' said Ramage.

'Pity,' said Blizzard, still perplexed. 'I'd have loved to hear it.'

'Guv,' said Colley, turning to Blizzard with a mischievous look. 'How do you fancy a little trip out?'

'You're the boss,' said the bemused detective.

'Excellent,' said Colley, standing up with a scrape of the chair. 'Then might I suggest you root out your wellies.'

·· CHAPTER seven ····

THE MEMORIES HUNG thick as cobwebs in Hut 23. And there were plenty of cobwebs in Hut 23. Standing wrinkling his nose in a musty atmosphere created by a mixture of dust and decay, tinged with decades of old engine oil and rotted animal feed, John Blizzard felt the memories strongly even though they were not his. Felt the presence of those who had gone, heard their voices and the song and banter of comradeship. Felt he knew the men who had once lived their lives out within the hut's walls, could see them reading, playing cards or writing letters home in the dim light. It was a strange feeling, as if he was standing to one side, allowed a tantalizing glimpse into the past. As if everything was being played to him on black-and-white film; a film to which he knew only part of the ending. Knew that its participants now lay cold and silent in Peter Reynolds' mortuary at the city hospital.

And always Blizzard felt the man's presence, stronger than before. Knew now why the events at the farm had so disturbed him. Knew what this was all about. Knew who it was about. Had known from the start. Knew why it was happening and why he felt these unfamiliar feelings. It was to do with what the Americans called 'closure'. Blizzard hated the word but had nevertheless felt that same need ever since he realized with a jolt on his previous birthday that he was now nearer fifty than forty. The realization, coupled with the death from cancer of two old school friends over the past two years and laced with his constant awareness that he was much older than Fee, had imbued the chief inspector with a sense of mortality for the first time in his life. It was a strange feeling, a sensation that somehow Fee had given him a reason to live that he did not have before, and had given him a desire to tidy up some loose ends. The dead man was a loose end and, in some way Blizzard could not yet understand, Hafton POW Camp was part of his story.

Not that Blizzard was about to divulge any of his thoughts in public. These were private thoughts and not even Fee, nor Colley, had been privy to them although both had noted the pronounced change in his demeanour since the bodies were found and had asked him about it at different times over the past few days. Even a concerned Arthur Ronald had asked him if he was all right but Blizzard had said nothing, even though he was uncomfortably aware of the change in himself, too. For a man who had long prided himself on a single-minded hard-headed approach to the job, such considerations were disturbing and even frightening. And distracting; and he did not like being distracted.

Such were his thoughts as he stood in Hut 23 and let the feelings wash over him. The hut stood at the furthest end of the camp complex. Reached by beating a muddy path through alder trees and straggly bushes, whose branches had scratched and clawed at the officers' coats and faces, the huts stood silent and empty, some with gaping holes in their sloping roofs, others with windows blackened and cracked. Peering in through one of them as they made their way towards Hut 23, Blizzard could just make out in the gloom crumbling walls with faded murals running along one side. Painted by the German prisoners, they included a rudimentary depiction of a river, the Rhine presumably, and a crude image of poorly drawn cows in green fields. Images of a home which fifteen of the men would never see again. Maybe Horst Knoefler never saw it either. Who could tell?

In the hut next to number 23, Blizzard saw the remnants of piled-up agricultural sacks and a rusted engine motor and another mural on a far wall, a faded image of Hitler, simply fashioned in black chalk yet sinister for all that as the Führer stood with his arm raised in the familiar salute. Blizzard, who had spent part of the weekend reading up about the camps, knew from the library books that such motifs at POW camps had been banned by the British military; found himself wondering at the mural's survival into the 1990s. Peering through the window, letting the others walk on to Hut 23, he felt there was something very real, very now, about the picture. For all it was a long time since the prisoners lived there, the chief inspector felt as if they had never left. Until the previous week, he reminded himself, fifteen of them hadn't.

Thoughts of the murdered man brought Blizzard back to the present as, flanked by Ross and Colley, who was looking at him intently, he now stood in Hut 23, the most ramshackle of the lot. Large gashes in the roof had allowed the rain to pour in over the years with the result that the walls were damp and mould-infested and half the timber floorboards had rotted away, creating a hole six feet long and as much wide. The surviving floor was littered with rotted wood and crumbs of plaster from the wall and the air was thick with damp; Blizzard could almost feel the spores of mould swirling about him. Realizing that the others – Doctor Hamer and Elspeth Roberts were there as well – were looking for him to say something, Blizzard dragged himself from his reverie.

'So how did you find it?' he asked Ross, looking down at the hole.

'Once we had done the graves, we started searching the huts,' explained the forensics chief, pointing to the floor, 'and found this.'

Blizzard crouched and peered down. The area beneath the floorboards had been opened out to create what appeared to be a hiding place beneath the remaining timbers. In one corner, not noticeable unless you looked for them, were a couple of duvets, pillows and the remnants of food wrappers and drink cartons. In another corner, deep in the shadows, was an ashtray with a number of stubbed-out butts and several empty beer bottles. Blizzard recognized the brand of beer immediately. One of his favourites. Brewed in Eastern Europe, if he was not mistaken; 5.4 per cent proof. A nice drop.

'Not exactly the kind of things you would expect to be left

over from a 1940s wartime camp, Graham,' said Blizzard, glancing at Ross.

'Indeed not, sir. We haven't had a chance to do a full examination – thought you would like to see it all first – but it does not take a genius to work out they are modern. I had a glance at one of the bottles. Says the beer was brewed two years ago.'

'So,' breathed Blizzard, 'what is it doing here?'

'Ordinarily, I would have thought it was left by the farmhands,' said Ross, 'but this is the worst of the huts. Huts 1 and 4, for example, have their roofs on and are nice and dry. In fact, we sheltered in them when the rain came on yesterday. If you were going to hunker down and knock back a couple of beers out of sight of the farmhouse, they would be much more comfortable.'

'No, I don't think this is a social thing,' said Blizzard, straightening up and grimacing as his knee emitted a cracking sound. 'No, this is a hiding place sure enough, Graham.'

'I agree,' nodded Ross.

Blizzard looked at Hamer and Roberts.

'Could this be anything to do with your people? Maybe enjoying a quick snifter,' and the chief inspector glanced at the bedding and added slyly, 'or something else while on duty?'

'No,' and Hamer shook his head vehemently. 'Definitely not.'

'Not archaeologists' style, eh?' said Blizzard, looking at Elspeth with a sardonic smile. 'Any explanations, Mrs Roberts?'

Determined not to be shown up this time, she also shook her head.

'No, Chief Inspector,' she said. 'None at all. It is most strange. As your officer here says, Hut 23 is in the worst condition of the lot.'

'How come you did not find the duvet and things?' asked Colley, who had been wandering round the hut, occasionally running a hand along its crumbling wall, but had now returned to stare into the hole.

'I am pretty sure they were not there when I last came in here,' said Roberts, a defensive tone in her voice.

'Which was when?' asked Colley.

'Three months ago.'

'Why so long?'

'This is a large job,' she explained, her body language suggesting she took the sergeant's comment personally. 'Each hut needs to be carefully chronicled and examined.'

'What's to examine?' asked the sergeant.

'When the camp was closed, some of the prisoners left personal possessions behind,' she said. 'We also discovered some fascinating material in one of the offices. That took us several weeks to examine and record. We would not have moved on to a detailed examination of this hut for several weeks.'

'So the stuff was put here sometime in the past three months,' said Blizzard.

'Not necessarily, guv,' said Ross. 'Could have been much longer. The archaeologists could simply have missed it when they first came in here. We only found it because we were looking for things out of the ordinary, remember.'

He paused but could resist the temptation no longer.

'As they say,' he said, starting to laugh, 'police discovered a hole and are looking into it.'

'Your scriptwriter is worse than his,' said Blizzard, gesturing to the grinning Colley.

'Sorry, guv,' chuckled Ross.

'So,' said the chief inspector, allowing the detectives time to enjoy the joke but suddenly serious when he noticed that neither Hamer nor Roberts was laughing. 'We have no idea at all when these things were placed there?'

'Not at this stage,' said Ross, covering up his smile.

'Bloody marvellous,' sighed Blizzard.

'We'll be able to narrow it down when we get the stuff back to the lab. Just a pity the archaeologists cannot be more precise.'

'We have been working as fast as we can,' said Elspeth quickly. 'It's not our fault.'

'It really isn't,' said Hamer, also bridling at the comment.

'For God's sake, don't be so bloody defensive!' exclaimed Blizzard, who had become increasingly irritated by the archaeologists' approach. 'I just need to get some answers! I am not blaming anyone. Yet.'

'Elspeth is just saying,' replied Hamer, slightly mollified. 'That we are working as fast as we can.'

'We have to, given the situation,' added Roberts.

'You mean us?' asked Blizzard sharply.

'Now who's being defensive?' said Hamer.

Blizzard glared at him.

'Your presence does not exactly help, Chief Inspector,' said Roberts, speaking quickly to head off further confrontation. 'But no, actually, I meant Mr Ramage. He has been most insistent right from the start that we finish as quickly as possible.'

'Has he now?' said the chief inspector. 'Why would he do that?'

'He said the terms of his agreement with the housebuilders included a clause that construction work start in early October or else they had the right to withdraw and he would have to repay the money they paid for the land. Our presence has already delayed that by several weeks because the boundary of the planned estate runs across the edge of the camp and we have consistently denied the workmen access to it.'

'He won't like that,' grunted Blizzard.

'Indeed not,' said Hamer. 'Not surprisingly, the housebuilders are beginning to ask him somewhat pointed questions and our presence here has angered him more and more, I fear. There have been several angry exchanges with him. Goodness knows what he thinks about you.'

'I think we already know,' said Blizzard.

'If you want to find out more,' began Roberts, then her voice tailed off and she looked at the floor.

'Go on,' said Blizzard, eyeing her keenly.

'It's nothing,' she mumbled.

'Mrs Roberts,' said the chief inspector with an edge in his

voice, 'I am sure I do not have to remind you that this is a murder investigation.'

'She told me not to say anything,' said Roberts, looking at him unhappily.

'Precisely the reason why you should tell us,' said Blizzard. 'And who, pray, is she?'

'Moira Savage.'

'The chair of the parish council?'

Roberts nodded uncomfortably.

'Where does she fit into this?' asked the chief inspector.

'We have been working together on some research.'

'What kind of research?'

'To do with the camp.'

'What to do with the camp?' asked Blizzard.

'I am saying nothing more,' said Elspeth Roberts uncomfortably. 'Just ask Moira about Henderson Ramage.'

'We will,' said an intrigued chief inspector, realizing he would get nothing more out of the archaeologist on the subject. 'Have you found out anything about our Herr Knoefler?'

'Very little,' said Roberts, grateful for the opportunity to change the subject and fishing a scrap of paper out of her anorak pocket. 'In fact, it is very strange.'

'Strange?'

'Yes. With most soldiers you can normally trace their war records pretty accurately. For instance, we know that Helmut Haller, the man lying next to him in the grave, joined the army in 1941. We know he was decorated twice and captured near Paris as the Allies pushed on through France on their way to Berlin. We even know that he had, at some point, been wounded by a bullet in the shoulder.'

'There is a mark on the skeleton,' nodded Ross. 'Reynolds confirmed it was a bullet wound.'

'And the man on the other side,' continued Robert, 'a Peter Schellinger, was from Dusseldorf. He signed up to a tank regiment in 1942 and was captured on the Dutch border in 1944 when his vehicle ran into a detachment of American troops.'

'How do you know all this?' asked Colley, impressed.

'They're both mentioned in the material we found in the camp office, which matches with papers we found in the reference library.'

'But nothing like that on Knoefler?' asked Blizzard.

'Nothing,' said Roberts, a perplexed expression on her face as she handed the chief inspector the piece of paper, a photocopy of a handwritten camp record. 'Nothing at all.'

Blizzard screwed up his eyes as he tried to decipher the handwritten scrawl snaking its way across the page.

'You're not wrong,' he commented after a few moments. 'It does seem somewhat sparse.'

'It's all we have,' said Roberts. 'Not that it is of much use, as you can see. It states when he arrived at the camp – mid-1944 – and when he left, but nothing more. No personal information. Not even a home address in Germany. And we have been unable to find out anything about where he spent the war or even with which unit he served. I don't understand it, it is as if Horst Knoefler never existed before he came to Hafton.'

'Perhaps, Mrs Roberts,' said Blizzard enigmatically, as he walked out of the hut into the crisp afternoon air, 'he didn't.'

·· CHAPTER eight ····

THE CHILL IN the streets of Hawkwith village late that afternoon was nothing compared to the ice forming in Moira Savage's front room as she sat on the sofa, surveying Blizzard and his sergeant with the kind of expression she might normally reserve for something unpleasant stuck to the bottom of her shoe. In Blizzard's jaundiced view, she typified the village perfectly and also represented the way that the nature of its residents had changed during its recent history.

Hawkwith had existed as a hamlet from the third century, its residents poor farm labourers dependent on the land and the changing seasons. There had, at one point, been a large manor house owned by the local squire but it had been destroyed by fire in the 1600s and had never been rebuilt. Blizzard, with his interest in industrial and social history, knew that Hawkwith had been on the verge of dying and that its salvation was the construction in 1851 of a textiles mill by a local entrepreneur. For thirty-five years, the mill's success meant Hawkwith was a bustling, prosperous and expanding community with more than 200 terraced cottages to house the many new workers.

Then in 1886, thanks in part to a series of ill-advised investments by its new owner, the mill closed, throwing 260 people out of work. Most of them headed into nearby Hafton to find jobs in the city's factories, and the terraces of Hawkwith fell derelict, eventually demolished in the 1920s. For forty years, Hawkwith reverted to type, a small, neglected place, the remaining streets tired, the village green faded, its monument to Queen Victoria crumbling and moss-ridden, the church and pub long since closed, the former demolished, the latter standing empty and dusty at the end of the village and a target for vandalism. Hawkwith become a ghost village as the people moved out.

Then came rebirth, sparked by the renaissance of Hafton when a major aviation plant was sited in the city in the late 1960s. Suddenly, there was no shortage of highly paid executives looking for places to live and Hawkwith found new favour and new life – and new houses. During the years that followed, the village became one of *the* places to live in the area, prosperous and well heeled, all big gates, pergolas and attitude. Moira Savage's home was one of the new ones. The imposing White House, as it was known, was built in 1969, set back from the village green behind a high fence and with ivy creeping across its walls. Everything abòut it, from the statues of lions in the immaculately landscaped front garden to the tasteful timber window frames recycled from much older properties, smacked of wealth. And the two detectives knew as they walked up the drive that wealth usually did not welcome the arrival on its doorstep of the police. What would the neighbours think? Blizzard, who lived in a nearby village, sometimes said the hostility was because of fear that the police would find all the skeletons in the cupboards.

Blizzard and Colley arrived at the house as dusk was falling, ringing the bell and waiting for almost a minute for an answer, almost, they felt as they shifted uncomfortably from one foot to another in the chill porch, as if they were being deliberately forced to wait. Eventually, Moira Savage opened the door and eyed them suspiciously, demanding to see their identification and reading every word written on the warrant cards with minute and deliberate interest as she peered above the rim of her metal-framed spectacles.

Then, reluctantly and with a pained sigh, she ushered them into the house, insisting that they take off their shoes at the front door and leading them into a large living-room, carpeted in cream and lined with high-class ornaments and expensive original paintings. Attempts at small-talk having failed, and the parish council chairwoman having not even offered them a cup of tea, they all sat in silence, the officers perched uncomfortably on the edge of the cream sofa, terrified lest they mark it in some way.

They guessed that Moira Savage, who was dressed in an austere blue blouse buttoned up to the top, over which was a thin white cardigan, and a sharp, black pencil-skirt, was aged in her mid-sixties. The sergeant eyed her with interest as he waited for her response to Blizzard's opening question. She reminded Colley of a hawk, the sergeant smiling inwardly as he realized that he had lapsed back into animal metaphors. He would have to get Jay to start teaching something else to her young pupils. But it was an understandable description, he thought as he viewed the angular features, the sharp nose and the thin lips, all topped off with a beautifully groomed hairstyle with that unmistakable hint of blue. Glancing into those eyes, he could almost see the shutters coming down. Welcome to Tory-ville, thought the sergeant gloomily.

'So, are you going to answer the question?' said Blizzard.

Quite what this pillar of the community was concealing intrigued him. Moira Savage was a well-known and much-respected figure in rural circles, not just chairman of Hawkwith Parish Council but a major mover in the W.I and W.R.V.S and, if some were to be believed, a certainty for the Honours List before long. Having constructed a fearsome reputation for not suffering fools gladly, if at all, she was now giving the very clear impression that the detectives' presence was an unnecessary and unwanted intrusion.

'I will not answer your question unless you tell me who suggested you come here,' said Moira in her cultured voice, the tone overtly hostile as she fixed the detectives with that icy stare again.

Here was a woman who was not going to be intimidated by a couple of police officers, thought Blizzard, and smiled slightly. Just the kind of challenge he relished, particularly given his innate dislike of the blue rinse brigade and his equally strong distaste for pushy women, a viewpoint that had led to the chief inspector being accused of misogyny on more than a few occasions by frustrated female colleagues, particularly in the Human Resources department at head-quarters. But, as Blizzard was at pains to stress to the long suffering Ronald whenever the complaints arrived, that was an HR thing, not a woman thing.

'I told you,' said Blizzard calmly, 'we do not divulge the names of....'

'I imagine it was that Harry Porter,' snorted Savage. 'He's just the kind of busybody that would do that.'

'Please, Mrs Savage,' said Blizzard but she ignored him.

'Or that Betsy Palmer. Oh, yes,' and the laugh was dry and bitter, 'she would just love to see me dragged off in irons to the police station. Step into my grave that one would.'

'An unfortunate turn of phrase,' murmured Blizzard. 'Besides, we are not here to arrest you. We just want....'

'Or that Elspeth Roberts, I always thought she was the type to....'

'Please, Mrs Savage,' said Blizzard, 'all we want is to know about you and Henderson Ramage.'

'I do not wish to discuss that horrible man!' snapped Moira.

'Will you just tell us what happened, for God's sake!' exclaimed Blizzard angrily.

The show of emotion seemed to work and, after staring at him for a moment, something in Moira Savage changed and she nodded meekly. Suddenly, there was an air of vulnerability they had not seen in her before and her features softened.

'Would you gentlemen like a cup of tea?' she sighed. 'This could take some time.'

Ten minutes later, as the detectives sipped from china cups and nibbled at biscuits, the atmosphere in the room had changed completely. Suddenly, Moira Savage looked as if she was ready to unburden herself of a dark secret. Whether it was Blizzard's harsh tone of voice, or the realization that the detectives would find out her secret anyway, Moira Savage had decided to co-operate, a relief to Blizzard, who knew from tough experience that buttoned-up Tory women were the hardest of nuts to crack if they set their minds to it. Give me a mindless thug any day, he thought. You could reason with mindless thugs.

'I apologize if I was a bit short earlier,' said Moira. 'It is just that this affair with the housing development has been somewhat fractious, as you can imagine.'

'But I thought everyone was against it?' asked Colley.

'Not everyone, alas, Sergeant,' said Moira, shaking her head sadly. 'When the idea was proposed four years ago, the parish council had a meeting about it. I have to be frank, I was shocked at what transpired. I expected complete support for my motion to oppose the development but that did not happen.'

'Why not?' asked Blizzard.

'The meeting turned into a heated affair and some harsh things were said. Mr Ramage made some highly personal comments about some of the councillors, myself included. In the end, we voted nine to two to oppose his plan. Mr Ramage stormed out, uttering some profanities as he did. It was all very unpleasant.'

'Is there not a touch of irony here, Mrs Savage?' said Blizzard and he looked around him. 'I mean, this house itself is fairly recent, surely?'

'They were different times, Chief Inspector,' said Moira sharply.

'Of course they were,' said Blizzard sardonically, ignoring her frosty look. 'So tell me, what were your reasons for opposing the plan?'

'The village would become too large,' and she became animated. 'Besides, the last thing we should be doing is taking away our countryside. Hafton is expanding rapidly enough as it is without losing more land around our villages. And the proposal includes the felling of a number of mature trees, which are habitats for wild birds.'

'Then there's the POW camp,' commented Colley.

'Yes, that as well. Although the housing would in theory skirt round the edge of the camp, we all know what happens: give it a year or so and there would be an application to build more. The only way they could expand the estate would be to bulldoze the huts and I have made no secret of the fact that I think the camp should be preserved.'

'Why?' asked the sergeant.

'I am sure it would make a tourist attraction,' said Moira. 'Perhaps we could expand it to celebrate the history of the Hafton Regiment as well.'

'Can't see it,' said Colley with shrug, then on noticing the chief inspector's look, he added, 'Sorry, guv, I just can't.'

'It's an important historical site, David,' said Blizzard. 'There's not many of these places left.'

'I am delighted to hear that you share my beliefs, Chief Inspector,' said Moira gratefully.

'So if this place is so important,' said Colley, 'how come at least two parish councillors backed Ramage's housing plan?'

'They were the younger ones,' she said with a smile which seemed to suggest that she tolerated their existence. 'They said that it was time the village moved into the twentieth century, said we needed some new blood. Clearly, they do not realize that until people like me and Brian arrived, this village was dying.'

'Brian?' asked the sergeant.

'My husband.'

'So I guess this has not been good for community spirit,' said Blizzard, conscious of the way tensions always ebbed and flowed in the village where he lived; ebbed and flowed in every small community.

'It has not, Chief Inspector,' replied Moira sadly. 'Although I have to say that the issue merely brought to the surface tensions that had been there for some time.'

'I can see that,' nodded Blizzard. 'But how does all of this impact on our inquiry, Mrs Savage?'

'I imagine whoever suggested you talk to me was referring to the threats, Chief Inspector.'

'Threats?' asked Blizzard, eyes gleaming, 'from Henderson Ramage?'

'Well, I say threats, maybe that is putting it a touch dramatically.'

'What happened?'

'I have always spoken out against the housing plan and I

sent a strongly worded submission to the Government inspector to consider at his inquiry. A somewhat short man called Baldridge. Ill-fitting suit. Didn't clean his teeth very well. You can tell a lot about people by the way they clean their teeth.'

'I'll bear that in mind,' said Blizzard.

'Anyway, someone did not like what I said because,' and she paused, surprising them as her self-contained façade crumbled, 'certain unpleasant things have happened.'

'Things?' asked Blizzard.

'Yes, one week a pick-up truck was parked across our drive for two or three days running, blocking us in. We could not get the car out and it caused a lot of problems. My husband attends a lot of meetings. He had to use,' and she paused for a moment as if about to reveal a terrible and sordid secret, 'taxis.'

'How terrible,' murmured Blizzard, earning himself a stern look over her spectacles. 'What is the world coming to?'

'And you believe it was Mr Ramage's truck?' asked Colley quickly, trying to avoid one of Blizzard's rows if at all possible.

'Oh, I know it was,' she nodded. 'I have seen him driving the filthy thing up to the farm.'

'Anything else happen?'

'Yes, one day, a Wednesday I think it was, I noticed two rather burly men standing on the other side of the green,' and she gestured through the window into the gathering gloom, 'by the Post Office. Just staring at the house. They did not do anything but the message was clear. Mr Ramage was trying to intimidate me.'

'And did it work?' asked Colley, doubtful that anything could intimidate this indomitable woman.

'It was certainly disturbing,' she said, voice trembling slightly. 'As were the phone calls.'

'Phone calls?' said Blizzard.

'Yes, late at night. They would start whenever I said something in public about the housing plan and go on for several weeks. Then they would stop. Then I would say something else and they would start again.'

'How long has this been going on?' asked Blizzard.

'More than three years.'

'Jesus,' said the chief inspector, struck yet again by how terrible things could happen behind well-constructed façades. 'Do you know who the phone calls were from?'

'Nothing is ever said but I knew. It's Henderson Ramage. He is a truly horrible man. It has all,' and she looked down at the floor, 'caused tensions within our marriage, I am afraid.'

'Tensions?'

'Yes. Last year, a couple of my husband's clients received letters saying that he was under investigation by the police for fraud.'

'What does he do for a living?' asked the sergeant.

'He owns Savage's land agents over in Burniston. The letters suggested that he had been misappropriating funds raised during the sale of land.'

'And I take it he was not under investigation?' asked Blizzard.

'Of course not,' said Moira, clearly appalled that he should even consider the suggestion. 'But it still caused Brian a lot of trouble. At least two clients that I know of switched to another firm. After that, my husband said he wanted me to drop my opposition to the housing plan. Said it was costing us money. That's Brian all over.'

'But you did not do as your husband said?' asked Blizzard.

'I can't do that, Chief Inspector,' said Moira. 'I love my husband but to give up on this issue would not be right. Not after so long fighting it.'

'Surely you have made your point, though,' said Colley. 'The planning inspector gave permission. That's the end of it, isn't it?'

'I cannot just let it end at that,' and she looked more animated than she had been throughout the entire interview. 'The housing estate will destroy the character of this village and it is my duty as parish council chairwoman to make my views known.'

'So, when was the last incident?' asked Colley.

'There had not been one for six or seven weeks, then,' and

she walked over to an antique bureau in the corner of the room and took out a piece of paper. 'This.'

She handed the paper over to the sergeant. Decorated with a crudely drawn gravestone, it read, 'You will lie where they lay if you do not shut up. RIP Miora', in capital letters clipped from a newspaper. Colley noted the misspelling of the name for future reference.

'When did this arrive?' asked the sergeant, handing it to Blizzard.

'The day the news broke about the discovery of the bodies,' she said. 'I told some people in the shop that perhaps the area could be designated an official war grave; I said that if that happened, we might be able to block the housing development.'

'Who did you say this to?' asked the chief inspector. 'Who was in the shop?'

'It doesn't really matter,' she shrugged. 'Word goes round villages like this in minutes. I might as well have put a poster on the church notice-board.'

'And have you followed up the idea?' asked Colley.

'Yes, I went to see Elspeth Roberts. I know her quite well now and she has been very supportive of my efforts to preserve the camp. I wanted to see if the idea was feasible. The note,' and she gestured to the piece of paper in Blizzard's hand, 'was on the mat when I got back home.'

'And who do you think sent it?' asked the chief inspector.

'Do you need to ask?' she said.

'Humour me.'

'I think someone told Henderson Ramage about my comments,' she said, adding quickly, 'but I have no proof that he is behind all this.'

'It's a remarkable coincidence if he isn't,' remarked Blizzard. 'From what we hear, he is indeed increasingly angry at all the delays on the site.'

'He's worried that the housing company will pull out,' nodded Moira. 'Getting them to do that is the main aim of our campaign now that the plan has been given official sanction by that nasty little inspector.'

'Why on earth did you not come to the police about this when it all started?' asked Blizzard in exasperation, glancing down at the note.

'What could you have done?'

'We would have investigated it.'

'Chief Inspector,' said Moira, voice stronger now, composure fully restored. 'I am a great supporter of the work the police do but, on this occasion, I fail to see what contacting you would have achieved.'

'Mrs Savage,' said Blizzard earnestly. 'People like Henderson Ramage rely on victims not contacting the police. You should have come to see us.'

'Yes, well there was a reason that I didn't,' and the vulnerability was back again as she turned haunted eyes on the detectives.

'Which was?' asked Blizzard.

'I am frightened, Mr Blizzard,' and she seemed close to tears. 'I know that Henderson Ramage is an unpleasant man and, if he heard that I had called the police in, who knows what he might have done next? It could only have made things worse.'

'Well, we're in now,' said the chief inspector. 'Like it or not.'

'Yes,' she said unhappily, 'I imagine you are.'

A few minutes later, the officers were walking to the car when Blizzard's mobile phone rang. He listened for a few moments, watched by Colley, then punched the air.

'Yes,' he breathed. 'Oh, yes.'

'You on a promise?' asked Colley.

'No, even better than that,' said Blizzard excitedly. 'That was my contact at the city council; the rail company has agreed to sell them Tenby Street station so we can turn it into a museum.'

'And am I pleased about this?' asked Colley, thinking of the dilapidated building.

'It's marvellous,' said Blizzard.

'Yeah,' said Colley, who had never understood the chief inspector's passion for railways, 'whatever. Personally, I would have thought being on a promise from young Fee was more exciting. Just think of those black trousers.'

'Well that just shows you what....' began Blizzard, then paused and looked at his sergeant thoughtfully. 'No, actually you're right, maybe I'll swing round her place later.'

'That's my boy,' said Colley.

·· CHAPTER nine ····

'PERHAPS THEY AREN'T going to come,' said Blizzard into the darkness.

'They'll come,' replied Fee Ellis from the back seat of the car, but her voice did not sound as confident as earlier in the evening.

'I hope so,' grunted Colley, shifting uncomfortably in the front passenger seat next to Blizzard. 'I'm missing the eighteenth repeat of *Prisoner Cell Block H* for this.'

Ellis leaned forward and cuffed him affectionately about the head.

As for Blizzard, he said, 'Given the time we've had of it with the POW camp, it would be very appropriate viewing.'

'Even with the wobbly sets,' replied Colley.

It was midnight, a week after the interview with Moira Savage, and the three officers had been sitting in Blizzard's ageing Ford Granada, parked in the shadows at Hafton's ferry terminal, for the best part of two hours. Stretching out in front of them, the quayside was virtually deserted, illuminated by harsh spotlights, the tarmac glistening from the drizzle that had fallen steadily throughout the evening. A hundred metres to the Granada's right was the ugly concrete control tower and they could see through the top-floor windows a couple of figures moving about in the half-light as they scanned the river for the approach of the ferry.

Beyond the tower, the officers could just make out the dark waters of the River Haft and the glinting reflections of the sprawling chemical complex on the south side, pinpricks of light on a winter's night. To the officers' left, over towards the main road into Hafton city centre, and on a slight rise, was the ferry terminal car park but there were only a few vehicles waiting, barely visible through the border of bedraggled bushes, their occupants concealed by the shadows thrown by the wan street lamps. All in all, it made for a damp and dismal sight.

But the reason the officers were there was far from dismal, promising a glittering prize at the end of the night. A tip-off from one of Ellis's informants had led to a hurriedly-organized joint police and Customs operation that promised to deal a major blow against one of the city's most troubling new crime trends. Over recent months, officers had noticed a growing number of Eastern European men hanging around street corners in bedsit-land, unkempt, thin and emaciated individuals, dressed in ill-fitting jeans and T-shirts and giving the appearance of not having washed for days. That they were illegal immigrants was easy to prove, brought over to Britain with no jobs to go to and no visible means of support. There was also growing evidence that they were largely responsible for the worrying, rising tide of street robberies in the city, seventeen in six weeks alone, one of which saw an elderly woman hospitalized after she was knocked to the ground when her handbag was snatched.

Detectives surmised that the robbers were either stealing to survive, or to order for the gang who had smuggled them into Britain. Arthur Ronald had made it clear that he wanted the situation brought back under control; no senior officer liked to see a spike in crime figures and the chief constable had already been asking pointed questions, as had the local evening newspaper. The superintendent tasked Blizzard with overseeing the initiative and the chief inspector ordered Detective Inspector Chris Ramsey to establish a squad, two detectives, two uniformed officers, under the command of a uniformed sergeant. They had had made significant inroads, thirteen offenders having been apprehended already, and the team was eagerly awaiting the first of the court cases. But for all the success, the problems continued and it was clear that more and more of the Eastern Europeans were arriving in

Hafton. The team needed to know who was bringing them in because action was needed to stem the tide.

Tide was the word because the tip-off that brought Blizzard and his officers to the ferry terminal came from a man who worked on the docks and who had seemed truly terrified when he had passed the information on to Ellis. They had met in a local park the day before. According to the man, who had known the constable when she worked on the east side of the city, a lorry was due to travel over on the last ferry that night, a Wednesday, ostensibly carrying a cargo of fruit bound for the local indoor market but really trans-porting a group of illegal immigrants being smuggled into the UK from the Continent by an organized gang. Attempts by Ellis to elicit the organizer's identity had been met with strenuous shakes of the head from the informant, amid dark hints that he had already placed his life in danger. These were major league criminals, he had warned before vanishing into the shadows.

It was more than enough to tantalize Ronald and Blizzard and they moved quickly. Protocol in such situations dictated that Customs take the lead, but Ronald had a good relation-ship with his counterpart at the ferry terminal – Gerry Hope was a former police sergeant – and they quickly agreed to mount a joint operation. So now, dotted around the deserted terminal, were ten Customs officers as well as cars containing police. Parked further back, concealed behind sheds next to the main road entrance, were the firearms and tactical support units to be deployed in case of emergency. Ronald and Blizzard had insisted they be there: in one of the incidents, a street robber had produced a handgun when challenged by a member of the public.

During their long vigil in the car, Blizzard had hardly said a word even though Colley and Ellis had made occasional attempts to start conversations. Although seemingly wrapped up in his own thoughts, Blizzard welcomed the action because in the week after the gathering in Hut 23, progress had been frustratingly slow on the Knoefler inquiry and he was coming under pressure from Ronald to produce a breakthrough.

Blizzard knew that really meant Ronald was under pressure from the chief constable to produce a breakthrough. But, pressure or not, nothing was forthcoming. Forensic examinations had revealed several sets of fingerprints on the beer bottles found in the hut, as well as traces of saliva on the cigarette butts, but none of them matched anyone known to Hafton police. Circulation of their details to other forces and Interpol had revealed nothing either; Blizzard was as far from identifying the interlopers as ever, although the thought that Hut 23 was somehow linked to the illegal people trafficking had grown in his mind ever since Ellis had reported her informant's words.

Adding to his frustrations, all attempts to track down anyone who knew Horst Knoefler had failed, even though police had named him at a press conference and revealed everything they knew about his life. Which was not much. In the days that followed, Blizzard had elaborated little on his thoughts when questioned by Ronald except to stick resolutely to his view that the German was a man who had wanted to disappear; whether his desire to disappear and his murder were linked or just coincidence remained to be established.

With Henderson Ramage released without charge, the frustrations had continued even further with Eddie Gayle. Tulley and Ellis had been watching the landlord for several days, but quickly convinced themselves that Gayle realized he was being trailed. Accordingly, he had been keeping his nose clean, steering clear of any of his criminal associates and retiring early to bed each night. And there had been no sign of Garry Horton. Released from prison three weeks previously, he had kept an equally low profile and had not been seen in any of his usual haunts. It had all been very frustrating so Blizzard was praying that the operation at the terminal produced something to deflect the questions away from him. At least for a day or two.

'What's that?' asked Colley, as he scanned the river and noticed a glow in the distance.

'That,' said Blizzard as the gigantic column of light edged

its way round a bend in the river, 'is the ferry, my boy. So, Fee, you still reckon our little friends are on board?'

'My informant seemed pretty convinced,' she nodded.

'I just hope we don't open it to reveal a truck-load of bananas,' grunted the chief inspector.

The radio crackled. It was Ronald, who was sitting in another car parked on the other side of the quayside, Gerry Hope alongside him. The men, who had worked together over on the Eastern side when Hope was a police officer, had been yarning about the old days and had not, at first, noticed the ferry come into view.

'You see it?' said a disembodied voice.

'We've got it, Arthur,' said Blizzard, watching as the ferry turned towards the terminal.

'Remember, let the Customs boys take the lead. They'll watch the lorry off the ferry and do what appears to be a routine search. We don't want to spook anyone. Once they find the illegals, we move in.'

'You can hold our coats,' they heard Hope say in the background.

'And your handbags,' grunted Blizzard.

They heard Hope's laughter over the airwaves. A few minutes later, the ferry was nudging its way into the terminal and the officers could see that for all its blazing lights, there were very few people on board. After it docked, they watched the small number of pedestrians straggle their way down the gangplank with their bags, then turned their attention to the vehicle bay door that was being slowly lowered. A few cars drove down the ramp and across the quayside followed by a couple of lorries, the second of which caught the officer's attention immediately. It was a large blue artic with a large picture of a banana and red German lettering on its mud-spattered side.

'Oh, yes, we have no bananas,' said Colley.

They watched the vehicle slowly rumble its way down the ramp. Gerry Hope had already checked with the captain of the ferry and confirmed that the vehicle had been registered in Hamburg and the detectives watched with interest as it edged out on to the tarmac and started moving towards them. Two of Hope's officers moved in calmly, one of them holding up a hand and instructing the vehicle to draw to a halt. The detectives could see the driver lean out of his cab window and a short conversation ensued after which he jumped down, revealing himself as a tall, lanky man with straggly brown hair. He was dressed in a red and white checked lumberjack's shirt, jeans and scuffed brown boots.

'Recognize him?' asked Blizzard.

'Difficult to see from here,' murmured Colley, screwing up his eyes.

The driver took the Customs officer round to the back of the lorry and began to unlock the rear door. All seemed calm then it all happened very quickly. Suddenly, the driver snapped out a hand and caught the Customs man full in the face, sending him crashing backwards to sprawl on the tarmac. The lorry driver produced a gun and pointed it at the Customs woman, who backed off, holding her hands up.

'Firearms go, go!' roared Blizzard into the radio and turned the key in the ignition, slamming the Granada into gear.

With a squeal of tyres, the car shot from the shadows – other vehicles did the same from the other side of the quay-side – and veered across the tarmac to where the lorry driver had leapt back into his cab, brandishing his weapon at the two Customs officers and shouting at them to keep back. With a guttural roar, the lorry engine sputtered into life and the artic set off with a clashing of gears, rocking and rolling as the driver jammed his foot down on the accelerator. As Blizzard's car sped into the lorry's path, a hand emerged from the cab window and to their horror the detectives could see that the artic driver was pointing the gun in their direction.

'Get down!' yelled Blizzard and turned the wheel franti-cally, sending the car into a wheel-spin as the lorry thundered past them.

Colley was gripping on to the dashboard as the car swerved but Ellis, who was not wearing a seatbelt, was hurled violently sideways, cracking her head against the window and slumping back on to the seat. Blizzard heard her give a grunt of pain but did not have time to react, instead concentrating on zig-zagging behind the lorry that was picking up speed as it thundered towards the terminal entrance, pursued by several other cars. Blizzard revved the engine and with its tyres squealing, brought the Granada alongside the artic. The driver leaned out and pointed the weapon again. This time, there was a crack and the whine of the bullet as it whistled over their heads and, with a dull smack, embedded itself in a corrugated-iron storage shed.

From the entrance of the terminal, a white car appeared, moving at great speed. It juddered to a halt in the lorry's path, and two officers in full flak gear leapt out and crouched, training their weapons on the approaching artic. For a second it appeared as if the lorry would slam into the police car then it veered off to the right, clipping a line of rubbish bins and sending them scattering across the tarmac. In the careering Granada ten metres behind, the detectives could see that the lorry driver was desperately battling to regain control of the articulated vehicle but, as he steered it once more towards the terminal exit, more armed officers appeared in his path. A single shot from a police weapon rang out, shattering the windscreen and the lorry veered wildly, the driver slumped across the steering wheel. The squealing artic ploughed into the grassy bank just beneath the car park, sending plumes of soil billowing into the air. For a second or two, it teetered on two wheels then all four wheels returned to earth with a crash, the vehicle shook violently and it was over.

By now, officers were converging from all sides, some in cars, some running, all coming to a halt as the firearms team edged closer, weapons at the ready. One of the team held up a hand to keep the others back while a colleague ripped open the cab door and trained his gun on the driver.

'Someone call an ambulance!' he shouted.

Other firearm officers edged round to the back of the lorry. A dazed Fee Ellis staggered out of the Granada and joined the other officers, leaning on Colley's arm as she tried desperately to regain her bearings yet eager to see if her informant's tip-off was correct. One of the firearms officers tentatively lowered the rear door of the artic. As his torch beam illuminated the inside, everyone could see, badly shaken after the collision, a dozen or so men cowering behind fruit crates. They were holding their hands up but the cautious firearms officers kept their weapons trained on them as they were led out one by one. Searches revealed none of the stowaways were armed and the firearms inspector nodded at Ronald.

'All yours, gents,' he said.

'Thank you, Barry,' said the superintendent.

'Well done, Fee, top notch tip-off,' said Colley, slapping her on the back.

'Ow,' she winced.

'You OK?' asked the sergeant.

'Yes, just give me a moment or two,' she said weakly.

Followed by Blizzard and Hope, the superintendent approached the group of men who were now standing next to the battered lorry, shivering in the chill night air and eyeing the police nervously. As the officers surveyed the men, all of whom were desperately thin and dressed in T-shirts and jeans, Blizzard noticed one who was different. Standing apart from the main group, he was an older man, maybe in his seventies, dressed in a black jumper and brown trousers and altogether more composed than his wide-eyed travelling companions. Before Blizzard had time to consider the point further, one of the younger stowaways stepped forward, produced a scrap of paper from his breast pocket, glanced down then looked at Arthur Ronald.

'Mr Garree Horton?' he asked hopefully in broken English.

Blizzard beamed.

·· CHAPTER ten ····

'I AM DELIGHTED you have agreed to talk to us,' said John Blizzard. 'You are the first person we have met who knows what Horst Knoefler is like.'

'Was like,' corrected Edward Cranmer. 'I have not seen him for fifty years.'

It was the morning after the events at the terminal and, although Abbey Road Police had been swarming with police and Customs officers since early on, none of the apprehended men had said anything. Having gratefully left Ronald to deal with the aftermath, Blizzard and Colley were sitting in a neat little living-room in one of the terraced houses a matter of minutes from the city centre. The house was situated just off a main road but although outside there was the usual noise and clatter of life, car engines revving, horns honking and buses groaning, the room was quiet, the only noises the gentle hiss of the gas fire and the ticking of a small clock on the mantlepiece.

Houseowner Edward Cranmer sat on the pale blue sofa, composed, calm, hands held together on his lap, and waiting for the next comment from the chief inspector. Blizzard was intrigued by him; up until now, Horst Knoefler had been an ephemeral person, a skeleton in a mortuary, a fleeting name scrawled on a prison camp register. Now, Cranmer could, as it were, put flesh on the bones and cast some light on the life of the man whose killer the detectives sought. And, boy, how they needed some light. So far, it had felt like picking their way through pitch darkness.

Cranmer was eighty-three, a thin, lanky man who exuded a

sense of fitness despite his advanced years. Like his house, he was neat and tidy. His thinning white hair was combed across his head, the strands, not one of which was out of place, allowing the detectives glimpses of mottling on the top of the skull, and he had shaved fastidiously, as he did every day, his slightly pointed chin smooth and stubble-free. He was wearing dark brown suit-trousers, a faded white shirt and a pale brown cardigan. The room mirrored his pride in appearance. The small table in the window was polished and shiny, the flowers fresh and watered, the standard lamp in the corner topped with a dust-free shade, the two armchairs and the sofa vigorously brushed. Blizzard sat in one of the armchairs, Colley in another, and perched on the sofa, next to Cranmer, was Elspeth Roberts, looking as nervous as ever. She it was who had insisted that Cranmer call the police that morning and the detectives were struck by the way she kept cropping up in their inquiries.

There was another man in the room. Leaning against the wall by the door and saying nothing, Tommy Cranmer, the old man's son, was a tall, muscular, well-built individual with strong features and a slightly snub nose. Judging his age was difficult, thought the sergeant. Late forties, early fifties, maybe. But he could not be sure. Whatever his age, the man clearly looked after himself. Ex-army, perhaps, mused Colley. And a bodybuilder, maybe. Or, more likely given the misshapen nose and his blue and yellow hooped shirt, a rugby player like the sergeant. Front row, mused Colley, none of them had straight noses.

For all his formidable appearance, Tommy seemed affable enough. Although it was not his house, he welcomed the detectives and busied himself in the kitchen, making tea that was served in green flower-patterned tea-cups and bringing in a plate of biscuits. Surreal really, thought Colley, as he reached for his cup, here they were enjoying tea and biscuits when they were about to discuss the horrible death of a man. Such was the job, he thought, biting into a digestive and realizing that in the rush of the morning, the detectives had forgotten to grab their customary bacon butty from the café down the road from the police station.

'I am not sure I can be of much assistance to you,' said Cranmer.

'You may know something that we don't,' said Blizzard. 'Frankly, that would not be difficult. Horst Knoefler is a real mystery man.'

'That's what I told him,' said Elspeth Roberts.

'How do you two know each other?' asked Colley, looking at her.

'I suddenly remembered that we talked right at the start of our excavations,' she said.

Blizzard raised a quizzical eyebrow.

'I wanted to see what the old place looked like after all these years,' explained Edward, his voice firm and confident, belying his years. 'It was not possible to visit before. In fact, I tried once a couple of years ago but the farmer told me to go away. A somewhat coarse man. Threatened to shoot me if I did not get off his land.'

'Sounds just like Henderson Ramage,' grunted Blizzard.

'That was the name,' nodded the old man. 'Anyway, when I read in the paper that the archaeologists had moved in, I asked if I could go with them one day.'

He smiled at Elspeth Roberts. 'They were kind enough to let me do so.'

'But why would you want to?' asked Blizzard.

'I learned a couple of years ago that I have heart problems, Chief Inspector,' said Cranmer. 'My doctor believes I may not last much longer and there are some things I want to do before I die.'

'But why the camp, of all places?'

'There is something about it, Chief Inspector,' said Cranmer. 'Such an atmospheric place. It draws you back. It has a sense of so many memories, don't you think?'

'It does indeed,' nodded Blizzard.

'And some of those memories are mine,' added the old man.

'You were a guard at the camp, I think?' asked Blizzard.

'Yes, I was.'

'How come you ended up there?'

'I started off the war as a sergeant in the Hafton Regiment. Such a sad day when they disbanded it a few years ago.'

'So what happened?' asked the chief inspector.

'It was such a long time ago,' said Cranmer, eyes adopting a far-away expression. 'Such a long time – and yet it is as if it happened only yesterday. I do not know if you are aware of this but The Haftons were one of the first British regiments ashore on D-Day. At Juno.'

Juno. One word, so many memories. Cranmer paused for a moment, transported back to the chaotic scenes on the beach, hearing again the explosions, the incessant rattle of machine guns and the cries of fallen comrades ringing in his ears, and seeing the scenes of carnage re-enacted in front of his eyes as if they were a film, a film which had been replayed time and time again in his quiet moments down the years.

'Terrible. Truly terrible,' he whispered at length, shaking his head and looking at the detectives with dark eyes. 'Such carnage. You can have no idea what it was like. No one can imagine it unless they were there.'

The detectives waited in respectful silence and after a few seconds, Cranmer recovered himself and continued with his story.

'My war did not last long after the landings,' he said. 'I was wounded near Caen.'

And he was back in the theatre of war again. The Allies were pushing inland through France after the successful D-Day landings and the German Army was starting to fall back. For the first time, the men of the Hafton Regiment could sense victory as they began the race for Berlin. Perhaps such a euphoric feeling after so many long years of despair bred complacency in the small group of infantrymen advancing down a country lane a few miles from the city of Caen, rifles cradled in their arms. Whatever the reason, within a few chaotic moments, four of them lay dead.

It was a bright, sunlit morning, the kind of morning when it was a joy to be alive, particularly after the slaughter on Juno Beach a few days before. Sensing no danger, they were chatting, cracking jokes, not hiding their presence. Perhaps they let their guard down and missed something, perhaps they were just unlucky. Whatever the reason, a rustling in nearby trees and a voice changed everything. An order. Barked. Harsh. The rat-rat-rat of the machine gun, spraying death along the lane, cutting down the men as they ran desperately for cover behind the nearby wall. Regrouping, a brief fire-fight, then the loud explosion as a grenade landed in the Germans' machine-gun nest. Fire, body parts, screams. Then silence and the surviving British soldiers advancing slowly along the lane, guns at the ready, peering nervously through the wafting smoke and seeing the ripped and twisted bodies of the Germans. All dead. Young men just like themselves. A few more widows, a few more orphans. There were British orphans and widows as well because when the men turned back they saw bloodstained green uniforms lying in the road.

'We lost four men that day,' said Cranmer, voice trembling slightly. 'Good men.'

He paused for a moment and his son walked over and placed an arm around the old man's shoulder. Colley watched with interest. Never judge a book by its cover, he thought as he watched this bull of a man comforting his father with such tenderness. Cranmer patted Tommy's hand appreciatively, looked up at his son and nodded, then returned his gaze to the detectives.

'I'm sorry,' the pensioner said, his face clouded. 'It's just that they were friends, Chief Inspector. I went to school with three of them – and I was born on the same day as Reggie Rostron. Our mums were in neighbouring beds down the infirmary.'

Cranmer shook his head.

'I saw all four of them die that day,' he said quietly. 'Absolutely senseless.'

'And yourself?' asked Blizzard.

'I took a bullet,' said Cranmer, patting his right shoulder and allowing himself a wry smile. 'Still gives me gyp, particularly in winter. Had to give up mountaineering last year. Pity, I'd planned to do K2.'

The detectives smiled at the quip. Tommy chuckled, relieved that his father had regained some of his spirits.

'Then what happened?' asked Blizzard.

'I was taken to the nearest field hospital. They patched me up and shipped me back home to Hafton. Moved back in with my parents, God bless them.'

'He's not telling it all,' said Tommy. 'Typical Dad. He got mentioned in dispatches for what he did that day.'

'Oh, Tommy, it was nothing....' began the old man.

'It's important, Dad,' insisted Tommy and looked at the detectives. 'I served with the Haftons and I know what Dad did. It's in the regimental history. When the German machine gun opened up, one of Dad's men fell, hit in the leg, and Dad carried him to safety under fire. That's how he got the bullet in his shoulder. If he had not done what he did, that soldier would have been killed.'

'Geordie would have done the same for me,' said the old man, looking down at the floor in embarrassment.

'You should be proud of what you did, Mr Cranmer,' said Blizzard, the image of the face in the faded black-and-white picture coming to mind again. 'You should always be proud of it.'

'Thank you,' said Cranmer, clearly affected by the chief inspector's words. 'Thank you.'

'So how come you ended up at the camp?' asked Colley.

'My comrades were dying on the frontline,' said Cranmer softly. 'There was no way I could sit back and do nothing. I tried to get back out to France but the doctors said my arm was too badly damaged so I volunteered to be a guard at Hafton POW Camp instead. At least I was doing something useful.'

'What kind of a place was it?' asked Blizzard.

'Like all the others, I suppose,' shrugged Cranmer. 'There were about 600 German prisoners there when I started. Most of them were happy their war had ended. They had lost the stomach for a fight, Chief Inspector. They knew the game was up. We could see it in their eyes. If you ask me, I'm not sure a lot of the ones in the camp wanted to fight in the first place. They were quite content to see out the war at Hafton. Well, most of them, anyway.'

'Most?' asked Blizzard, recalling the crude image of Hitler that he had seen scrawled on the hut wall.

'Yes, one or two who still carried the flag, rabble-rousers, Nazis, still believed that Hitler would triumph,' and he shook his head in disbelief. 'It was obvious to everyone but them that the war was over but they just didn't get the message.'

'What happened to them?' asked Colley.

'They're not the ones in those graves if that's what you're thinking,' replied Cranmer. '*We* didn't do that kind of thing.'

'We know that,' said Colley. 'So, what did happen to the awkward prisoners?'

'They were shipped off to other camps.'

'There were special high-security camps for their type,' said Blizzard, recalling his recent reading on the subject. 'The idea was to keep them away from the rest of the prisoners, stop them fermenting trouble.'

'We never saw them again,' nodded Cranmer.

'Was Knoefler one of the troublemakers?' asked Blizzard.

'Him?' and Cranmer shook his head. 'No, not him. Good as gold, was Horst. Most of them were.'

'How come you remember him?' asked Colley. 'I mean, like you said, there were hundreds of them there.'

'Demon chess player,' smiled Cranmer. 'I thought I was good but Horst, he was really something. We used to play a lot and I think I only beat him three times. He used to do this devilish move with his bishops and a rook. Got me every time.'

'So, what was he like?' asked Colley. 'I mean, as a man?'

'Quiet chap. Very courteous even though we were on opposing sides. We got on OK. It was the same with most of the prisoners.'

'We are struggling to find out what happened to Horst before he came to the camp. Any ideas where he had been fighting?' asked Colley.

'He never talked about any of that,' said Cranmer. 'I never asked him and he never asked me. Didn't seem to matter. Both our wars were over.'

'Did anything happen at the camp that might explain why he was killed?' asked the chief inspector.

'Not that I can recall,' and Cranmer shook his head. 'To be honest, life was all very uneventful, Chief Inspector. Most of them just wanted the war to end and be shipped home to their families. It was not in their interest to cause trouble.'

'And what about before the war? Do you know anything about his life then?'

'Not much,' said Cranmer. 'I think he said he came from Hamburg. Funny, really, whenever I asked him, he changed the subject.'

'Any idea why?' asked Colley.

'Well, there was one thing,' said the old man cautiously.

'Go on,' replied Blizzard as Cranmer paused for a moment.

'Well, you should not speak ill of the dead,' said Cranmer, lowering his voice a touch, almost as if the German could hear him from beyond the grave, 'but I think Horst was a bit of a spiv in civvy street.'

'Spiv?'

'Yes. You name it, he could get it when he was in the camp,' and Cranmer chuckled. 'Horst could get hold of the kind of chocolate I hadn't seen for years. God knows where he got it from. Anyway, one night, just a few weeks before the war ended, we were sitting outside his hut, sharing a cigarette after a game of chess – he'd got the ciggies as well as I recall – and he told me he might be in trouble when he went home.'

'Did he say why?' asked Blizzard.

'Said he was wanted by the police.'

'Now that is interesting,' breathed the chief inspector. 'Did he say why they were after him?'

'Said he had been selling stuff on the black market. Said he had a lot to be grateful to Adolf Hitler for.'

'What do you think he meant by that?' asked Colley.

'He gave the impression that when war broke out, he was about to be arrested. Joining the army was his way out. When he saw how interested I was in his story, he clammed up. Told me I must not say anything to anyone. It was the only time I saw him looked worried.'

'And did you say anything?'

'No, I didn't.'

'Not even to a commanding officer?' said Blizzard, raising an eyebrow. 'Or the local police?'

'Do you think the police would have been interested in some German black market racketeer with a neat line in ciggies and bars of chocolate?'

'Plenty of Hafton spivs to worry about,' said Colley.

'Exactly,' said Cranmer. 'Although you would know more about that than I would. Anyway, all I know is that we never spoke of it again.'

'Did you see Horst after the war?' asked Colley.

'No,' and the old man shook his head again. 'When it was all over, we went our separate ways. The camp stayed open for a few months after the end of the war but I left and got a job at a local engineering factory. I never went back.'

'Any idea what happened to Horst when he was released?' asked Blizzard.

'None, I am afraid.'

'You never met up?'

'No. If the truth be told, I felt guilty about how friendly we had been with the POWs. I felt I had let down the lads that died that day near Caen. And all the others. So when the war finished, so did our relationship.'

'But did you not come to think of him as a friend?' asked Colley. 'At least in some way?'

'No,' said the old man, eyes suddenly burning bright, 'not a friend, Sergeant. A human being, yes, but not a friend. It's never really over, you see.'

'It certainly isn't,' murmured Blizzard.

'So how come you did not come forward when we named Horst Knoefler at the press conference?' asked Colley.

'Couldn't see the point, really,' shrugged Cranmer. 'It was fifty years ago and I haven't seen him since the day I left the camp. What use could I be? It was Elspeth here that suggested I contact you.'

'I thought he might know something of use,' she said. 'It took me a while to track his address down. I hope I did the right thing.'

'You did,' said Blizzard. 'Oh, did you find out anything

about Moira Savage's idea? Could the camp become an official war grave?'

'I don't really think so,' she said cautiously. 'For a start, I understand several of the families in Germany have already requested that their relatives be shipped home.'

'They have,' nodded Blizzard. 'But, in theory, it could become a war grave if some of the bodies stayed in Hafton?'

'That would be for others to decide,' she said. 'You think it's a good idea, don't you, Edward?'

'I do actually. Most of them were decent blokes. They deserve a proper resting place. But ...' and he fixed the detectives with a quizzical expression, 'I am still a bit confused. What on earth could any of this have to do with Horst's death?'

'What indeed?' murmured Blizzard, glancing out of the window and noticing without much surprise that it had started to rain again. 'What indeed?'

They left the house a few minutes later and on their way to the car, Blizzard said, 'I'll drop you off at the factory, there's something I need to do.'

'Not going off on one of your tangents again, are you?' asked Colley suspiciously.

'No, it's nothing to do with the inquiry,' said Blizzard, adding as he noticed the sergeant's sceptical expression. 'Honest.'

·· CHAPTER eleven ····

AN HOUR LATER, having dropped Colley off at Abbey Road, Blizzard was standing in the wrecked shell that was Tenby Street railway station. Through his passion for local industrial history, Blizzard knew all about the station, which dated back to a time when the growth of the railway in Hafton was rapid, linking the city with the rest of northern England. Constructed half a mile from the city centre, the station was opened in one of the western suburbs in 1847 to cater for the huge expansion in population as the textile mills sprung up in Hafton during the 1800s. For the best part of the century that followed, Tenby Street station remained a busy place but its fortunes changed in the decades following the Second World War. Services stopping there were gradually reduced and in the 1960s, Dr Beeching swung his axe and most of the district's other stations were closed. Tenby Street survived but only just, becoming an unmanned halt. By 1973, only one train a day ran through the station.

The decision to turn it into an unmanned halt took a terrible toll. Tenby Street deteriorated, becoming a target for vandals and arsonists, and its increasingly fragile state meant it was unable to resist the ravages of the harsh northern winters, eventually becoming derelict. In time, the trains rattled straight past without stopping and the building's fate seemed settled when the station was earmarked for demolition. That was when the Hafton railway society, led by an appalled John Blizzard intervened, arguing that the building's historical importance meant it should be preserved.

The intervention meant the station's fortunes seemed about to change for the better again and society members had drawn up a proposal for a railway museum with the Silver Flyer at its heart. Now, Blizzard stood in the musty station, visualizing what the loco would look like on the main platform, and waited for the man from the city council to arrive. Glancing around at the platform stained with pigeon droppings, at the deserted and darkened ticket booths and into the shadows of the neglected offices through doors that hung off rusting hinges, he shook his head at the thought of all that history being lost for ever. The scrape of a shoe broke into his reverie and he turned and smiled.

'Malcolm,' he said, extending a hand.

Malcolm Watt shook the hand enthusiastically. A slim, earnest young man, dressed in green cords and a yellow shirt with green tie, he was the council's tourism officer.

'How's it going?' he asked.

'Fine,' said Blizzard, 'especially since the news that the council is going to turn this into a railway museum.'

'Hey, hey, hey, not so fast,' said Watt, as they walked along the platform, watched by the beady-eyed pigeons perching on the rusty rafters above. 'It's still just a proposal from my department – well, I say department, there's me and the kettle – and it still has to go to full council.'

'Yeah, but several of the councillors are old railmen. They'll back it, surely?'

'They are and they will,' nodded Watt, 'but it's not that easy. You know councils, they're always squeezed for cash and we reckon it would cost at least £15m to turn this place around.'

'That much?' said Blizzard with a low whistle.

''Fraid so,' and he glanced up at the mouldering ceiling. 'I mean, just look at the place. And, sad to say, I'm not sure the council has that kind of money.'

'So are you saying the railway museum might not go ahead?' asked the chief inspector anxiously.

'I'm saying it's a brilliant idea but sometimes that's not everything. Surely I don't have to tell you, of all people, what politicians are like?' and he smiled knowingly.

Blizzard, who had fallen out with more than a few councillors in his time, pondered the thought for a moment and nodded. They had reached the end of the platform by now and he stared gloomily out over the nearby wasteland, once occupied by terraces of houses that had long since been demolished. It was Malcolm Watt who spoke next.

'How are you getting on with Elspeth Roberts?' he asked, turning and starting to walk back down the platform.

'You know her?'

'Yeah. Which council officer do you think first realized what old Willy Ramage had on his land?'

'You discovered the huts?' asked Blizzard in amazement.

'Rediscovered them, really. I just went up there one day – I was with the planning department in those days – and there they were. Everyone had forgotten about them. I was gobsmacked.'

'I'm sure you were. So, when did you meet Elspeth?'

'We knew each other at university. I was studying planning and she was doing archaeology. In fact,' and he looked slightly embarrassed, 'we even went out a couple of times.'

Blizzard raised a quizzical eyebrow.

'Didn't work, though,' said Watt sadly. 'Anyhow, moving on rapidly. When the university team was called in to survey the camp I rang her up again. Went out for a drink with her.'

'I thought she was married?'

'It was purely platonic. Anyway, that's beside the point. Elspeth is passionate about her work and really keen to see the POW camp saved. She'd do anything in her power to achieve that.'

'And what do you think?' asked Blizzard.

'Actually, I prefer the railway museum idea,' said Watt, 'but what I think does not come into it.'

'Meaning?'

'Four or five months ago, just after I had got the tourism officer's job, a number of opposition councillors came to see me.'

'What did they want?'

'It was all very hush-hush but they reckoned the camp

would make a good tourist attraction and wanted my support in lobbying for the council to spend money on converting it.'

'Why were they suddenly so interested?'

'Several of them were new ones, younger people just elected to the council. A couple of them had relatives who had been in the Hafton Regiment; I think they saw it as a chance to celebrate the history of the Haftons. Oh, and as chance to make a name for themselves.'

'Sounds like Moira Savage got to them,' grunted Blizzard.

'Let's just say she is an energetic and persuasive woman when she has the bit between her teeth. And, like I said, the councillors who came to see me *were* Conservatives. But what I am saying is....'

'I know what you're saying, that you're not sure the council can support the camp and this place.'

'Unfortunately, that is the case,' and Watt looked at the chief inspector apologetically. 'Mind, until all this thing blew up at the farm, the railway museum still had a chance; the last thing Labour was going to do was back anything put forward by the Tories. But the discovery of the bodies put a different spin on it and there are quite a few Labour councillors prepared to entertain the idea now. And, remember, there's an election coming up.'

'So?'

'Celebrating the Hafton Regiment will play well to the electorate.'

'But can't you put a word in for this place?' and the chief inspector glanced around him. 'It needs a few friends right now.'

'I will try but you have not got a hell of a lot of friends in city hall right now. You're not exactly the most diplomatic of men.'

'Politics,' snorted Blizzard.

'I hate it as well,' nodded Watt, 'but you really should learn to play the game better if you want to get things done.'

And when he spoke, John Blizzard was struck by how much like Arthur Ronald he sounded.

·· CHAPTER twelve ····

'ARE YOU OK?' asked Blizzard, looking at Fee with concern.

It was early afternoon and having returned to Abbey Road Police Station after his meeting at the railway station, the chief inspector was sitting with Fee Ellis in the deserted CID squad room, waiting for other officers to arrive for a briefing. Blizzard had walked in to see her sitting at her desk, holding her head in her hands. Now looking into her face, which was pale and adorned with a livid black eye, his expression underlined his worry. It also illustrated for him yet again the difficulties of working together. At the time their relationship had started, Ronald had suggested that Ellis be transferred to another department but she protested, desperate not to see her fledgling CID career killed off before it started. Blizzard, who could see both viewpoints, had assured Ronald that they could maintain a professional distance at work. Reluctantly, Ronald had relented but the couple knew they were on probation. So far, it had worked well, except for those times when she put her life at risk in the line of duty, as had happened at the ferry terminal the night before.

Blizzard knew that was all part of the job – he had faced down enough men with knives and guns in his time – but it did not make it any easier for him. The first time it struck home was when he heard that she had disarmed a man brandishing a wooden stave during a drugs operation on one of the division's toughest housing estates. Blizzard had tried desperately to appear unconcerned when Colley was telling him about it with great enthusiasm but the chief inspector nevertheless felt his heart pounding. It was not a pleasant experience and coping with it did not get any easier; the demands of policing Western Division did not allow it to get any easier. Now, surveying her black eye and weary expression, Blizzard was feeling that uncomfortable sensation again.

'Perhaps you should go off duty,' he suggested.

'Don't be such a fusspot,' said Ellis with a forced smile. 'I'm perfectly fine as long as I don't nod my head.'

'Why not?' asked the chief inspector quickly.

'It makes a strange rattling noise.'

'Have you seen the doc?'

'I shouldn't worry,' she said. 'My friends have been saying for ages that I must have a screw loose to go out with an old fogey like you. This just proves it.'

He stared at her, not sure whether to be relieved that she was not badly hurt or offended by the comment. When he saw the smile creep over her face, he settled for the pained expression he normally reserved for one of Colley's bad jokes.

'You,' said the detective constable, 'are just too easy to string along, Mr Blizzard. And you worry about me too much.'

'OK, point taken,' he said and gave her arm an affectionate squeeze.

'Eh, eh, eh, he's never that nice to me,' said a voice and they turned to see Colley walking in with a wide grin on his face. 'I normally just to have to settle for a quick kiss – and no tongues, mind.'

'A thought that conjures up so many negative images,' replied Blizzard. 'But let's be honest, you are not as attractive as the constable here.'

Ellis blushed but said nothing as, with a murmur of voices, more officers filed into the room and Blizzard switched once again into professional mode, stood up and walked over to the desk at the front of the room. Colley, settling himself down in his customary position in the corner, tipping back on his chair, feet resting on the desk, winked at the chief inspector. Blizzard feigned not to see it.

'So, ladies and gentlemen,' said Blizzard, looking at the gathering expectantly, 'let us start to make some sense of all this.'

There was much to make sense of. It had been a busy day at Abbey Road Police Station and, on his return to the police station, the chief inspector had roamed the corridors, seeking out officers and demanding updates. His urgency had communicated itself to the investigators; they knew that the longer they went without breakthroughs in the Knoefler case, the greater the pressure from on high became. And the greater the pressure from the chief constable became, the grumpier John Blizzard became. Forget the chief constable and Arthur Ronald, everyone knew that John Blizzard was the one to worry about. That was why the events at the ferry terminal had proved so useful, giving the impression that progress was being made somewhere and alleviating, if only temporarily, the chief inspector's frustrations by relieving some of the pressure on him.

'Gerry,' said Blizzard, looking at the Customs chief. 'Please give me some answers.'

Hope, a burly man with thinning black hair and a fleshy face complete with black moustache, was sitting at one of the desks. Dressed in a dark suit, he had a slightly dishevelled look and Colley was struck by the similarity between him and Blizzard. Now with dark bags under his blue eyes after a long night, and precious little sleep, Hope considered his response.

'OK,' he said at length. 'This is what I think we know after this morning's interviews. Well, maybe interviews is putting it a bit strongly because none of these characters speak English and we have had to wait for interpreters to arrive.'

'Have they told you anything?' asked Blizzard.

'From what we can gather, they all come from Eastern Europe. Quite a few of them are Polish, one's Hungarian and we reckon there's a couple of Czechs. It would fit; we have suspected for a while that they are being smuggled from Eastern Europe through Germany. This is the first time we have had proof.'

'Virtually all of our street robbers are Eastern European,' said Blizzard. 'Any ID on this lot?'

'They had nothing at all on them. No money, nothing.'

'Who is the old guy?' asked Blizzard, recalling the white-haired man he had seen standing next to the lorry the night before.

'That's the superintendent,' quipped Colley as, with impeccable timing, Ronald walked in and looked at them in bemusement as the room erupted in raucous laughter.

'I won't ask,' said Ronald, looking at the grinning faces, dragging up a chair and sitting down next to Blizzard.

'Best not to,' said the chief inspector. 'So who is the old guy, Gerry?'

'No idea. Won't talk to us.'

'OK. So where does Garry Horton fit into it?'

'It seems clear that he was their link in this country,' said Hope. 'That was the name on the piece of paper they had, which serves to strengthen our belief that they are being brought in by a gang based in the city rather than the West Midlands, as we at first thought.'

'It could also explain why Eddie Gayle has been keeping a low profile in recent days,' said Detective Sergeant Dave Tulley, a stocky man with fleshy cheeks and a shock of tousled black hair. 'Given that Horton works for him, it could mean that Eddie Gayle is behind all this.'

'It could indeed,' nodded Blizzard with a gleam in his eye. 'The last thing any of them wanted was being hauled in again just as a delivery was due. That's presumably why they went to ground.'

'And there is a decent link with Henderson Ramage,' said Graham Ross. 'We are pretty sure that some of the illegals were being kept at Hut 23 before being shipped out somewhere else. Since Ramage owns Green Meadow Farm, that puts him in the frame as well – and if Ramage is in the frame then so is Eddie Gayle.'

'Maybe,' said Ronald doubtfully. 'But it's a big step up for Eddie, surely? We have had no indication that he was into people-smuggling before, have we? I mean, what if Horton and Ramage are working for someone else on this one?'

'Na,' said Tulley firmly. 'Horton is Gayle's man through and through, sir. He hasn't got the brains to find anyone else.'

'OK, so where is Horton?' asked Ronald.

'Nobody is sure,' said Tulley and he nodded at Ellis. 'We have been checking all his usual haunts but no one has seen him since he got out of the clink. Eddie Gayle seems to have disappeared off the face of the earth as well. And, frankly, there is a lot of ground to cover with just the two of us, particularly, since I reckon the constable here should really take some time off.'

'Why?' asked Blizzard, trying not to sound concerned.

'The rattling of her head is really irritating when you are trying to do the crossword,' said Tulley.

Gentle laughter and an embarrassed smile from Ellis.

'I appreciate the concern,' she said, then noticing the sceptical glances of her colleagues, added earnestly, 'I'm OK. Really I am.'

'OK,' nodded Blizzard, then turned to DI Ramsey. 'Chris, this inquiry is getting more complicated all the time, how many more officers can you let me have?'

Ramsey pondered. Aged in his early thirties, he was slim and tall with short-cropped brown hair, an angular face, a prominent nose and a thin mouth not particularly given to laughing. He was dressed as immaculately as ever, in a grey suit with a perfectly matching powder-blue tie, and black shoes. A conscientious, thorough and precise, if unspectacular, detective, he was the one who drew up the rosters and allocated the manpower. It was a role that suited his methodical mind and one that sometimes brought the pragmatic DI into conflict with Blizzard.

'Not that many, guv,' said Ramsey after rapidly doing the arithmetic in his head.

'Come on, Chris,' sighed Blizzard. 'Not this again.'

'You know the score, guv,' replied Ramsey defensively. 'We've got those ram-raids over on the Larchgrove and those indecent assaults at Hadrian Walk. And an attempted murder over in Raglan Street, the guy who was attacked with the baseball bat. That needs sorting p.d.q before his mates escalate things. They're angling for revenge and that area is sensitive enough without something like this getting out of hand. You told me that.'

'Yes, I know but—'

'And we had nine burglaries overnight,' said Ramsey, cutting across the exasperated chief inspector as he got into his stride. 'And you know as well as I do that last month the chief constable publicly pledged that all break-ins would be investigated inside twenty-four hours. It's difficult enough doing that without losing more officers.'

'Yes, I know but—' began Blizzard again.

'You can have three,' said Ramsey. 'And, frankly, that's stretching it.'

'That all?' asked Blizzard, pursing his lips.

'I can't shit them out of my arse,' snapped Ramsey.

Everyone in the room looked at him with surprise; it took a lot to make Chris Ramsey swear.

'OK, OK, point taken,' sighed Blizzard. 'Let me have them anyway. Arthur, any chance uniform would lend us a couple of bodies?'

'I can ask,' said the superintendent dubiously, 'but they're really stretched at the moment. I can have a word with Barry Glenhorn over in East Division, maybe he can let us have a couple of his detectives instead.'

'But will they be sober?' said a sly voice which sounded remarkably like Colley's although when everyone looked at him, his face bore an innocent expression.

'I think,' said Ronald tartly as the chuckles rippled round the room, 'that a little more respect for your colleagues would be in order.'

Then, relenting as he realized that the official line sounded ridiculous in front of the officers, he added, 'Pissed or not.'

'Well, whoever we get,' said Blizzard, 'I want us to spend the next couple of days tapping up every informant we know and let's bring in some of the bad lads. I want to turn the heat up on Gayle and Horton. They've got to be somewhere.'

Hey up, thought Colley, the chief inspector's favourite tree line could not be far away.

'Let's shake some trees and see if they fall out,' said Blizzard, not noticing the small smile on Colley's face, and turning to Tulley. 'You're in charge of organizing that. Oh, and can you get on to Hamburg police, see if they know anything about Knoefler's activities before the war?'

'OK, guv, but what am I looking for?'

'Sounds like he was a black market racketeer. Could be something or nothing but worth a look all the same.'

'Right-oh, guv. Er, will they speak English?'

'You don't so it won't be a problem,' said Blizzard, getting a laugh for the comment and turning to the forensics chief. 'Graham, anything else?'

'Yeah, like I said, I am pretty sure that Hut 23 is where the illegals are kept when they come in. A couple of the ones lifted last night had the same fags we found in the hut and we found some of the same beer stacked behind the lorry driver's seat.'

'How is the driver?' asked Ronald.

'He'll live,' said Hope. 'Turns out it was not the bullet that knocked him out but hitting his head on the steering wheel.'

'I know how he feels,' murmured Ellis.

'Shouldn't you be at home, Constable?' asked Ronald, looking at her with concern. 'You did take a hell of a whack.'

'No, I'm fine,' said Ellis, and noticing his doubtful look, added, 'Honest, guv. I just wish people would stop asking about my health!'

'Well, if you're sure,' said Ronald.

'I am,' she said firmly.

'So, have we got anything on the driver?' asked Blizzard, turning back to Hope. 'Is he one of our eastern chums as well?'

'Yes, East Hafton,' said the Customs man. 'He's called Karl Robinson.'

'I know him,' said Tulley. 'Daft lad, do anything for money. And I did hear that he was working for Eddie Gayle at one point. Running errands, that kind of thing.'

'And we all know Eddie's errands,' said Blizzard grimly.

'It does strengthen the theory that the people-trafficking is organized out of Hafton and that Eddie Gayle is pulling the strings,' commented Ronald, glancing at the chief inspector.

'It does indeed. Tulley, do you think one of your lot can fit in an interview with Robinson as well?' Blizzard asked his sergeant then glancing at Hope. 'Assuming Customs are OK with that?'

'Yeah,' said Hope, flapping a hand in agreement. 'I can always go and search some old dear's bag for illegal shampoo or something.'

'Good,' said Blizzard, turning to the DI. 'Chris, are you and the robbery team still OK working with the Customs boys on last night's op?'

'No problem,' nodded Ramsey.

'Thank you,' said Blizzard, conscious of the need for diplomacy after their spat. 'You're doing some good work there. See if you can link the bunch that came in last night with the gangs doing our street robberies.'

'Right-oh, guv,' and he nodded his appreciation at the gesture.

'OK,' said Blizzard. 'I think that's about it for now. Get out there and make something happen. Oh, David....'

He glanced at Colley as the others officers stood up and started to make their way out of the room.

'Guv?' said the sergeant, flipping his legs off the desk and walking over to the front of the room.

'What about Moira Savage's story?'

'Seems to check out. Other people in the village confirmed bits of it. Some saw the truck, others heard about the bogus complaint against her husband and Moira told a couple of them about the phone calls.'

'And hubby was not on the rob?'

'Not that we know of, but I'm waiting for some calls back on him.'

'And no link between Henderson Ramage and Brian Savage?'

'We're still checking that as well. One or two interesting leads but nothing definite yet.'

'Well, whoever's behind the threats, Moira has hacked them off big time,' said Blizzard, heading out of the squad room.

'Ramage has got to be the most likely candidate, guv,' said Colley, following him into the corridor. 'Most people I talked to in the village seemed pretty supportive of Moira. Even those who disagreed with her don't look particularly dodgy.'

'Nevertheless,' said Blizzard, 'it does give us an excuse to bring Henderson Ramage in again, does it not? Somehow, I think he has been giving a whole new meaning to farm diversification.'

·· CHAPTER thirteen ····

'DID YOUR FAMILY lose anyone in the war, John?' asked Jay Priest, looking at Blizzard.

'All these detectives,' said the chief inspector, nodding at Colley and Fee Ellis with a gentle smile on his face, 'and it takes a teacher to ask the right question.'

'It's dealing with guilty-looking children every day that does it,' chuckled Jay.

'I take it you are referring to Colley,' replied Blizzard.

'Something like that.'

It was shortly before eleven on Saturday evening and they were sitting in the terraced house which Colley had shared for the best part of ten years with his girlfriend, a willowy redhead in her early thirties who taught at one of the city's primary schools. Over previous years, the regular gathering had been a threesome, the couple playing host to the chief inspector every other month, he doing the same on a somewhat more occasional basis. But since the arrival on the scene of Fee Ellis, it had become a foursome and, after the inevitable initial awkwardness the first night they tried it, the arrangement had worked out well, to the relief of all concerned. Jay and Fee quickly became friends – united in their exasperation at their menfolk – and Blizzard and Colley had always had an easy relationship.

That evening, after eating their meal of pasta – Blizzard loved Italian food – they were sitting in the living-room with its pastel shades and rustic prints, the soft light afforded by a couple of table lamps and the flickering fake coal fire. Mellow jazz music was playing quietly in the background and

Blizzard was lounging in an armchair, glass of wine in hand, Colley was in another chair with a pint of bitter, and Jay and Fee were sitting on the sofa, sipping port and nibbling at chocolates. For Blizzard, although shoptalk was banned at these nights, the gathering had always played an important part in not just his life but also the investigative process, allowing him an escape from the pressures and frustrations of major inquiries.

And this one had more than its fair share of those. There were still far more questions than answers. Despite the arrival of extra officers on to the team, the detectives had not been able to track down Eddie Gayle, Garry Horton or Henderson Ramage, informants suggesting that the men had all vanished in the hours after the ferry terminal operation, possibly leaving the city. Even if they had not fled, Hafton was the kind of place whose dark recesses had afforded many a guilty man a hiding place down the years. They could easily have concealed themselves amid the warren of terraced streets just outside the city centre, in the sprawling expanses of the housing estates or in the poisonous alleyways and landings of the blocks of flats. But, hiding or not, each of the men would have been sitting with ears straining for the sound at the door that told them that John Blizzard had come calling. He usually did and did not normally offer the courtesy of a ring on the front doorbell.

But sometimes it took time and the remainder of the week had been full of delays and frustrations for the chief inspector. Attempts to speed up the process in further interviews with the men apprehended at the ferry terminal had proved fruitless. Not even the eager interpreter had been able to persuade them to speak. As for the older white-haired man captured at the same time, he had proved even more intransigent, not scared or intimidated and refusing even to give his name; attempts to identify him had so far come to nothing. As a result, the group had been taken to a Home Office holding centre an hour's drive from Hafton to await deportation, taking their secrets with them.

So it was a downcast John Blizzard that headed for Colley's

house that Saturday night. However, three hours, and several drinks, later he was in a much more relaxed and mellow mood and found himself, to his surprise, ready to talk. It was often the case with their evenings: something about Jay and Colley somehow encouraged him to be more frank than he had ever been before, even with Fee from whom he had now had few secrets. Considering Jay's question, Blizzard surveyed the sergeant and his girlfriend fondly and prepared to unburden himself. Taking another sip of wine, he smiled slightly; perhaps they were taking the wrong tack with the Eastern Europeans, he thought, perhaps all he had to do was ply with them with a decent Italian red and a nice plate of pasta.

'So did you lose someone?' asked Jay, repeating the question.

'Yes,' Blizzard said softly, nodding at her. 'Yes, we did.'

Now, all eyes were turned on him, sensing that somehow this was the reason for his strange behaviour at the graveside and the cause of his distracted demeanour in the days that had followed. Colley fervently hoped it was, because experience had taught him that a distracted John Blizzard did not think clearly when he was investigating cases. Free his mind of the clutter and the chief inspector honed in like a laser on the salient points. That was why he often went to work on the Old Lady during difficult inquiries, to find peace amid the tangled metal and rusty old tools. And, in Colley's view, something to clear his mind was exactly what was needed now, so he waited and watched his friend intently. And hoped.

'My uncle,' continued Blizzard.

'On which side?' asked Jay.

'He was my mother's brother,' replied Blizzard, taking a sip of wine.

The chief inspector stared into the flickering firelight, transported for a moment to stand once more by the graveside at the farm, seeing again, through the swirling mists, the man's face, seeing that crooked smile in the photograph, hearing once more the clatter of battle and the rattle of death. And in those seconds in the cosy living-room he felt grief and bereavement and loss as acutely as he had during those first moments at the farm. It was the sensation that had surprised him then and it was the sensation that surprised him now. We will remember them at the going down of the sun, he thought. And in that moment, John Blizzard remembered the man. And decided it was time for others to remember him as well.

'Frank William Robinson,' he said, adding with a chuckle. 'Frank 2 they used to call him.'

'Frank 2?' asked Colley.

'Yeah, there was another Frank lived in the village, a couple of months older than my uncle, so they called them Frank 1 and Frank 2. Daft really, Frank 1 had the brightest red hair you ever had seen, they could not have been more different if they had tried.'

As they smiled at the thought, Blizzard stood up and walked out into the hallway, returning a moment later with his wallet, which he opened, producing a crumpled black-and-white photograph, handling it gently as though it was delicate silk which could tear at any moment. Unfolding it carefully, as he had a thousand times over the past year, he showed it to them. The first time anyone outside his family had seen it.

'That's him,' he said.

They looked with fascination at the image of a handsome young man, dressed in soldier's uniform and standing in a summer garden, stared at the dark hair cropped short and immaculately groomed, at the angular and prominent cheekbones and at the laughing eyes. They looked at the smile and suddenly knew why it was a picture which so affected John Blizzard. It was almost as if Frank knew they were looking at him and in that moment, he reached out to each of them down the years as he had to his nephew John Blizzard. It was an uncanny and powerful feeling and they started to understand why John Blizzard had been so affected by it.

Standing next to Frank was an attractive young woman dressed in blouse and pleated skirt, a women with curly dark hair, a pleasant rounded face and a happy smile. The proud smile of motherhood. The woman was holding Frank's arm but what drew the eye most of all was the reason for their smiles, the baby which he held as if it was a piece of precious china that might break. Jay caught Colley's eye for a second and gave a half-smile.

'Who's the sprog?' asked Colley quickly, embarrassed that Fee had caught the look.

'My brother,' said Blizzard, sadness in his eyes.

'You have a brother?' exclaimed the sergeant in amazement.

'Had a brother, David,' said Blizzard. 'Charlie. He died three months after this picture was taken. Ironic really. He died of influenza. He would have been fifty something now.'

'And the woman?' asked Jay.

'My mother. Frank's sister. That's where the picture came from. When my mother went into the home last year I was going through her things and came across this at the bottom of a battered old box. I'd never seen it before. For some reason, she had never shown it to me. I have asked her about it several times but she doesn't say anything. It obviously still upsets her and she won't have it in her room. Too painful, I suppose. Seeing it certainly gave me a jolt, I can tell you,' and he paused. 'It is all I have of them. All my mother has of them.'

'So you never met your uncle?' asked Fee.

'No,' and Blizzard glanced down at the picture and shook his head sadly. 'Within a year of this picture being taken, he was dead. They were both dead.'

'What happened?' asked Fee, moving over to kneel by the armchair and reaching across to take his hand.

'His troop ship sank in the Azores in 1942,' said Blizzard. 'He was with the Hafton Regiment at the time. They never found his body.'

'That's awful,' said Jay.

'Yes. His wife – Clarrie she was called – waited and waited then one day, more than a year later, the telegram arrived, saying he was lost,' and Blizzard shook his head again, a faraway look coming into his eyes. 'We can only imagine what

Frank's final minutes were like. Or perhaps it is better that
we don't.'

'No wonder you have been acting oddly over the past few
days,' said Colley.

'Yeah, sorry about that. It never really bothered me before.
Everyone else moved on after his death, Clarrie remarried
after the war, they were together for forty years before she
died, and had a very happy marriage, my parents had me in
1950 and no one really talked about Charlie. Folks just got on
with their lives. That's what they did in those days. They
didn't have all this poncy therapy. Of course, I always wished
that I could have met my uncle but it was no big deal,' and he
paused. 'But I think it was the link with my brother that
really got to me.'

'I can understand that,' nodded Colley, recalling the many
good times he and his own brother had shared down the
years.

'It was finding that picture that started it. Then, a few days
later, having my 46th birthday seemed to make it worse. Too
near fifty, I guess. The feeling of loss has somehow grown
stronger over recent months. I tried to stop thinking that
way, told myself I was being daft, but when they found those
soldiers' bodies at the farm, I don't know, I thought of poor
Frank and I thought of my little brother....' and his voice
tailed off. 'And then I think of all the things he and I could
have done together.'

There was an awkward silence for a moment as Blizzard
gathered his thoughts.

'Somehow the grave at the farm has assumed an importance for me. I have gone back a couple of times,' and he
noticed the sergeant's surprised expression. 'Sorry, David, I
should have told you, but I didn't go back because of the case,
it's just that in a strange way it makes me feel closer to them.
As if they are there with me.'

And he looked down at Fee with an embarrassed smile.

'Stupid really.'

'No, it's not,' said Fee quietly, squeezing his hand. 'We all
need to know where we come from, John.'

'Yes,' said Blizzard quietly, nodding at her and squeezing her hand back. 'Yes, I think we do.'

And he turned away to look into the firelight again. He did not want them to see the tears glistening in his eyes.

·· CHAPTER fourteen ····

HIS MIND CLEARED by his admissions the night before and his mood significantly lightened, Blizzard sweated off his hangover the next morning on a ten-mile bike ride with Fee. It was the kind of crisp and bright morning when it was a joy to be alive. The ice glistened on the hedgerows and the sun glinted off the tarmac, beneath wisps of blue sky that heralded a welcome end to a fortnight in which endless winter days had followed endless winter nights.

So, as the couple rode through the country lanes surrounding the chief inspector's home, chatting idly about nothing in particular, Blizzard felt his alcohol-induced headache gradually dissipating and his spirits rising for the first time in weeks. That it should happen on a bike would have amazed many that knew him before Fee walked into his life. A year earlier and it would have amazed him as well because for many years, the chief inspector had a harboured a deep dislike of exercise and regarded those who took part in it with great suspicion.

All that had changed eighteen months before when he hosted a press conference at Abbey Road and was horrified at the photograph that appeared in the newspaper that evening. When Colley pointed it out, Blizzard's feeble attempts to blame the double chin on a trick of the light or a bad camera angle only served to make the chief inspector realize that he had to lose some weight. If the truth be told, and despite his vociferous comments on the subject of exercise, Blizzard did not really need much convincing. On more recent occasions than he cared to remember, he had found himself struggling badly when having to chase after suspects, depending instead on the speed and agility of Colley and other colleagues to run down their quarry. Each time, it had taken the best part of an hour for his breathing to return to normal.

So, three times a week, and very self-consciously at first, Blizzard had started going to the police leisure centre before work to shed a few pounds in the swimming pool, swearing the reception staff to secrecy lest word got out. The visits did remain a secret – for all of three minutes. A detective sergeant from Eastern Division spotted Blizzard emerging damp-haired from the changing room that first morning and that was that. By the end of the day, everyone in Abbey Road knew about it. And someone – the culprit was never found although Colley spent the day with a sly look on his face – left a yellow rubber duck on the chief inspector's desk when he popped out to the coffee machine.

Despite his new fitness pledge, Blizzard had nevertheless been perturbed to discover Fee's love of cycling and in the first few months of their relationship had stoutly resisted whenever she tried to interest him in joining her on her rides. Stout was the word, though, because his swimming only led to him losing a few pounds so, reluctantly, and after a lot of gentle badgering from Fee, he accompanied her into town one day and purchased a bike. The experience was deeply embarrassing for the chief inspector, who, glancing round at the mixture of excited small children squeaking at Barbie and Commando bikes and the lean lycra-clad racing types, felt desperately out of place. And old.

Adding to his discomfort was the impossibly thin young man who sold him the machine while asking pointed questions about Blizzard's level of fitness, ostensibly so he could select the right bicycle but really, in the detective's jaundiced view, so he could take the mickey out of him. The final straw for Blizzard was when, having completed the sale, the young man asked the chief inspector if he wanted the saddle adjusting. Muttering something dark about adjusting the teenager's 'sodding saddle', Blizzard glowered at him and wheeled the bike out of the shop without a further word, followed by a chuckling Fee and watched by the grinning young shopworker.

Blizzard wished he could say that his first bike ride since schooldays was a pleasant experience but he hated every minute of it and fell off twice, once into a hedge near his house, watched with some amusement by a neighbour who was cutting the grass, and a second time into a water-filled ditch. By the end of the ride, Blizzard was wringing wet and aching in places he did not think he had places and had vowed never to mount another bicycle. He had even suffered the indignity of having to ask Fee to stop on several occasions to allow him to catch her up and catch his breath. Eventually, however, Fee's gentle coaxing, in the tone of voice she would have normally reserved for a small child, did the trick and Blizzard started to complain less each time he went out. And although he would never admit it to anyone, he quite enjoyed the experience despite the obligatory grumbling. It did help him lose a few pounds but his love of alcohol and his enthusiasm for making his own pizzas ensured that he remained what he liked to call 'chunky'. No one else at Abbey Road dared to call him anything else. At least, not in his presence.

So, Blizzard enjoyed his Sunday morning ride that day, he and Fee chatting comfortably about anything that wasn't linked to policing as they rode along the winding lanes to the west of Hafton, appreciating the unaccustomed warmth as the sun burnt away the mist, sending clouds of steam rising from the road surface. Yet always, behind the idle conversation, Blizzard was thinking about the case and starting to come to some conclusions. Feeling as if somehow a great weight had been removed from his shoulders at Colley's house the night before, he soon found himself in a cheerful mood and after the bike ride, the couple went back to his house, changed and went out for lunch at the village pub. Then they drove into the city, where Blizzard spent a couple of hours with his mother in the residential home, talking properly about Charlie for the first time. Fee visited a friend, spending the entire time talking about John Blizzard. The couple met up again just after four and went back to Fee's terraced house near the city centre for a light tea, sitting by the fire in her cosy living-room as the late afternoon gloom closed in. Then Blizzard went to view the battered body of Moira Savage.

The call from Colley came shortly after six and within twenty minutes, the chief inspector and Ellis were driving through the same roads along which they had cycled that morning, the grim expression on their faces contrasting sharply with the happy smiles of a few hours before. The end to a perfect day, Blizzard thought morosely. But his mind had little time to dwell on such prosaic notions because, as so often happened when murders occurred, he felt himself coming alive. He knew it sounded insensitive, and Blizzard did not expect non-police people to understand, but murder brought out the best in him, sharpening his instincts. Instincts that he felt had been dulled over the past fortnight by his preoccupations with his own thoughts.

Now, though, the chief inspector saw things more clearly, perhaps for the first time during the inquiry. Knew now the significance of something Colley had told him the previous Friday so that, even before he arrived at Moira Savage's house, things were slotting into place and he had determined on a course of action.

'I've missed something,' said Blizzard as he manoeuvred the car into the dark country lane leading to Hawkwith.

'What do you mean?' asked Fee, trying to sound casual and conceal her apprehension at what they might find when they got there; the sergeant had said it was bad and the sergeant tended not to exaggerate these kind of things.

'Something Colley mentioned. I didn't listen hard enough,' said Blizzard enigmatically, then lapsed into silence, declining to elaborate further.

Driving past the flashing lights of the police cars stationed at the entrance to Hawkwith village, he headed along the narrow road along one side of the green and pulled up outside Moira Savage's house. Leaving Ellis to hook up with Sergeant Tulley a little further along the green, Blizzard edged his way through the crowd of curious villagers that had gathered. Brusquely ignoring their questions and ordering a uniformed constable to move them back from the house, he pushed open the gate and walked up the drive, noticing through the illuminated living-room window that Graham Ross was already there, briefing a couple of his forensic team. Colley was standing on the doorstep, mobile phone clapped to his ear. Seeing the chief inspector approaching, he ended the call and slipped the phone into his anorak pocket.

'Sorry about this, guv,' he said, walking down the drive to meet him.

'No worries,' said the chief inspector. 'All I was doing was snuggling up to a devastatingly attractive blonde and wondering when I could decently suggest that it might be bedtime.'

'Not that bird from HR?' grinned Colley.

'No, it was not,' said Blizzard with a smile then nodded at the sergeant's pocket. 'Who was on the phone?'

'Jay.'

'Another dinner ruined, eh,' said Blizzard with a wry smile.

'Something like that.'

'So, what have we got?' asked the chief inspector, following his sergeant into the hallway.

'It's a bit of mess,' said Colley, pushing open the door to the living-room.

'Tell me something I don't know,' grunted Blizzard.

He stood and surveyed the scene for a few moments. Colley was not wrong. The chief inspector had seen plenty of deaths in his time but somehow that never made it any easier whenever he was confronted by a new one. There was something about the smell that triggered off instinctive feelings of unease in him, that and the realization that just a short time before on the very spot where he stood, someone had committed the ultimate act of outrage against a fellow human being. And the death of Moira Savage was more of an outrage than most.

She had been beaten to death in an attack whose level of violence Blizzard had rarely seen. Moira Savage lay on the floor by the mantelpiece, her head having been smashed in with a heavy object. One eyes was closed and caked in blood, her nose was split and several of her teeth had been knocked out. The blood had poured down her front, soaking into the once-white blouse and tweed skirt, staining them crimson, and flecking her shoes. Blood had also spattered the nearby wall, the pattern ranged across the pale floral wallpaper. It had been a truly brutal attack.

'Who found her?' asked the chief inspector, shaking his head.

'A neighbour,' said Colley. 'Called in about half-five to borrow a bottle of milk. 'Found the front door open. Came in here.'

'And where is hubby?' asked Blizzard pointedly, looking back into the hallway.

'Away for a few days. Some kind of conference in Torquay apparently.'

'How convenient,' murmured Blizzard.

'And I thought you were not listening,' murmured Colley.

'I always listen,' said Blizzard. 'It just didn't quite click into place on Friday. I owe you an apology.'

'No, you don't.'

There was an awkward silence.

'I take it someone has contacted him?' asked Blizzard.

'Yeah, one of the neighbours. He's on his way back. Reckons he'll arrive about midnight.'

'That's a lot of turns round the ring road,' said Blizzard sardonically. 'He'll be very dizzy by the time he gets home.'

He turned to the forensics chief, who was crouching by the body and surveying the wounds.

'So, what have we got, Graham?' asked the chief inspector.

'It's a nasty one.'

'That's why he had to go through all that extra training,' grunted Blizzard. 'They have to pass a paper in Stating The Bleeding Obvious before they can work on forensics. You'd get on well with Elspeth Roberts.'

'Sorry, guv,' grinned Ross, standing up and instinctively running a hand through his beautifully coiffured hair.

'Don't worry, you look lovely,' said Blizzard, scowling at the gesture. 'So what was she killed with?'

'Not sure. Something heavy.'

'A poker perhaps?' asked the chief inspector, nodding at the hearth. 'There's not one there and these kinds of people always have one for show.'

'Maybe,' said Ross cautiously. 'Reynolds will be able to tell us more when he does the PM but, whatever it was, I am pretty sure it is not in the house now. We've looked everywhere, haven't we, Dave?'

Colley nodded.

'Then look again,' said Blizzard, turning to the sergeant. 'Anyone see anything?'

'Tulley's doing door-to-door but nothing so far,' said Colley, glancing out of the window and noticing Ellis and the sergeant talking to a small group of villagers on the green.

'Well,' said the chief inspector, walking over to stand next to him and staring sourly at the gathering at the front gate. 'Someone out there must know why someone wanted to kill her. What about those who opposed her in the parish council meetings? Remind me where we got with them on Friday, David.'

'Na, it's none of them,' said Colley. 'No way are they the type to murder her. I mean, one of them was Harold Brown. He's a solicitor, for God's sake.'

'Oh, that's all right then,' said Blizzard acerbically, then nodded at his sergeant. 'But you're right, they're not killers and this is not about them. No, whoever it was, they hated Moira Savage enough to bash her brains out and that means there was more at stake than a little falling out among neighbours. And that means we have to look for the person with the strongest motive.'

'And that means,' said Colley, taking up the train of thought, 'those behind the sale of the land at Green Meadow Farm.'

'And if that is the case,' said Ross, 'Henderson Ramage has got to be in the frame, surely?'

'You know,' nodded Blizzard, walking out into the hallway,

'I think he just might be. Ah, Mrs Roberts, what a pleasant surprise. You seem to turn up everywhere like a bad penny.'

The historian was standing at the front door, an anxious look on her face.

'She wants to come in, sir,' said the uniformed constable who was keeping guard. 'I told her she couldn't.'

'It's OK,' nodded the chief inspector. 'Might I suggest we go into the kitchen, Mrs Roberts. It is not very pleasant in the living-room.'

They sat down at the kitchen table and Blizzard waited for her to speak. She was very upset and had been crying.

'I just heard,' she said at last.

'How?'

'One of her neighbours rang me,' and she broke down in tears. 'Oh, God, it's terrible!'

'I didn't know you were that close,' said Blizzard, slightly puzzled.

'We weren't,' she said, suddenly producing a piece of paper from her anorak pocket. 'But I'm terrified that I am going to be next!'

Blizzard took the paper. Decorated with the same crudely drawn gravestone they had seen in the threatening note sent to Moira Savage, it simply said, in letters snipped from a newspaper: 'I warned you to keep your nose out. RIP, Bitch.'

'You know, Mrs Roberts,' said the chief inspector. 'I think you might just be right.'

· · CHAPTER fifteen · · · ·

'I HOPE YOU know what you are doing, John,' said Arthur Ronald doubtfully as they sat in his office shortly before midnight, sipping mugs of tea and occasionally reaching for digestives from the open packet on the desk.

'You're not sure then?'

'I know Brian Savage from my days in Burniston and he's a decent bloke. Member of the Freemasons, past president of Rotary, that sort of thing.'

'Oh, I'll release him immediately then,' said Blizzard, unable to conceal the mockery in his voice. 'And there was me thinking it was wrong that he's been lying his bloody head off since we lifted him.'

Ronald looked at him unhappily. This was one of those moments where he felt the burden of responsibility at its heaviest. The return of Brian Savage to Hawkwith had placed the officers in an extremely difficult situation. Convinced by his lies that the land agent was implicated in the death of his wife, Blizzard had been arguing vociferously that he should be arrested. Ronald, on the other hand, acutely conscious of how it would play in the media if Savage turned out to be an innocent victim, was more circumspect, particularly since he knew that the chief constable always took a keen interest when fellow Lodge members were in trouble. Ronald sighed; he knew that such considerations tended not to register particularly highly on John Blizzard's radar. If at all. The chief inspector's ability to cut through vested interests was one of the reasons Ronald respected his friend as a detective and at the same time one of the reasons he found working with him so challenging.

'You know I didn't mean it that way,' said Ronald, trying again to reason with the chief inspector. 'I'm just saying, what if he's not guilty?'

'Then he would have to explain his lies.'

'Granted, but what if there is another reason for his misleading his wife? Maybe he's having an affair.'

'It is always a possibility,' nodded Blizzard. 'She'd be enough to drive any man bonkers.'

'All I'm saying is go easy on him until you are sure. He has just lost his wife.'

'Yeah, but that could be because he killed her,' said Blizzard. Noticing Ronald's pained look and holding up his hands, he added, 'OK, OK, we'll make it a nice little chat to start with.'

'Go carefully, John,' warned Ronald. 'I know what your nice little chats are like.'

Blizzard smiled broadly – he loved having a reputation – and heaved himself out of the chair to head for the interview room, where an anxious Brian Savage had been waiting with Colley for several minutes. Walking into the room, the chief inspector looked at the land agent for a moment then sat down behind his desk and, recalling Ronald's words, tried to smile at him. It didn't really work and the smile resembled something more like a grimace, serving only to make Brian Savage look even more worried. Next to him, his lawyer, a smartly dressed young woman shuffled her papers importantly.

'Thank you for coming in, Mr Savage,' said Blizzard, trying to retain a semblance of civility. 'I know this is difficult for you.'

'Can't it wait?' asked the lawyer. 'My client's wife has just been murdered, for goodness' sake.'

'I appreciate that, Miss Hewitt,' said Blizzard, 'but I really do need some questions answered if I am to work out who killed her. The first few hours after a murder are crucial.'

The lawyer said nothing but glanced at Savage, who sat with his head in a whirl of shock and confusion. Having returned to Hawkwith shortly after 11.30, he had been met at the door of his home by a stern-faced Colley, who had informed him he would not be allowed in his own house and had taken him immediately to the station. Guided to the interview room and given a cup of tea, Savage had sat for several minutes, watching the clock on the wall moving inexorably towards midnight. Now, he eyed the chief inspector and his sergeant uneasily. Something about Blizzard's tone of voice and his body language alarmed Savage and had driven away the tears he had shed for his wife. Now there was a need for clearer thinking. The detectives' words had been the right ones, sorry for his loss, that kind of thing, but their voices suggested something more. And the sergeant had been far from forthcoming on the car journey into the city. Now, the land agent was desperately worried that they had discovered his secret.

Blizzard and Colley, for their part, were watching him intently. It never failed to amaze them how the oppressive atmosphere of the interview room got to even the most composed of characters. Brian Savage was a man who normally cut an imposing figure but was now battling to retain control. A tall, lean man he had short, neat hair, still largely brown with only a few flecks of grey even though he was in his mid-sixties. His face was thin with high cheekbones, the eyes green, the nose prominent and the mouth thin with a slight tendency to curl downwards. He was dressed casually, yet smartly, in a tweed jacket, black pullover and dark slacks.

'You see,' said Blizzard, trying to sound as relaxed as he could as he reached out to flick on the tape machine, 'we have been finding out some interesting things about you, Mr Savage.'

The land agent looked at him anxiously.

'Like what?' he asked guardedly in his cultured voice.

'Like there is no conference in Torquay,' said Blizzard, watching for a reaction. 'Well, not unless you count a gathering of midwives and somehow I don't think that's quite your thing, Brian.'

'And what's more,' said Colley, 'your car never left the county this afternoon.'

Savage's jaw dropped open as he suddenly realized the extent of police inquiries into his movements.

'I don't know what you mean,' he said, trying to sound calm but failing dismally.

'Oh, I think you do,' said Blizzard, leaning forward across the desk, voice changing suddenly to razor-wire sharp. 'You see, after your wife was murdered, we put out an APB on your vehicle and one of the traffic lads from Northern Division recalled seeing your Bentley parked up outside a guest house in Halcrombe for most of the afternoon.'

'He must be mistaken,' said Savage.

'Actually he wasn't. He's a classic car buff and has been considering buying one. We clearly pay our constables too much. There are not that many Bentleys in this area so he stopped to look at it. Said it was there at 2 p.m. and still there are 6.30 when he came back that way, when you were supposed to be in Torquay. Care to explain that, Mr Savage?'

Savage looked at him with mounting horror.

'There's something else that intrigued us,' said Blizzard, allowing himself a thin smile as he took control of the situation. 'See, over the past few days, the sergeant here has been doing some digging – he's good at that – and he discovered that your company has links with one Henderson Ramage and the sale of his land at Green Meadow Farm.'

'So we handled the sale,' said Savage, now well and truly rattled. 'So what?'

'More than handled the sale, surely,' said Colley. 'You and Ramage were partners on this one. In fact, you smoothed the deal with a friend of yours who runs a housebuilding company. As I understand it, your cut was ten per cent of the not inconsiderable profits.'

'Oh, Jesus,' gasped Savage, the true seriousness of his position hitting him for the first time.

'And then,' said Blizzard, the edge still in his voice. 'Someone in the village threatened to wreck it all, started kicking up a fuss, rallying the locals, speaking out in meetings, firing off letters, even campaigning to make it a war grave so the development was blocked. And this was not any old villager, Mr Savage, this was your wife, the indomitable Moira.'

'And now she's dead,' added Colley. 'Isn't that strange?'

'Mr Savage,' said Blizzard, turning piercing eyes on the perspiring land agent. 'I think it is about time you started telling us what has been happening because, from where I am sitting, it looks like you had a pretty strong motive to see Moira dispatched to a better world.'

Savage hesitated for a moment then nodded weakly.

'You'd find out anyway,' he said hoarsely.

'We usually do,' said Blizzard. 'We don't like secrets. I take it your wife did not know about the arrangement with Henderson Ramage?'

'No,' and Savage shook his head vigorously. 'We kept the company's name out of it. Moira would have killed me if she found out.'

He paused in horror when he realized what he had said.

'Oh, Jesus,' he said, burying his head in his hands and starting to cry. 'Oh, Jesus, what have I done?'

'I don't know,' said Blizzard. 'What have you done, Mr Savage?'

'I think,' said Miss Hewitt, 'that my client has said too much and I really do need time to....'

'They weren't supposed to kill her,' moaned Savage.

'Who weren't?' asked Blizzard quickly.

'Ramage and his bully boys,' said Savage vehemently, lifting his head and staring hard at Blizzard. 'He's an evil man!'

'He is indeed and you certainly do make strange bedfellows. Why on earth did you go in with him?' asked the chief inspector.

'I really do think—' began the lawyer.

'Well, I really do think your client should talk to us without you clucking on in the background,' snapped Blizzard, silencing the solicitor with a look. 'Now, please answer the question, Mr Savage. Why on earth did you get involved with Henderson Ramage?'

'The business has not been doing as well as everyone

thinks,' sighed Savage after glancing at his lawyer, who shrugged. 'Land prices have been dropping in this area for several years and more of the farmers are holding off until the market turns. I needed something quick and Henderson Ramage provided it.'

'So what was the plan? Turn the screws on your wife to scare her off?'

'Something like that,' nodded Savage weakly, the fight going out of him again. 'I had tried to tell her to stop campaigning so many times but she wouldn't listen.'

'And she wouldn't be scared off either, would she?'

'She just would not quit,' said Savage bitterly. 'That was Moira all over. Said no bully boy would keep her quiet.'

'Well, he has now,' said Blizzard thinly. 'So what happened? I assume that when she started banging on to anyone who would listen about the idea of a consecrated war grave, that was the final straw for Ramage?'

'He rang me a couple of days ago,' nodded Savage. 'He was absolutely furious. Said she had to be silenced because the housing company was threatening to pull out and take its money back. I said I would have another word with her but he said he would handle it; told me to invent an excuse to get out of the way.'

'And came round and killed her,' said Blizzard flatly.

'Yes.' The voice was hoarse now, virtually a whisper.

'While you spent the afternoon in a guest house.'

'Yes,' said Savage miserably.

'Why did you take the Bentley?' asked Colley curiously. 'Surely you must have realized someone would have noticed it. It's not exactly low profile, is it?'

'Moira would have thought it odd if I didn't take it to Torquay. I always drive it on long trips and I could not afford to raise her suspicions. I tried to park it round the back of the guest house but someone had dumped a skip there so I had to park it on the front.'

He looked at them helplessly.

'I never thought he do would this,' he said, his voice breaking. 'It's a nightmare.'

'It is indeed,' nodded Blizzard and he walked from the room and headed along the corridor towards Ronald's office.

'Well?' asked the superintendent hopefully as the chief inspector walked in. 'All sorted?'

'Depends what you mean by sorted,' said Blizzard, sitting down heavily in a chair and suddenly feeling very weary. 'Put it this way, there might be a vacancy in Brian Savage's Lodge soon.'

'Brilliant,' groaned Ronald and closed his eyes.

'Hey,' said Blizzard, looking at his friend with mischief in his eyes as if the thought had just occurred to him. 'They might let you in, Arthur.'

'Not after your little performance tonight,' said Ronald gloomily. 'Or over the past few years for that matter.'

'Don't worry about it,' said Blizzard, standing up and heading back out of the office. 'I'll nip down to B & Q tomorrow and get you a trowel anyway.'

Ronald could hear him chuckling all the way down the dimly lit corridor on his way back to the interview room.

·· CHAPTER sixteen ····

FOR BLIZZARD, DRIVING home from Abbey Road in the early hours of the morning having ensured that Brian Savage was locked up for the night, many things were still unclear as he turned them over in his mind. Each time, he thought, as raindrops started to spit against the windscreen and he turned the wipers on, he came up against the same basic problem, the link between the killing of Moira Savage and Horst Knoefler. Or rather, the lack of a link. Half of the equation was easy. The chief inspector could understand why Moira Savage had been killed; she was standing in the way of a lucrative bit of business for Henderson Ramage. Colley had suggested that the sale of such a prime site might have netted him something in the region of £10m. Even after Brian Savage's cut, that was a large amount of money to earn and an even larger amount to lose because of one woman's campaigning. And that added up to motive in Blizzard's eyes.

Not so easy when it came to Savage, though, because the chief inspector was convinced that he did not mean for his wife to be killed; his shock at her murder was too genuine for that, felt the chief inspector. There was no way that Savage could ever have really thought that Ramage's hired thugs would go that far. In his more generous moments, Blizzard could even convince himself that Henderson Ramage did not mean her to be killed either. It was perfectly feasible to imagine how things might have got out of hand when the heavies arrived at the house, their arrival cloaked in late afternoon darkness. Maybe the plan to surprise her backfired, maybe she saw them, cried out, tried to reach the telephone to call the police, maybe she fought back – there was evidence of a struggle – maybe the thugs panicked. It sounded reasonable; Blizzard had seen too many victims more dead than alive to doubt what such men could do if they lost control. It was a fine line to tread and, inevitably, sometimes they stepped over it.

But Horst Knoefler, how did he fit into things? mused the chief inspector as he left the deserted city streets and headed out towards the village where he lived. Perhaps, and this idea was the one that simply would not be dislodged, he did not fit into things at all. Perhaps it was all just a big coincidence. Nothing to do with the furore over the POW camp's future but something deep in his criminal past in pre-war Hamburg. Or was it something else, someone he had angered during his business life? In Blizzard's experience, men did not get as wealthy as Horst Knoefler without standing on a few hands on the climb to the pinnacle. But if so, why did Knoefler's killer dump him in the grave? No, thought Blizzard with a shake of the head as he pulled up to his front drive, cut the lights, got out and dragged his black binbags out for the morning collection, the answer lay in the damp soil of Green Meadow Farm. Of that he was sure.

It was the dramatic turn of events an hour's drive inland, as Blizzard was struggling to get to sleep, that hurled the theory about pre-war Hamburg criminals on to centre stage. The event happened at the makeshift holding camp where the Eastern Europeans apprehended at the ferry terminal were taken after their questioning finished. A former RAF airfield, the site had been appropriated by the Home Office eighteen months previously as the number of illegal immigrants in northern England spiralled. The idea was that the centre, with its ageing huts and weed-infested runways, would be the temporary holding place for people awaiting completion of the deportation process. However, not everyone agreed with the idea of sitting tight and as Blizzard was dozing fitfully, events were taking a distinctly sinister turn.

It meant another brief night for the chief inspector, the call from Gerry Hope coming shortly before 4.30 a.m. What Hope had to say snapped Blizzard wide awake. Two hours before, a white transit van pulled up on the furthest perimeter of the camp and three men wearing black balaclava masks hacked their way through the high wire fence with industrial cutters. The van slammed through the remainder of the fence and drove at high speed towards the huts where the deportees were being held.

A couple of the soldiers on guard, alerted by the revving of the engine, ran across to intercept the van, which slewed to a halt just metres from them. More gang members leapt out and, having opened fire on the soldiers with sawn-off shotguns, smashed their way into the nearest hut. Clearly waiting for their arrival, the group from the ferry terminal revealed day clothes beneath their pyjamas and rushed out into the night air. The raiders left the younger men to make their own way out but grabbed the older man and bundled him into the van, which screeched away across the grass and out through the gaping hole in the fence and into the night. It was all over in three minutes, a highly professional operation and one that smacked of organized crime. By the time the local police arrived, they were long gone. Hope rang Blizzard during his journey back from the camp, where he had been summoned to survey the scene, and now, shortly after six, the two men were sitting in the chief inspector's office in a largely deserted Abbey Road Police station. Outside, all was pitch black, dawn still a long way off, and they had settled down with mugs of tea.

'I'm getting too old for this getting up early lark,' muttered Hope, taking a sip and hoping it would banish the thick-headed feeling.

'Me, too,' nodded Blizzard, glancing up at the office clock.

The office door swung open and in breezed David Colley. He was dressed as immaculately as ever in a dark suit, dark blue tie done up and shoes shiny, in stark contrast to Hope in his crumpled grey jacket and mud-spattered dark trousers and Blizzard in a hurriedly thrown-on suit with an unfastened tie draped round his neck.

'Morning, girls,' said Colley cheerily.

'Is he always like this?' asked Hope morosely.

'Yeah,' grunted Blizzard, glancing at his bright-eyed sergeant. 'I blame the amphetamines.'

'Anyone want a top-up?' said Colley, nodding at their mugs.

Shakes of the head, so he disappeared and they could hear the clink of cups further down the corridor then the sergeant returning, whistling cheerfully.

'Too bloody happy,' growled Hope, fatigue seeping through his bones.

'So,' said Colley, entering the office, slumping in a chair and taking an appreciative sip of tea. 'There's a great big floppy-eared mammal bounding around somewhere, gents.'

'There is indeed,' nodded Hope, fascinated by the image which popped into his head of a huge rabbit bouncing across the airfield runway. 'They definitely knew who they were after and where he was.'

'And they only took the old fella?' asked Colley.

'Yeah.'

'By force?'

'No,' and Hope shook his head. 'One of the guards said he seemed to know they were coming and that he got into the van voluntarily. Even hugged one of the rescuers.'

'And the other illegals, what happened to them?' asked the sergeant.

'The gang just left them to make their own escape,' said Hope. 'The local cops have got most of them now. Three are missing, that's all. And they won't get far, I don't imagine. But it wasn't about them, I'm sure about that.'

'So, what the hell *is* it about, Gerry?' asked Blizzard, glancing at the unshaven Customs man. 'What is so special about the old fella?'

'Well,' said Hope, opening his battered brown briefcase, 'I may be able to shed some light on that. You see, I reckon what happened earlier is something to do with your Knoefler fellow.'

'Really?' and Blizzard sat forward with a look of intense interest on his face.

'Could be the link we've been looking for, guv,' said Colley.

'It could indeed,' said Hope, handing over a couple of news-paper cuttings.

Blizzard examined them in silence for a moment or two before handing them to the sergeant and looking at the Customs officer quizzically.

'Where did you find them?' asked Blizzard.

'They belonged to the old bloke. After the break-out, we searched the hut and found them hidden in the bedstead. The guards had missed them.'

'How?'

'It's the old metal type where you can screw the top off the legs and he had stuffed them down there. Must have forgotten them in the rush to escape, or perhaps he thought we would never find them.'

'German newspapers,' said Blizzard.

'Yeah,' said Hope. 'The story appeared over there the day after you gave that press conference when you said Horst Knoefler was the man in the grave. And see how the word Hafton has been ringed in red pen on both articles.'

'It's certainly very interesting,' said Blizzard, glancing at his sergeant. 'What do you reckon, David, is our man in the truck a relative of Horst Knoefler?'

'He's certainly a similar age,' nodded Colley. 'Brothers maybe?'

'Could be,' said Blizzard.

'And there's more,' said Hope with a triumphant look on his face, rooting around in his briefcase again, fishing out a piece of paper and winking at Colley. 'I always like to keep the best till last. Sort of a big finale.'

'I always said Customs were a bunch of drama queens,' grunted Blizzard.

'It's true,' nodded Colley, with a mischievous expression on his face, 'he does always say that.'

'Don't be surprised if your bags get searched next time you go to Italy,' said Hope to Blizzard, but the detectives knew that he was not annoyed.

'So what have you got?' asked the chief inspector.

'Well, I was going to talk to you last night but your control room said you were busy with the murder over at Hawkwith.'

'Just a bit,' grunted Blizzard.

'Nice to know someone else is having a shite time.'

'I appreciate the sentiment. What were you going to tell me?'

'I got a fax late yesterday from an old mate of mine,' said Hope. 'Lad called Arnie Bellshaw. We started together over in Eastern Division when I was a copper. Arnie married a German girl and moved over there, works as a detective with the *poliss* in Hamburg these days.'

'Well, I hope you got further with him than Tulley did with the people he rang,' said Blizzard morosely. 'They hadn't even heard of Horst Knoefler. So much for German sodding efficiency.'

'I'm not surprised they hadn't,' said Hope.

'What makes you say that?'

'All will become clear. Anyway, I sent Arnie a photograph of our mystery old fella from the truck a few days ago. He came back to me yesterday after one of his informants recognized the bloke.'

'So who is he?' asked Blizzard.

'None other than Franz Hasse,' said Hope, handing the fax to the chief inspector.

'The name rings a bell,' said Blizzard.

'Drug trafficker.'

'Of course,' said Blizzard with a low whistle. 'I should have remembered; I saw a circular about him when I was in drugs squad; he operated out of Germany, didn't he?'

'Yeah, Hamburg,' nodded Hope.

'But I thought everyone reckoned he was out of the picture these days.'

'Hang on,' said Colley. 'Who is he?'

'Big-time criminal,' said Hope. 'Retired or not, we are very interested in him, as are Interpol. In fact, everyone will be fighting each other to get their hands on him.'

'Pity you've lost him then,' said Blizzard sardonically.

'Er, yes, indeed,' said Hope, an unhappy look creeping over his face.

'So who is he again?' asked Colley, glancing down at the fax handed over by the chief inspector.

'There's warrants out in half a dozen countries for him, Germany, Holland, France and the like,' said Hope. 'Oh, and Spain. Franz Hasse started out as a black market racketeer in Hamburg before the Second World War. You name it, Franz could get hold of it for you.'

'Now that is interesting,' murmured Blizzard, 'because that is exactly what Edward Cranmer said about Horst Knoefler.'

'Yeah, that could well explain a lot,' nodded Hope. 'See, apparently, Franz was in business with his brother, one Martin Hasse. Well, during the war, Martin goes off to do his duty for barmy Adolf but Franz bribes a local official to get out of war service, stays behind and builds up the criminal empire. By 1945, he's the kingpin in Hamburg and moving into heavy league stuff.'

'Like?' asked Blizzard.

'Well, there were a lot of lads came out of the army with their weapons and Hasse ran a black market selling their guns to criminal gangs all over Europe. Apparently he was responsible for a series of nasty armed robberies in Germany as well. Couple of bank tellers and a cop got shot dead during one of them in Hamburg in February 1946.'

'So, if Horst was really Hasse's brother, it's not surprising that he did not want to go home,' said Colley. 'The last thing he wanted was to be linked to a cop-killer.'

'Indeed,' said Hope. 'Anyhow, in the seventies, Franz Hasse moved into drugs, heroin mainly. Linked up with a couple of Turkish gangs, took out a couple of rival operations. All nasty stuff, lots of shooting. By the end of the seventies, police forces from all over Europe were looking for him.'

'But not here?' asked Colley.

'No, there was never any indication that he was pushing into the UK.'

'How come no one managed to arrest him?' asked the sergeant.

'According to Arnie, the cops have been close to him a few times but he keeps slipping through their fingers.'

'I can think of someone else like that,' grunted Blizzard, a vision of Eddie Gayle in his mind. 'So how come no one collared Franz?'

'Kept moving,' said Hope. 'There were a few police raids but he always managed to get out in time. Got down a hotel fire escape on one of them, leapt into a passing lorry. In another one, the police arrived at a villa on the Costa del Sol but he got away by boat. One of his henchmen shot a copper dead as they made their getaway. Arnie says the word is that Franz has people on the inside keeping him one step ahead of the game.'

'Cops?' asked Blizzard.

''Fraid so.'

'So how come you did not clock who he was at the terminal?' asked Colley.

'I simply didn't make the connection,' said Hope.

'Neither did I,' murmured Blizzard.

'Not sure there was a reason to,' said Hope. 'The interpreter thought he was Polish. What's more, Franz Hasse has never had his fingerprints taken, there's no up-to-date official picture of him, and like you said, everyone thought he had retired. There's been no evidence of him being involved in crime for at least fifteen years – he's well past seventy now – and the last time anyone heard anything about him, he was in Spain. That's why I did not make the connection until I saw the newspaper cutting and by then it was too late.'

He looked at them hopefully. 'Does that sound convincing?'

'Very good,' said Blizzard reassuringly. 'It'll play really well at the official inquiry before they stick our arses out of the window to dry.'

'So,' said Colley, 'if he was yesterday's man, how come he turned up in the back of a truck at Hafton Terminal?'

'Good question,' said Hope.

'It's got to be something to do with organized crime,' said Blizzard. 'The breakout last night had all the hallmarks. It certainly looks slick enough and they knew exactly where to go. Someone must have told them where he was.'

And he looked at Hope.

'Again.'

'Yeah,' said Hope, returning the gaze evenly, 'and it won't take long for people to start saying the tip-off came from Customs or one of your lot.'

'I just hope your lot are watertight,' said the chief inspector, mulling over the implications.

'Are yours?' riposted the Customs man calmly.

'Point taken,' nodded Blizzard then brightened up. 'Mind, the leak could be someone at the holding camp.'

'Whoever it was, there's a lot of top brass stamping around wanting answers,' said Hope. 'Give it twenty-four hours and we won't be able to move for sodding clipboards. And the Military Police are already clumping about in their size fifteens.'

'Get away,' grunted Blizzard.

'Everyone is terrified it will hit the press,' said Hope.

'I am sure they are,' said Blizzard. 'They'd have a field day. This is the kind of thing that ends ministers' careers.'

'Yeah,' nodded Hope. 'In fact, one of the chinless Home Office wonders rang me when I was at the camp – Sebastian Faffar-Faffaffar or something equally poncy – to say the Home Secretary had started an official investigation and that he wanted answers. Be warned, this is bringing a lot of shite down on our heads.'

'Brilliant,' groaned Blizzard. 'That's all we need.'

'So I suggest you keep your legs clean.'

Blizzard glanced at the Customs man's mud-flecked trousers.

'And you,' he said with a wry grin.

'So,' said Colley, nodding at the newspaper cuttings on the desk, 'can we prove Horst Knoefler was really Martin Hasse in an earlier life?'

'There is nothing concrete,' said Hope, 'but I think there has to be a good chance. Why else would Franz have the cuttings on him?'

'Indeed,' said Blizzard, cradling his mug of now lukewarm tea. 'So, how does this sound? When war breaks out in 1939, our Martin joins up to escape the German plod. At some point, he realizes the war is lost and he cannot go home because the plod will lift him and his brother has become Public Enemy Number One. So, he changes his name to Horst Knoefler; the *poliss* would not be looking for anyone of that name.'

'That makes sense,' said Colley, 'and it explains why Hafton POW Camp had no background information on Horst Knoefler. Like you said that day in Hut 23, he did not exist.'

'Indeed,' nodded Blizzard. 'And it's war so nobody cares anyway. Then what happens? The war ends, Knoefler realizes this is his golden opportunity. He can't go home, maybe he did not want to go home, maybe he had changed. Anyway, he decides to stay in Britain, marries a British girl, puts his past behind him and turns legit. To all intents and purposes, Martin Hasse is dead and buried – as it were.'

'But brother Franz knows his new identity,' said Colley, 'and when he reads in the newspaper that Horst is dead, he comes over here to find out what happened. Maybe, he thinks someone has done his brother in to get even with him over something. Franz has got plenty of enemies, I imagine.'

'Could be,' said Blizzard.

'And he can't travel the usual way in case some of Gerry's lads spot him at an airport or whatever,' continued Colley. 'So, he goes illegally with the banana boys.'

'Probably his own route,' said Hope. 'Arnie says that since this broke, cops in Hamburg have turned the heat up and discovered that Franz has gone back into business running a people-trafficking scam with a couple of Spanish shysters. They do all the work and he bankrolls them. Nice little earner for all concerned.'

'And it looks like Garry Horton is his contact over here,' said Blizzard, eyes gleaming, 'which drags Eddie Gayle kicking and screaming on to centre stage. I like it, Gerry. I like it a lot.'

'It certainly sounds OK,' said Hope. 'But there is just one

problem – who killed Martin Hasse or Horst Knoefler or whatever we decide to call him?'

'You,' sighed Blizzard, 'always have to ruin a good thing.'

·· CHAPTER seventeen ····

'I DON'T WANT to appear unhelpful,' said Edward Cranmer as he looked uncomfortably at the detectives sitting on his sofa, 'but I am not really sure I want to assist you any further.'

It was shortly after ten that morning and Blizzard and Colley had arranged to meet Elspeth Roberts and the old man at his terraced house to see if they could throw any more light on events at Hawkwith. Edward's son Tommy was there as well, dressed in overalls having taken time off his job as a garage mechanic. He sat on a chair in the window and looked increasingly worried at his father's demeanour.

'Why not?' asked Blizzard.

'People keep getting killed,' said Cranmer. 'First, poor Horst, or whatever you think he was called, and now Moira Savage. I may be an old fossil, Chief Inspector, but I have no desire to go the way they did.'

His son nodded vigorously and Elspeth Roberts just looked unhappy, severely shaken by the death threat she had received the day before and increasingly frightened at the waters in which she found herself swimming. It had been a difficult and shocking journey for a woman whose life had been spent ensconced in the ivory corridors of university life. Suddenly, all her writings about death and mayhem, produced without thinking, dispassionately, academically, and always without questioning the real impact of such tragedies on people's lives, had become horribly real. The experience had disturbed her deeply.

For Blizzard, noting her discomfort, it reinforced yet again his reservations about academia. The chief inspector was well known within the force for the way he entertained grave suspicions about some of the officers with whom he worked; the ones who had been fast-tracked from university but whom he regarded as too far divorced from the realities of the street to be truly effective. It was not, as some suggested, envy from a man who never attended university, rather that John Blizzard had always judged officers entirely on their ability to do the job. Although he readily acknowledged that some graduates turned into excellent officers, for which he gave them due respect, too many, in his view, floundered badly when it mattered and the chief inspector had displayed little time for their shortcomings down the years.

It was a viewpoint that brought him into conflict with some fellow senior officers from time to time, even with Ronald who, as a university graduate himself, felt duty bound to defend those who had taken the same route. Blizzard always won the argument, though, pointing out that Ronald had experienced the sharp end of policing and done his time on the frontline before promotion came beckoning. Ronald's respect was earned, not given, the chief inspector had said on many occasions. Instead, said Blizzard, his concerns were with those who were 'wet behind the ears and had hardly been in the force ten minutes, then they're divisional bloody commander'. Ronald, never showing it but always flattered that Blizzard held him in such high regard, also had to admit, if only to himself, that the chief inspector was sometimes right on such occasions.

The way Elspeth Roberts was reacting to her situation only served to underline Blizzard's prejudices. Now, having completed his perusal of her, he looked away, a thin smile on his face, and studied Edward Cranmer.

'All we want to know,' said Blizzard, 'is if you knew Horst Knoefler was really called Martin Hasse?'

'I have told you all I know,' said the old man, his voice firm. 'As far as I was concerned, Horst Knoefler was who he said he was. Now, I really would like you to go.'

'But did he say anything that might suggest his real name?' insisted the chief inspector.

'Please, Mr Blizzard,' said Tommy, half getting to his feet. 'Dad has said all he is going to tell you. This has upset us all. Dad knew Moira Savage and....'

'How did he know her?' asked Blizzard.

'I was one of the people who signed her petition to save the POW camp,' said Cranmer. 'Two or three years ago. And I went to a couple of her meetings about the housing plan.'

'Why?'

'I agreed with Moira that the camp should be preserved. I wanted to help her if I could. But now,' and his voice tailed off, 'now, I am frightened.'

'And it takes a lot to scare Dad,' said Tommy. 'Like, he went through the war and that.'

'But what scares you now, Edward?' asked Blizzard keenly.

'This does not seem to have been a random killing, Chief Inspector,' said the veteran. 'What if this madman is looking for other people who supported Moira?'

Mindful of the death threats against her, Elspeth nodded her head.

'Did Moira ever tell you she was being threatened?' asked Colley.

'I knew there had been some unpleasant things happen to her,' said the old man cautiously, 'but that's about it. We were hardly close friends, Sergeant. We had tea at her house a couple of times, saw each other after a meeting once, but that was about the extent of it.'

Cranmer paused and shook his head in disbelief.

'Such a terrible tragedy,' he said. 'She was such a nice woman.'

'Indeed,' said Blizzard impatiently. 'But to go back to Horst. Are you sure he never—'

'Please,' said Tommy, walking over to stand by his father and fixing the detectives with a hard stare. 'We really are serious about this, Chief Inspector. People are being killed and Dad really does not want to be involved. He has a bad heart and the doctor has said he must avoid anything that makes it worse. Please, go.'

Blizzard eyed him for a moment but one glance at the

worried expression on the old man's face and the genuine concern on that of his son was enough to convince him.

'I am sorry,' he said, standing up. 'I was forgetting myself. We will go.'

'Thank you,' said Edward Cranmer, also standing up and extending a mottled hand. 'This really has upset me.'

'I can understand that,' nodded Blizzard, shaking the hand and walking into the hallway.

As Tommy opened the door, Blizzard turned back to Edward Cranmer, who was standing in the doorway to the living-room, watching the detectives go with a relieved look on his face.

'Just one thing,' said the chief inspector. 'Have you ever received threats, Mr Cranmer? Is that why you are so frightened?'

'No. No, I haven't.'

'And he doesn't want to start getting them now,' said Tommy firmly, gesturing to the open door. 'Go, please.'

Moments later, the detectives and Elspeth Roberts were walking along the congested little terraced street to their cars parked at the far end.

'And how are you?' asked Colley, having noted her increasingly anxious demeanour throughout the meeting.

'Terrified,' she said.

'Understandable,' nodded Blizzard. 'Well, hopefully our forensics boys can get something off the piece of paper with the death threat on.'

'What did you make of Edward, Mrs Roberts?' asked Colley. 'He seemed only too eager to get rid of us.'

'People are very worried, Sergeant,' said Elspeth, turning frightened eyes on the officers. 'When it was just a murder four years ago, no one was particularly worried. It seemed a long time ago. Now, with Moira having gone, people are thinking who will be next.'

'People?' asked Blizzard. 'Like who?'

'Everyone who has worked on the site is frightened,' and she stopped walking and looked at the officers. 'Some of them knew Moira and we are widely seen as supporting her campaign to save the camp, remember. Doctor Hamer has already ordered extra security for us.'

'Mrs Roberts,' said Colley firmly, 'there is nothing to link your work with the murders. For a start, as far as we know, Horst Knoefler and Moira Savage did not even know each other existed.'

'I would not be so sure,' said Elspeth, reaching into her jacket pocket and producing a piece of paper.

'What is that?' asked Blizzard.

'I went through my old documents last night,' she said. 'To see if I had missed anything. I found this. They were some of the people who wrote to Moira to support her when she started her campaign to save the camp.'

'How come you have it?' asked Colley, taking it from her.

'She gave it to me a few months ago. I had forgotten I had it.'

'Why would she give it to you?' asked the sergeant.

'She thought it might help me.'

'Help you do what?' asked the sergeant, glancing down, his eyes widening as he read the note. Wordlessly, he handed the piece of paper to the chief inspector.

'Moira knew I was researching the history of the camp. She said I might be able to interview the people on that list for my final report. I don't suppose for a minute it was an entirely selfless act. I imagine she hoped that if I concluded that the camp was an important historical monument, it would help her fight to block the housing development.'

Blizzard said nothing; he was staring at the piece of paper in astonishment.

'Jesus,' he breathed.

Written on top of the list in Moira Savage's scrawling hand was the name Horst Knoefler.

· · CHAPTER eighteen · · · ·

'THE ANSWER IS here, I know it is,' said Blizzard.

They were standing at the side of the empty grave at Green Meadow Farm. It was mid-afternoon and the winter gloom was already closing in again. After a busy day, Blizzard had felt himself drawn back to the graveside for reasons he could not fully understand. All he knew was that he felt a powerful compunction to stand there once more. So, now he stood, staring down at the damp earth and the rain-covered blue tarpaulin stretched across the hole.

Next to him, David Colley glanced around at the foggy fields, turned up his anorak collar and shivered. Through cold, he told himself sternly, nothing more, no spooks for him. Nevertheless, he had finally to admit it, there was something about the place and this time he could feel it, too. Could feel for the first time the sensations that had so unnerved the chief inspector that first day, the sensations that the lads who stayed guard there in the early days of the inquiry had talked about in hushed, almost embarrassed tones. Colley recalled their relief when Blizzard announced there was no further need for a round-the-clock guard. Up until now, Colley had dismissed it as fanciful talk but, standing at the grave and feeling the chill fingers of the mist caressing him, he was not so sure. Not that he was going to show it to the chief inspector. One of them had to keep his wits about him.

'What do you mean the answer's here?' asked the sergeant, trying to sound casual.

'This place is trying to tell me something, David.'

'So, what is it saying?' said Colley. 'All I can hear is that sodding wood pigeon.'

'Really?' asked Blizzard, turning to look at him intently. 'Is that all you sense here?'

'Yes.'

'Honestly?'

The chief inspector's look made Colley feel uncomfortable and, finally, he admitted defeat.

'OK,' he said reluctantly. 'There's something weird about this place. Happy?'

'So let's play its game,' said Blizzard, surveying the barren fields. 'Let's try to listen to what it is saying.'

'Oh, come on, guv, this isn't about bloody ghosts,' began Colley, but the chief inspector silenced him with a look.

'I know it's not,' he said softly, staring over at the fields and the distant copse rapidly vanishing into the murk. 'But have you never stood at a murder scene and felt it talk to you?'

Colley hesitated then nodded as he recalled, as if it were yesterday, long minutes standing in a murdered 6-year-old girl's bedroom, her walls covered with posters of puppies and horses, the floor littered with dolls and felt-pens, long minutes in which he had stood in silence and fancied he almost heard her speak to him. Almost heard her voice hanging in the air, small and clear. The sergeant had thought about it many times in recent weeks since he and Jay had decided to try for a family. It was every parent's greatest fear, he had thought, and now as he stood and looked at the chief inspector, he recalled the emotions of that little girl's bedroom.

'Yeah, I have,' he sighed.

'It's what makes you a good detective,' nodded Blizzard. 'Believe it, David, this place talks to me. This is where it all started, here, in this very spot.'

'OK,' said Colley. 'Talk.'

'Thank you. Let's look at what we know. This is where Horst Knoefler died, or at least where his body was dumped, then four years later,' said Blizzard, thinking aloud. 'Moira Savage is killed less than half a mile from here.'

'OK,' nodded Colley.

'And they are linked by this place, David. Nowhere else. Moira was prepared to use the bodies to block the housing development, Horst Knoefler was a prisoner in the camp and wanted to see it preserved as well and Elspeth Roberts works here and she gets a death threat.'

'Yeah, but I really don't think we should read too much into that,' said Colley, jerking out of his reverie of a few moments ago. 'There is no evidence that Horst Knoefler, or Hasse or whatever he's called, ever met Moira Savage. All we have is his name on her list.'

'Granted,' nodded Blizzard. 'But whatever happened, their deaths are connected to this place in some way, are they not? It's a circle that we have to complete.'

'But perhaps it's not a circle,' ventured the sergeant.

'Go on,' said Blizzard. This time it was his turn to listen.

'Maybe there is no link,' said the sergeant. 'Maybe we are creating one where it does not exist.'

'But that would mean we are looking for two murderers.'

'I thought that was the idea, though,' said Colley. 'What did you say this morning, guv? That you fancied Henderson Ramage for Moira's murder but not for Knoefler. He was something different – that's what you said.'

'I know,' nodded the chief inspector, 'but that was before I came back here.'

There were a few moments of silence as the detectives stood alone with their thoughts. Colley pondered the situation: Blizzard's instincts were to be respected and many a time he had pursued a line of inquiry that seemed forlorn only for it to lead investigators to the answer. But instinct could be wrong; had been wrong before, would be wrong again, could be wrong now. Colley knew that and Blizzard knew that, hence their confusion.

'So where does that leave us?' asked the sergeant at length, stamping his feet as the cold started to wheedle its way into his bones.

'I'm not sure,' said Blizzard, looking out over the fields again, as if seeking inspiration. 'But I tell you, David, this place is trying to tell me something.'

'Well, I wish it would bloody hurry up,' said Colley, flapping his arms. 'I'm freezing my knackers off out here.'

'OK,' chuckled Blizzard, clapping the sergeant on the shoulder and heading across the field. 'Let's go and see if we can prevail on your nice Mr Harvey to give us a cup of tea.'

'Yeah,' said Colley enthusiastically. 'And his missis does a madge fruit cake.'

'Madge?' asked Blizzard, shooting him a look as they approached the gate. 'I thought she was called Jane.'

'Yes, she is,' said Colley, looking surprised. 'I told you that half an hour ago. Is your memory going, guv?'

'No, it isn't. What the hell does madge mean?'

'It's Colley-speak,' grinned the sergeant. 'Short for magical.'

'Short for bloody bonkers,' grunted Blizzard.

Colley beamed at him. They were approaching the welcoming lights of the farmhouse and as they did so, a figure appeared from behind the barn and started walking rapidly down the track towards them.

'That's Robin Harvey,' said Colley, peering through the mist.

'Does he always look that worried?' asked Blizzard.

'I've never seem him this bad.'

'Can I have a word?' asked Harvey, walking up and lowering his voice conspiratorially, even though the surrounding fields were desolate and empty. 'I think there's something you should know.'

'See,' said Blizzard, turning to his sergeant with a triumphant look on his face. 'I told you this place would talk to me. All you have to do is listen.'

·· CHAPTER nineteen ····

'YOUR GERMAN WAS here.'

The detectives looked in amazement at the dishevelled figure of farmhand Dennis Hoare. After their meeting on the track, Robin Harvey had taken them into his cosy kitchen where they were confronted by Hoare's cowed figure. Colley recognized him as one of the farmworkers he had seen on previous visits to Green Meadow. The sergeant remembered him because every time he approached Hoare, he looked uncomfortable. At the time, the sergeant had attributed it to the usual suspicion of police felt by many people, particularly in rural areas. You got used to reactions like that; it had taken Jay's parents of two years to feel fully comfortable with him and even now, her father would say something indiscreet then clap a hand to his mouth as if he should have stayed silent. For his own peace of mind, Colley had run a check on Dennis Hoare and discovered a clean record. He had also asked around his colleagues, and officers over at Burniston, and no one recognized the name so the sergeant had dismissed him from his thoughts. How wrong could you be, he thought uneasily.

Hoare sat at the kitchen table, head bowed. He did not make an appealing sight. Aged in his mid-thirties, his lanky brown hair was uncombed and scruffy, his gaunt features grimy from a day's work and he had not shaved for several days. His skin was weatherbeaten and cracked after a lifetime working outdoors. He was dressed in jeans and a green pullover and his battered cap rested on the table. But it was his eyes that made the strongest impact on the detectives. Deep pools of fear.

Hoare's appearance was in sharp contrast to his boss. Robin Harvey was a fresh-faced man in his late twenties, brown hair neatly combed, beard immaculately clipped and eyes bright but betraying concern; he had found himself thrust into the centre of the detectives' inquiry and for a man who only wanted to farm and to ensure he could look after his wife and two small children, that was difficult to handle.

After making the detectives a welcome mug of tea, his wife took the children in into the living-room and Colley could hear, because the sturdy wooden door was not quite closed, the sound of the television. He allowed himself a small smile; *Thomas the Tank Engine* if he was not mistaken. Such things were of interest to him now since he and Jay had agreed to try for a baby. Colley had not told anyone this, not even Blizzard. He was still not sure how the chief inspector would react and Colley could understand it if he received one of those disapproving looks from his friend. Indeed, the sergeant's own view had long accorded with the chief inspector's, that his unsocial hours and hazardous profession did not sit neatly alongside fatherhood but Jay had argued strongly for many months. Her clock was ticking and greater forces than a lowly sergeant were at work. In the end, the forces won, as they always do, and Colley relented, if reluctantly.

When he gave his agreement, Jay had kissed him softly on the forehead and said he would never regret it and that he would make an excellent father. Looking anew since then at the bleary-eyed new parents working at Abbey Road, Colley still needed to be convinced. All these thoughts momentarily crowded into his mind as he heard the *Thomas the Tank Engine* music from the video which Harvey's young children were watching. Colley smiled as he heard them shout out at the screen as their favourite characters appeared. James, that was the red engine, he thought instinctively.

Sitting next to him, Blizzard was not occupied with such thoughts and he eyed the crumpled figure of Dennis Hoare with keen interest.

'I take it you mean Horst Knoefler was here?' he asked, using the name the farmhand would recognize.

'Yeah,' and Hoare nodded.

'When?'

'Four years ago.'

'How did you know it was him?'

'I overhead Mr Ramage call him that.'

'Which one?'

'Henderson.'

'I assume his father was dead by then?'

'Na,' and Hoare shook his head. 'He were kill't a few days later. That's how I remember it were four years ago.'

Blizzard and Colley exchanged glances.

'So exactly when was this?' asked Colley, banishing thoughts of Thomas from his mind and concentrating on the job in hand. 'What month?'

'Spring. It were nearly lambing time.'

'What happened?' asked Blizzard.

'They were walking in the field near the grave, talking like.'

'Who were?' asked the chief inspector.

'Henderson Ramage and the German.'

'How come you saw them?'

'I were there to bring a sack of summat out of one of the huts and were walking along the other side of the hedge. That's when I heard Henderson call him Knoefler.'

'Did you hear what they were talking about?' asked Colley.

'Only a bit,' and as Hoare nodded his head, a lock of lank hair flopped over his eyes. 'They waz talking business, like. The German fella, he said he wanted to buy some of the land.'

'Which bit?' asked Blizzard.

'The field where them prisoners are buried.'

'Are you sure?' asked Blizzard sharply.

'Yeah. Definitely.'

'Why would he want to do that?' asked the sergeant.

'Said he didn't want to see the bodies covered in houses. Said it weren't respectful.'

159

'How did he know about the housing plan?'

'Henderson made no secret of it. There'd been quite a few blokes in suits looking round the place.'

'And what did Ramage say when Knoefler told him this?' asked Blizzard.

'I don't fair know but he didn't sound very pleased. Said he could get more money from housing. Then Henderson, he sees me, and runs after me. He shouts at me, like. Trying to find out what I had heard. I said I never heard owt. He said I must never tell anyone like.'

'And you didn't?' asked Colley.

'Na.'

'Not even me,' said Robin Harvey, shaking his head at the thought of what had been happening on his farm without his knowledge.

'Why not?' asked Colley, looking hard at Hoare.

'Henderson said he would kill me if I did,' and the fear was back in the farmhand's eyes. 'You don't argue with him.'

'No, indeed,' said Blizzard. 'So, what happened next?'

'I got out of there, went back to the barn, tried to forget it ever happened.'

'And,' asked Blizzard, an edge to his voice, 'did you see Horst Knoefler leave the farm, Mr Hoare?'

The farmhand hesitated. The tension thickened in the air with every second that he delayed his reply. The detectives knew what was holding him back; they could almost smell his fear.

'Mr Hoare,' said Blizzard sharply. 'Answer the question.'

'Na,' said the farmhand at last. 'Na, I didn't.'

'Thank you,' said Blizzard softly, and glanced at Colley. 'Circle squared, I think, Sergeant.'

'There's one more thing,' said Hoare suddenly.

'More?' asked Blizzard.

'Yeah,' nodded the farmhand. 'There were rows.'

'Between whom?' asked Blizzard.

'Old man Ramage and Henderson. Terrible rows, they were. One time, when they was standing in the barn arguing, Henderson hits him, busted his lip. Sent him flying, it did,' and he shook his head. 'Nasty business it were, seeing father and son at each other like that.'

'What were the rows about?' asked Colley.

'His father didn't want to sell the land,' said Hoare, speaking rapidly, 'but Henderson said they could get a lot of money. The old man, he said no; said the farm had been in his family for a long time and it were going to stay there. Said the Ramages were farmers and that was that. When he found out that Henderson had been inviting folks to look at the land behind his back, he were furious.'

'And that is when Henderson hit his father?' asked Colley.

'Yeah,' Hoare nodded, adding after a pause to collect his thoughts. 'Then, after it happened, Willy jumps up and shouts that Henderson would only sell the land over his dead body.'

'Are you sure that's what he said?' asked Blizzard sharply.

'Yeah. Yeah, that's what he said. More shouted it, like. He were furious. I'd not seen the old fella that angry before.'

'Then what did he do?'

'Stormed off without saying owt. When Henderson saw me, he said he'd kill me if I spoke about it. He weren't messing, neither. Then his father gets shot,' and the farmhand allowed himself a strange kind of smile, his teeth yellowed and crooked. 'You work it out, Mr Blizzard.'

'Jesus,' breathed Blizzard. 'You know what you're saying, Dennis?'

'Don't I just,' said the farmhand bitterly. 'I ain't slept proper for four years worrying about it. Then when that Knoefler fellow were found, well....'

'But,' pointed out Colley, 'the inquest decided Willy Ramage's death was misadventure, that he fell on to his gun, probably after the dog bumped into him.'

'Pha!,' exclaimed Hoare. 'Your detective inspector, Wheatley or whatever they called him, he believed anything anyone told him. He were on a different planet.'

'What do you mean?' asked Blizzard.

'Them townies knew nowt. That dog had been walking out on the lands with Willy for years, do you really think a pheasant or owt like that would spook him? Everyone knows it weren't no dog that shot old Willy,' and Hoare gave a dark chuckle, his leer exposing his crooked teeth again. 'I mean, can you really see that happening?'

'No,' said Blizzard, eyeing him morosely. 'I don't suppose I can.'

·· CHAPTER twenty ····

'YOU WANT TO do what?' asked Ronald, sitting forward on his chair and gaping at the detectives in astonishment.

'You heard me, Arthur,' said Blizzard coolly. 'I want to re-open the investigation into the death of Willy Ramage.'

It was six o'clock that night and after a hurried discussion in the car on the way back from Green Meadow Farm, Blizzard and Colley had been united in their proposed course of action and were now sitting in the chief superintendent's office at Abbey Road, trying to convince him to agree. Outside, in the darkness of another Hafton winter's night, the wind was getting up and the officers could hear the rain driving ever harder against the window in the silence that had descended on the room. The detectives were not surprised that Ronald's reaction had been less than enthusiastic; such a course of action was fraught with potential difficulties.

'But why?' asked Ronald plaintively after a few seconds of pondering the bombshell.

'The RSPCA has been on, sir,' said Colley, his face deadpan. 'They think the dog was unfairly convicted. A case of wuff justice, as it were.'

Ronald stared at him for a second then at Blizzard's equally impassive face.

'This is some sort of stupid joke, yes?' asked the superintendent hopefully.

'It is a stupid joke,' nodded Blizzard, winking at the sergeant, 'but actually we do want to reinvestigate the death.'

'But why, for Pete's sake?' asked the exasperated superintendent.

'Actually, it's more for Willy's sake,' said Blizzard drily.

'But I thought that was all done and dusted years ago. The coroner brought in a misadventure verdict.'

'He did,' said Blizzard. 'But we think he was wrong. That is why we want the case reopened.'

'You'd need good cause, John.'

'We have good cause. We believe there is a link between the deaths of Horst Knoefler, Moira Savage and Willy Ramage.'

'And you'd need new evidence to re-examine it,' warned Ronald, uncomfortably conscious how obstructive he must be sounding to the detectives.

'We've got new evidence,' said the chief inspector coolly, understanding the superintendent's reluctance. 'A farmhand has come forward to say that father and son argued bitterly. Henderson wanted to flog the land off for as much as he could, his dad wanted to keep it all for farming. Henderson even attacked him over it.'

'And Willy told his son he would have to kill him to get permission,' noted Colley. 'A few days later, he was as dead as the proverbial.'

'And I'd have to clear it with Burniston,' sighed Ronald, as if he had not heard the detectives' words. 'And the coroner.'

'Then clear it with them,' said Blizzard. 'But tell them we want to do the inquiry from here because it fits in with the Knoefler inquiry. I don't want anyone at Burniston doing it.'

'And the chief constable will need telling,' added Ronald unhappily.

'Then tell him.'

'Look, is this really necessary, John?' and Ronald looked at him with dark eyes. 'I mean, really? You're not just doing this for devilment?'

'Arthur,' said Blizzard, an edge in his voice, not something that often happened when he discussed matters with his friend. 'I know why you don't want this to happen and I know it puts you in a difficult position.'

'Too right it does,' said Ronald gloomily. 'Danny Wheatley is destined for great things. The word is he will be promoted to chief inspector and brought on to the chief constable's team when he comes out of traffic next month. There's even talk that he will be after my job before long.'

'God forbid,' murmured Blizzard.

'So, the chief will not exactly be delighted when he hears you want to reopen one of his blue-eyed boy's biggest cases.'

'I know all that,' said Blizzard, 'but if we think Danny Wheatley got it wrong over Willy Ramage, then it's our duty to check it out, whoever gets hurt, surely? Unless I am mistaken, that's our job. Isn't it?'

Ronald, who was torn as so often between the need for diplomatic relations and self-preservation and the need to do the right thing, thought for a moment then came down instinctively on the side on which he always came down. Blizzard knew he would, Colley knew he would, Ronald knew he would, but they played the game anyway.

'OK,' nodded the superintendent. 'But, be warned, John, there'll be a lot of shit coming down on your head over this.'

'And yours,' said Blizzard coolly.

'Don't I know it. I can't see the Burniston commander welcoming this for starters. You know what Michael Giles is like; you're hardly top of his Christmas card list after that dust-up you had with him last year.'

'I know but you've made the right decision,' said Blizzard earnestly. 'That's what makes you different from those other muppets.'

'Thanks,' said Ronald, genuinely appreciating the comment but still uncomfortable at the thought of the difficult days to come. 'I imagine you want to do the inquiry yourself?'

'No,' and Blizzard gave a wry smile. 'Somehow I think that would make things worse. Besides, Tulley has turned up some new lines worth chasing on the Knoefler case.'

'Then who will you get to do it?'

'I was thinking of Chris Ramsey.'

'Why?' asked Ronald, although the tone of his voice suggested he approved.

'He's a DI, a solid officer, people respect him and he doesn't carry the baggage I do. Besides, doesn't he know Danny Wheatley?' and he glanced at Colley. 'I thought you said they started out as rookies together over at Halcrombe Street? Maybe Danny will open up to Chris a bit more.'

'OK,' said Ronald. 'But listen, John, watch Chris Ramsey's back all the time. I don't want him cut adrift over this one.'

'I watch all their backs,' said Blizzard. 'You know that, Arthur.'

'Yes, I know,' said Ronald, 'but you have to realize there's a lot of important people in headquarters that like Danny Wheatley.'

'It's a DBN thing,' said Blizzard sardonically.

'DBN?' asked Ronald bleakly.

'Department of Brown Nosing, sir,' explained Colley.

'Maybe so,' said Ronald, 'but whatever you think of him, Danny Wheatley is well and truly on the way up.'

'He must be,' nodded Blizzard. 'They've started calling him Daniel on the memos.'

'For God's sake, will you take this seriously, John!' exclaimed Ronald. 'This is as delicate as it gets. There's a lot at stake for all of us. And don't forget that I was the commander at Burniston when all this happened.'

'Yes, I know,' nodded Blizzard. 'And the last thing I want to do is get anyone in trouble, certainly not you. Or Danny, for that matter. He's a good officer and no one wants him to have got it right over Willy Ramage more than me but if the force has made a mistake, we have to sort it out. You know that, Arthur.'

'Yes, I know,' sighed Ronald. 'I know.'

'And if the chief gives you a hard time over it, remind him that the third line in that "pledge to the public thing" he published last month banged on about accountability.'

'Somehow I might not mention that,' said Ronald, fixing the officers with a stern look. 'But be careful; if word of this gets out, it could do a lot of damage to Danny Wheatley's career.'

'Oh, I shouldn't worry about Danny,' said Blizzard airily as he stood up and reached for his jacket. 'I'm sure there's some traffic bollards for him to sort out somewhere.'

'Yeah,' said Colley, following him out of the office. 'There was one on top of the bus stop outside my house last night. He can start there.'

And they walked out of the office, watched in exasperation by the superintendent. Brave? Stupid? Reckless? he asked himself. No, and with a shake of the head he glanced out of the window and sighed heavily, just good. In the higher circles in which he moved, Ronald had found himself increasingly depressed at the lack of integrity he encountered among some police officers. Only some of them, mind, he reminded himself sharply as his mind wandered, but it was there all the same. SPS, Blizzard called it. Slippery Pole Syndrome. And, thought Ronald, difficult as they might be to work with sometimes, give him Blizzard and Colley any day. He allowed himself a smile as he heard the two officers heading down the corridor; Ronald couldn't remember the last time he had heard the chief inspector whistling. If ever.

· · CHAPTER twenty-one · · · ·

NIGHT HAD FALLEN over the city again as John Blizzard made his way wearily across the wasteland the next evening, illuminating his way with a torch and peering into the shadows, the broken glass crunching beneath his feet as ever. Behind him, beyond the ramshackle tall brick wall abutting the municipal car park, the orange city centre lights twinkled and he could hear the low hum of traffic and the occasional blast of a car horn. Over to his left, and behind him now, the large glass windows of the main railway station were brightly illuminated and the platforms inside were bustling with early evening commuters. But here on the wasteland, Blizzard felt cut off from all that, as if he was in a different world. It was a sensation that he enjoyed and, for many years, the engine shed had proved a refuge when he needed time to think as fire and fury broke above his head. Which was why he had come now.

It had been a busy and testing day because, as Ronald had predicted, the news that Blizzard wanted to reopen the Willy Ramage case had caused major problems in headquarters that morning. Ronald had slept little overnight, turning the facts over and over in his mind, but whichever way he looked at it, Blizzard had a point. The superintendent realized that he had no alternative but to edge out along that limb once again for his chief inspector. Ronald hoped to dear God that his friend's instincts were right. So, he was in work early and, having stared at the phone on his desk for a pensive moment or two, he sighed and made the call.

Over the next two hours, he received a string of calls,

culminating in a summons to see the chief constable, who made it clear that he was dismayed that the judgement of the officer he was about to promote to his personal staff, and about whom a press release was already being prepared, was being called so spectacularly into question. As Ronald had warned, Danny Wheatley had friends in high places and it proved an uncomfortable half hour in the chief's office for the superintendent, the most uncomfortable he had endured since taking the job at Abbey Road. Nevertheless, he resolutely stuck to his case. During that time, the instinct for justice outweighed the instinct for self-preservation and, more than once as he listened to the chief constable's rant, Ronald heard Blizzard's words echoing round his head. At one point, Ronald even heard himself repeating them. 'But if the force has made a mistake, we have to sort it out. You know that, sir,' he said.

For all that, though, at one point, it looked as if his request might be rejected as the angry chief constable dramatically hurled his pen across the desk, narrowly missing the startled superintendent. The pen clattered into the bin and the noise alerted the deputy chief constable, who had been deliberately loitering outside the office, waiting for the right moment to intervene. It was an intervention that swung the argument. Relatively new to the post, having been appointed from one of the Yorkshire forces, Ken Bright was a no-nonsense hardened career detective, a burly dark-haired man in his late forties, a veteran of numerous murder inquiries, a man who talked straight, expected police officers to lock villains up and who had worked his way up through the ranks the hard way. A man, as Blizzard had said on more than one occasion, who knew what the job was all about. Indeed, many officers had expressed surprise that the chief should allow such a markedly different character to take on the job as his deputy.

Bright now proved his worth again, arguing forcefully that there was no alternative to reopening the Willy Ramage case. Clearly irritated that his deputy had so blatantly taken sides against him, the chief constable had pursed his lips then reluctantly nodded his assent. 'You owe me one,' Bright had said to Ronald as they walked along the corridor afterwards. 'And so does John Blizzard. Just make sure the bastard's right.'

Throughout all this, Blizzard had deliberately kept out of the way, not difficult given that there was so much to organize. One pressing matter was Brian Savage. Despite his admissions, there was no corroborating evidence to link him to the murder of his wife so the detectives had bailed him pending further inquiries. As part of keeping out of the way, the chief inspector found time to visit the ferry terminal for an impromptu meeting with Gerry Hope, ostensibly to update himself on the search for the missing Franz Hasse.

Sitting in his shabby office, cluttered with case files and cardboard boxes and with several dirty coffee cups ranged across the desk, Hope looked somewhat hangdog. He explained that the pressure from the Home Office to find out who leaked details of the villain's whereabouts to his rescuers was growing, intensified by the fact that the German had now gone to ground so no one could ask him. That did not surprise Hope; the Customs man was convinced that he would not risk escaping the country through an airport or ferry terminal but would make his own arrangements after lying low for several days. Compounding the situation had been a leak to a local freelance reporter whose exclusive story had been picked up by the national media. Hope and Blizzard discussed the situation for the best part of an hour.

Shortly after three that afternoon and back at Abbey Road, Blizzard was summoned into Ronald's office to be informed that the chief constable had reluctantly given permission for Ramsey to reinvestigate the shooting of Willy Ramage. When told of his new task by the chief inspector an hour later, Ramsey had not been particularly enthusiastic at the prospect – he and Danny Wheatley went back many years – but, professional that he was, he agreed to take on the job. Blizzard sometimes struggled with Ramsey's straight-laced ways, and his passion for administrative matters, but in that moment, he felt nothing but admiration for the detective inspector. Not that he told him so.

So now, the city hall clock having just struck seven, Blizzard was walking towards the railway shed to spend some time with the Old Lady and gather his thoughts. Many a crime had been solved in the hours he spent struggling with recalcitrant bolts or standing back to look at the engine and lose himself in dreams of the day when she would steam again. Fumbling about in his anorak pocket for the keys, Blizzard was startled by the scraping of a shoe and whirled round as a figure emerged from the side of the engine shed.

'Who's there?' he called out, trying to conceal the alarm in his voice and shining his torch into the darkness.

'The Fat Controller,' said a voice. 'Arthur said I might find you here.'

Recovering from the surprise, Blizzard peered into the steam.

'Ken?' he said, as the deputy chief constable stepped out of the shadows and into the chief inspector's torch beam. 'What are you doing here?'

'I needed to see you,' said Bright.

'You'd better come in then,' said Blizzard, unlocking the shed.

A few minutes later, they were sitting on battered old stools in the shed, cradling warming mugs of tea and surveying the old locomotive.

'She's a beauty,' said Bright. 'Or at least she will be when you've finished.'

'How come so appreciative?'

'My father drove engines round the colliery near my home when I was kid. Sometimes he let me go on the footplate. Don't supposed he was allowed to but no one ever seemed to mind. I loved it. Happy days,' and he sighed wistfully.

'Yeah,' nodded Blizzard, recalling his own childhood fascination with steam. 'You know, you are the first copper I have ever heard say anything nice about steam engines. Colley says I'm crackers.'

'He might have a point,' said Bright, and his voice had suddenly changed.

'Go on,' said Blizzard, 'I know you are not here to talk steam engines, spit it out.'

'OK,' nodded Bright. 'For a start, we never had this meeting.'

'OK.'

'And, frankly, I should not be here.'

'But you are.'

'Yes,' and Bright took a sip of tea before looking earnestly at the chief inspector. 'Listen, John, there is some heavy shit coming down and I am afraid it may be about to drop on your head.'

'Meaning?' said Blizzard, although he already knew the answer.

'This Willy Ramage business. There are people in head-quarters want to see you out of the door over it.'

'Tell me something I don't know,' grunted Blizzard. 'It's been like that for years.'

'Yes, but this time it's different,' said Bright.

'Because of Danny Wheatley?' asked Blizzard incredulously. 'Why, for God's sake?'

'He has been earmarked for great things. The chief sees an attack on Danny as an attack on him.'

'Maybe he does, but if Danny got it wrong, then surely we have to look at it again?' exclaimed Blizzard in exasperation. 'That's what I said to Arthur and I imagine that is what he said to the chief. And you agree with that; I heard what you did today and I'm grateful for the support.'

'Yes, I do agree,' nodded Bright. 'But I'm not sure the chief sees it that way. Look at it from his point of view; he's about to promote Danny Wheatley to his personal staff and if it turns out he made a gaffe over the Ramage death, the chief will have to change his mind. You can imagine what that will say about the chief's judgement.'

'Yes, but—'

'And, he is already under pressure over Brian Savage.'

'Oh, come on!' exclaimed Blizzard. 'Surely, you're not saying that because they're in the Freemasons together, the chief wants this case dropped?'

'No,' and Bright shook his head. 'No, he's too good a copper for that. Don't look like that, John, the chief may have many faults but he's not as bad as some people paint him. You might be surprised to hear that he backed you over Savage. He actually thinks you are a decent detective.'

'Really?' asked Blizzard, slightly mollified.

'Yes, but when you let Savage out, the first thing he did was ring the chief and protest his innocence. And he wasn't the first; the chief has had a few calls from Lodge members since Savage's arrest, saying that they are angry at the way he has been dealt with.'

'For God's sake,' protested Blizzard. 'He set up his wife for a beating.'

'I know, and the chief told him that,' said Bright, 'but all I'm saying is go careful. You have bruised plenty of egos in your time and there are some senior officers who would like nothing better than to see you drummed out of the force. This could give them just the weapon they need.'

'And you?' asked Blizzard shrewdly. 'Do you want to see me drummed out of the force?'

'You know the answer to that, John. If I had my way you'd be bloody chief constable by now,' and Bright chuckled. 'When I had retired, of course.'

'Thanks for that,' said Blizzard, genuinely touched by the support.

'Besides, there's something else,' said Bright.

'Top up?' and Blizzard nodded to the kettle.

'Aye, thanks,' and they stopped talking for a few moments as the chief inspector filled up their mugs with hot water and rooted round in a rusty old cupboard for a new box of teabags.

'So what's the something else?' asked Blizzard once they were settled again. 'This business with Franz Hasse, I imagine?'

'Yeah,' nodded Bright. 'The Home Office is turning the heat up. There's hell on, and all the publicity about them letting one of Europe's most wanted villains slip through our fingers has caused a lot of embarrassment in Whitehall.'

'I believe the *Sun*'s headline was Brea-Kraut,' said Blizzard with the ghost of a smile.

'It was,' nodded Bright, allowing himself a smile as well. 'But this is heavy-duty stuff. The Opposition is kicking up a big fuss over it and there's even talk that the Home Secretary might have to resign unless he can come up with some good answers pretty soon. And he may have to go even if he can't.'

'Why?'

'Apparently, there's a document floating around which shows that he was warned months ago that the detention centre was not secure. If the press get hold of that, he's dead in the water.'

'Whoops,' said Blizzard. 'But how does this affect me, Ken? I accept we didn't clock him when he was caught but neither did anyone else and he wasn't in our custody when he escaped.'

'No, but the inquiry is looking for a scapegoat, John. Someone tipped off the gang where to find Franz Hasse and someone tipped off the press. If the inquiry finds that the leak came from within Western CID, you can imagine what that will mean.'

'Yes, I can,' said Blizzard grimly.

'And did it?' asked Bright intently.

'Did it what?'

'Did it come from inside your CID?'

'I would not have thought so,' said Blizzard then looked sharply at Bright, alerted by something in his voice. 'Have you heard something?'

'No.'

'Then are you saying the inquiry might decide that the leak came from us anyway?'

'I'm not sure,' said Bright, downing the last of his tea. 'But if someone decides a scapegoat is needed, you or Gerry Hope are sitting ducks. I happen to know that Gerry Hope is held in high regard by his boss; can you say the same for the chief constable?'

'Well, it is a long time since we played golf together,' said Blizzard drily.

'Exactly.'

'Jesus Christ,' said Blizzard, looking up at him in dismay. 'Would the chief really stitch me up like that?'

'Who knows,' and Bright shrugged. 'Depends how high the stakes are. All I'm doing is laying it out for you.'

'God, I hate politics,' sighed the chief inspector.

'Yeah, so do I but sometimes you have to play the game.'

'So what do I do now?' asked Blizzard, the question genuine, the voice showing how rattled he was.

'Well, as I see it, you've got two choices,' said Bright standing up and heading for the door.

'Go on.'

'Number one,' said the deputy, glancing back at him with a thin smile, 'is roll your trouser leg up, stick a hankie on your head and start learning the funny dance.'

'No thanks,' said Blizzard, chuckling at the quip despite the seriousness of the situation.

'Thought not,' said Bright, grimacing as the door groaned when he wrenched it open. 'Then your only alternative is to bring this business to an end as quickly as you can. Thanks for the tea.'

And he walked out into the night. Behind him, John Blizzard sat in the chill of the engine shed and stared blankly at the locomotive. Suddenly, he felt very alone.

·· CHAPTER twenty-two ····

JOHN BLIZZARD WAS not one to admit defeat easily and early the next morning, the POW camp spoke to him in tones that were strong and clear. Its language was the language of hate and it resonated down the ages. Blizzard heard it after a disturbed night punctuated by nightmares about dead soldiers and gaping graves; the chief inspector had finally jerked awake at 4 a.m., sweating profusely, heart pounding, hands clammy. Finding himself unable to get back to sleep, and with his racing mind guaranteeing that rest was impossible, he took a hurried shower and drove to Abbey Road Police Station.

For the next two hours, he sat in his office, reviewing all the evidence and the reports from his team, while sipping endless mugs of tea. Unusually for him, he put sugar in them, sensing that he would need all his energies for the day ahead. The reports did not make for pretty reading. The pathologist Peter Reynolds had been able to glean little of use from the body of Moira Savage, and Graham Ross and his forensic officers had likewise drawn a blank in their search of her house; the murder weapon remained elusive. It all meant that, for the moment, Brian Savage was in the clear despite his admission over his relationship with Henderson Ramage. Exhaustive checks into Savage's background had confirmed much of his story but without firm evidence that Ramage or one of his heavies killed Moira, police were reluctant at this stage to charge her bereaved husband with anything. All they had was an uncorroborated confession and there was no way the CPS could buy that. Brian Savage would have to wait, thought Blizzard.

There was little better news on other fronts. The toiling Tulley had produced virtually nothing new on the Horst Knoefler/Martin Hasse case. They knew more about him now but whole areas of the German's life remained as mysterious as ever, although it was clear that concealed somewhere was a secret dark enough to drive someone to murder. As it stood, thought Blizzard, Henderson Ramage remained the prime suspect, largely because of Dennis Hoare's testimony about the two men's stormy meeting at Green Meadow Farm four years earlier. Perhaps Knoefler insisted that he be sold the land, pushed his luck, lost his temper, perhaps Ramage struck out at him, killed him by accident. No, and Blizzard shook his head, Moira Savage was not killed accidentally, nor was Willy Ramage or Horst Knoefler. No, Henderson Ramage was not unlucky, he was violent. But, with the farmer still missing, the inquiry was in danger of running into the doldrums, thought Blizzard gloomily as he tossed the last of the reports on to the desk, and sat staring out of the window into the inky blackness of the morning.

The more he thought and the more he looked down at the files scattered around his desk, the chief inspector felt ever more strongly that just one piece of the jigsaw was missing, one piece of information that would complete the picture. He felt ever more sure that he was looking at it, which was when one of the statements on the desk caught his attention and he heard again words that had been uttered during one of their earlier interviews. He did not know why they came back then but they did and they spoke to the chief inspector in a way they had not done before.

Blizzard reached for the report of the interview and started reading. What if, he asked himself, he had been approaching this the wrong way? What if he was not looking in the right direction? What if the answer was beneath his nose all the time? What if, and he did not know where this thought came from either, the answer came from beneath his feet as he stood at the graveside, at that first moment just thirty-six hours after the bodies were unearthed at the farm? Something that had gone unnoticed amid the detectives' desire to see

Henderson Ramage, Eddie Gayle and Garry Horton locked up, that had been masked by the revelations about Moira Savage and her contact with Horst Knoefler/Martin Hasse, and hidden by the discoveries about his brother's criminal history.

'Jesus Christ,' breathed the chief inspector, letting the file drop on to the desk once more. 'Perhaps *they* didn't do that kind of thing.'

Just then, the custody sergeant walked into the office, clutching a brown envelope. Blizzard smiled at him; they went back many years.

'Sorry, John,' said the sergeant, looking surprised and glancing up at the clock that read 6.35 a.m., 'didn't know you were in. How long have you been here?'

'You don't want to know, Frank.'

'What brought you in?'

'Couldn't sleep.'

'I keep telling you, hot milk and whisky, mate. But go easy on the milk, don't want to overdo things.'

'Thanks,' chuckled Blizzard. 'What kind of a night have you had?'

'So-so,' said the sergeant, slumping in a chair wearily. 'Couple of drunks brought in for fighting about eleven-ish, then another three after a brawl at the Red Dragon, oh, and traffic lifted a drink-driver just after midnight....'

'Nice to see they do some good,' grunted Blizzard.

'Yeah, well, you're not exactly the most popular person with traffic right now after what you're doing to Danny Wheatley.'

'But I thought half of traffic don't like him?' asked Blizzard in surprise. 'Why the hell would they care if I make him look stupid?'

'Think it through,' said the sergeant. 'If you wreck his chances of promotion, they'll be stuck with him.'

'Bloody marvellous,' sighed Blizzard. 'Damned if I do, damned if I don't. Anyway, you sorted the drink-driver out with your customary sensitivity?'

'Summat like that,' chuckled the sergeant, then gave a disbelieving shake of the head. 'He were completely off his face. Three and a half times the legal limit and crashed into a lamppost. Lad could hardly stand he'd downed so much booze. He fell over three times on his way to the cell. Then I'd just got him sorted when young Robbie Jakes comes in with a bloke he nicked trying to sell drugs outside the Manor Row shops.'

'He's a good young officer, he is,' nodded Blizzard. 'I quite fancy him for a stint on CID, actually. I'll have a word with him later. That's the third dealer lifted outside the shops this month; might be time for a Blizzard blitz.'

He nodded at the envelope.

'What's that?' he asked.

'Oh, aye, Bernie asked me to bring it along. Some lady brought it into the front office late last night. Bernie was a bit busy with a knob-head who had lost his wallet at the time and asked me to deliver it. In all the chaos last night, I forgot it. That why I didn't bring it in earlier. Sorry.'

'No need to apologize to me,' said Blizzard. 'You know that.'

The chief inspector was about to open the envelope when his phone rang. He listened grimly to the message from the control room operator for a few moments then stood up and reached for his jacket.

'Sorry, Frank,' he said. 'Duty calls.'

'Doesn't it always,' murmured the custody sergeant and ambled off to make a cup of tea.

Half an hour later, Blizzard was striding up the track to Green Meadow Farm, where he could see, through the blackness of the morning, the flashing lights of the police patrol cars in front of the farmhouse. Colley detached himself from the small knot of people standing in the farmyard and, a tall figure silhouetted by the lights, walked briskly towards the chief inspector.

'Where was he found?' asked Blizzard.

'In there,' said Colley, gesturing to the barn, turning and falling into step with the chief inspector.

'What happened?' asked Blizzard, as they made their way across the muddy farmyard.

'Robin Harvey found him,' said Colley. 'He always takes a short cut through on his way to the milking shed.'

They walked into the gloom of the barn and the sergeant flashed his torch across to the baled hay at the end of the building.

'That's where he was lying,' he said.

Dennis Hoare had been found with a severe head injury, his blood staining the straw on the floor maroon. The paramedics had applied immediate first aid and he had been rushed off to the city hospital, hovering between life and death. As the officers stood and surveyed the scene, Hoare was undergoing emergency brain surgery.

'Did Harvey see anyone?' asked Blizzard.

'No, no one. But I reckon he's holding something back, guv.'

'Harvey? I thought you said he was clean,' said the surprised chief inspector.

'I reckon he is but I'm pretty sure he knows more than he is letting on. He's just got that look about him. Like he's frightened.'

'We need to turn the screw on him, then. Any idea when Hoare was attacked?'

'The paramedics reckon a couple of hours ago.'

'Any idea why he was in the barn?'

'No to that as well,' and Colley shook his head. 'According to Harvey, he was not due to begin work until ten today. He'd worked a couple of late nights so Harvey gave him a lie in.'

'So what brought him here?' asked Blizzard, turning and walking out of the barn.

'No idea,' shrugged Colley. 'Nothing makes any sense any more, guv.'

'I wouldn't be so sure about that,' said Blizzard enigmatically.

It was then that the chief inspector remembered the envelope in his pocket and fished it out.

'Here,' he said as he ripped it open, 'shine a light on this, will you?'

'What is it?' asked Colley, flashing the torch.

'Left by some woman last night,' and Blizzard glanced down, noticing the name scrawled on the top of the note. 'Ah, it's from Elspeth Roberts.'

'What does she want?'

'Once we knew Horst Knoefler was a fake name, I asked her if she could find out anything about Martin Hasse's war record, and—' but suddenly Blizzard's voice tailed off as he read.

'What is it?' asked Colley, aware that the chief inspector had gone pale. 'What's the problem, guv?'

'This time,' said Blizzard softly. 'It is over. It has to be. For all of us.'

Colley grabbed the note from him and started reading. After going through it twice, he looked at the chief inspector with a perplexed expression on his face. But Blizzard was not there; he had been transported to a wild place, the man's place, and heard again the roar and clatter, felt the panic as the man fought for his life, heard the death rattle of his final breath. Saw the pain in his face – many faces this time, many struggles for life. The pain that comes with fear. The fear of men who knew they could never go home, would never see their loved ones again, would never feel the warmth of the evening summer sun on their back or feel the trusting embrace of a child. And in that moment, as the first glimmer of the morning light streaked the horizon above the copse, John Blizzard remembered them all. And finally understood.

'Clarissa?' asked the sergeant, glancing up from the piece of paper in puzzlement. 'Who the hell is Clarissa?'

'Clarissa,' said Blizzard, 'is a who and not a she – and she is what this is all about.'

'I still don't get it,' said the bemused sergeant, looking down at the piece of paper again. 'And surely there is no way that—'

'No time for explanations now. Listen, get Tulley or someone to wrap things up here, will you?'

'Why, where are we going?' asked Colley, following him along the track.

'There's a couple of things I need to check,' said the chief inspector. 'Then we are going to put an end to all this, once and for all.'

'But—'

'I'll explain when we get back to the factory,' said Blizzard, as he reached into his coat pocket for his car keys. 'Come on, Sergeant, time to lay some ghosts to rest.'

·· CHAPTER twenty-three ····

IT WAS SHORTLY after 9.30 that morning when Edward Cranmer opened his front door and looked at Blizzard and Colley standing in the street. There was no surprise on his face.

'I have been expecting you,' he said calmly, surveying their grim expressions.

'I know,' replied Blizzard.

Cranmer glanced at the two stern-faced uniformed officers who were standing at a discreet distance a little further down the street.

'Did you really need to come mob-handed?' he asked.

'You never know in these situations,' said Blizzard as he and Colley walked into the hallway and through into the living-room.

'How did you find out?' asked Cranmer, then gestured to the sofa, courteous as ever. 'Please, do sit, gentlemen.'

'Thank you,' said Blizzard. 'It was *Clarissa*.'

'Ah,' nodded the old man, lowering himself into one of the armchairs and looking at Blizzard with a knowing smile. 'Then, surely, you must know that your Uncle Frank was on board the *Clarissa* the night she was torpedoed?'

'Yes, I do,' nodded Blizzard.

'Then you, of all people, must understand, Chief Inspector.'

'Not sure I do,' said Blizzard. 'At least, not everything. Not yet.'

'He had to pay for what he did.' The old man's voice was calm, the gaze steady, blue and clear.

'But in such a brutal way?' asked Blizzard, shaking his head again. 'I mean, was there no other way?'

'Do you know what he did?' asked Cranmer.

'Just what I read in books.'

'The reality was much worse,' and Cranmer's eyes were moist. 'You cannot imagine.'

'No, but was it worth killing for?' asked the chief inspector.

'A promise is a promise.'

'You don't believe that,' said Blizzard, eyeing him intently.

'Not really. Besides, times change. It all happ—'

'No,' and the old man shook his head vigorously. 'No, I owed it to them. To all of them. It doesn't matter when it happened. Surely you of all people understand that, Chief Inspector?'

'Maybe,' said Blizzard.

'I promised,' repeated the man, voice breaking. 'I promised that night. I have fought it for years but it had to be done.'

'Are you going somewhere, Mr Cranmer?' asked Colley, noticing a couple of suitcases hidden behind the sofa.

'Yes,' nodded the man, regaining his composure.

'Where are you going?'

'Anywhere. Somewhere you cannot find us,' and Cranmer's face assumed a sad expression as he tapped his chest. 'I am not long for this world, Sergeant. We are going somewhere where the sun can shine on my last days. Were going, I suppose now.'

'You're not going anywhere,' nodded Blizzard.

'No,' and the man shook his head sadly. 'No, I imagine not. I wonder, do you mind if I ask how you made the link between me and *Clarissa*?'

'Elspeth Roberts worked it out. Stumbled across the passenger list in the local history library.'

'She was the one who told me about Frank as well,' nodded Cranmer. 'I told her she would not be able to keep her mouth shut.'

'When was this?' asked Blizzard sharply.

'This morning. She came round, tried to get me to give myself up to you. Said you might go easy on me if I co-operated.'

'So where is she now?' asked Blizzard anxiously.

'She's with him,' and the man eyed him coolly.

'Jesus Christ!' exclaimed the chief inspector, jumping to his feet. 'Why?'

'She was a loose end.'

'What do you mean?' snapped Blizzard, already half way to the door.

'She knows too much,' said Cranmer and he shrugged on seeing the detectives' horrified expressions. 'Like I told you before, it's never over. Not really.'

'Where are they?' demanded Blizzard.

'Up at the farm. After all,' and Cranmer smiled at them, 'there's a grave ready dug, isn't there?'

· · CHAPTER twenty-four · · · ·

THE TWO DETECTIVES sped through the city streets in the chief inspector's Granada, Blizzard weaving in and out of traffic, flashing his headlights and honking his horn to ensure that vehicles moved out of the way. Before long, they were out in the countryside, Blizzard hurling the car round sharp corners, the squeal of the tyres cutting through the morning silence. Neither man spoke to each other much on the journey but both realized that any delay in arriving at Green Meadow Farm could condemn Elspeth Roberts to death and, as they drove, Blizzard rapped out orders over the radio and they listened to the constant, urgent chatter over the airwaves as other police officers converged on the scene. During the journey, Colley tried fruitlessly on his mobile phone to contact Robin Harvey, eventually giving up in exasperation when there was no answer from the farmhouse.

It was starting to rain under leaden skies as the detectives' car edged its way up the track to the farm and slowed to a halt next to the gate leading into the fields. The detectives got out and stood for a moment to survey the farmhouse a hundred metres ahead of them. All seemed peaceful.

'What do you think?' asked Colley, sensing his heart pounding. 'Could be in the house.'

'No, the grave,' said Blizzard, gesturing to the path leading across the fields. 'Has to be. Remember what Edward said about the grave being already dug.'

The detectives set off at a run. As they brushed through damp grass along the field margins, they could hear the wail of sirens in the distance as police officers headed for Green

Meadow for the second time that morning. Blizzard and Colley ran in silence for several minutes through the sodden fields. For all Blizzard's new-found fitness, Colley still easily outstripped him and it was the sergeant who first spotted the motionless figure. Glancing to his right over the hedge into the field, Colley saw him, dressed in a military jacket and standing still and silent as he stared into the grave. Colley could see that the tarpaulin had been pulled back.

Hearing the sergeant's warning shout, the man looked up and gave a startled cry. As Colley flipped himself over the gate and jumped down into the field, the man started to run across the damp earth of the field, heading towards the copse. Noticing that he was holding a wooden club down by his side, Colley slowed to a walk as he moved to intercept his quarry. As he saw Colley approaching, the man wielded the club above his head.

'Keep back!' he shouted. 'I'll do you!'

'Come on, Tommy,' said Colley, coming to a halt and eyeing Edward Cranmer's son cautiously. 'What good would that do?'

'Too late for that, I've gone too far,' said Tommy, and he nodded at the figure of John Blizzard, who had appeared at the gate and was pausing for a moment or two to catch his breath. 'Your chief inspector knows that.'

Hearing the click of the gate as Blizzard entered the field, the sergeant turned and was about to shout something to the chief inspector when Tommy Cranmer struck. Moving with remarkable agility for a big man, he ran forward and swung the bat at the sergeant. Caught off-guard, Colley instinctively threw up an arm and tried to duck out of the way but the bat caught him a glancing blow on the elbow and he screamed out in pain. Staggering backwards, he sunk to his knees, groaning as he clutched his right arm. Cranmer advanced a couple of paces and stood over him for a moment then glanced at the approaching Blizzard.

'Keep back!' he snarled. 'I'll do him. I will, you know.'

'Leave him be!' shouted the chief inspector.

'Sorry,' shrugged Cranmer, looking down at Colley and raising his bat. 'Like I said, I've gone too far.'

Colley looked up at him in horror, which was when John Blizzard found new reserves of strength, gave a holler and ran the last few metres between them before hurling himself into Cranmer. The big man lurched backwards and stumbled, dropping the bat, and Blizzard was on him in a second. For a few moments, they struggled on the ground then Cranmer lashed out a fist and caught the chief inspector a ferocious blow to the side of the head. Blizzard let go of his quarry and rolled over, temporarily unsure where he was, and Cranmer grabbed for his bat. Colley staggered to his feet only to be caught by another swingeing blow from the club, this time across the side of the head, sending him crashing to the ground again, his mind a galaxy of stars.

'Bastard!' hissed the sergeant through gritted teeth, as Cranmer started to run across the field.

'You OK?' asked Blizzard, rubbing his ear and shaking his head to clear his thoughts.

'Yeah,' nodded Colley, face twisted with pain and blood dribbling from a gash on his cheek. 'Never been better.'

He reached out a hand to the chief inspector and the two men hauled themselves shakily to their feet. Breaking into a run after Cranmer, the detectives noticed that over to their left, sprinting along the hedge, were several uniformed officers followed by Fee Ellis, who was catching them up rapidly. Behind her was the toiling, more rotund, figure of Dave Tulley.

'Check the grave!' shouted Blizzard, pointing.

One of the uniform officers raised a hand and veered off in the other direction. Ahead of the two detectives, Cranmer halted and stood and surveyed his pursuers for a moment before plunging into the copse, disappearing for a few moments in the gloom beneath the interlocking branches of the trees. Running unsteadily, Blizzard and Colley were the first to follow him into the woodland, stopping and looking about wildly for a moment as they tried desperately to spot him. Then the sergeant gave a cry as a movement caught his eye.

'There!' he shouted, as Tommy Cranmer appeared on the far side of the copse.

It was then, on the edge of the next field, that the big man caught his foot in a creeper, stumbled and fell.

'Come on!' shouted Blizzard.

They crashed through the undergrowth, ignoring the grasping barbs of branches and bushes as they closed in on their man. Now only a few metres ahead of them and having scrabbled to his feet, Tommy Cranmer turned and wielded his club again.

'That's enough,' he rasped, 'or I promise, I'll kill the both of you.'

Blizzard, still catching his breath, and Colley, acutely aware of the stabbing pain in his head and the dull ache of his arm, eyed him for a moment, pondering their next move.

'Let me deal with it,' said the chief inspector, stepping forward.

Behind them, there was the noise of Fee Ellis and other officers entering the woodland, and further in the distance, the sound of more police sirens drifting across the morning air.

'Come on, Tommy,' said Blizzard. 'There's nowhere to run.'

Tommy Cranmer glanced past the chief inspector and saw that the perspiring Tulley had also reached the copse. Over to his left, he was vaguely aware of other shapes running across the field to cut him off. Blizzard held up a hand and all the pursuers ground to a halt, waiting for the chief inspector to make the next move. Cranmer eyed Blizzard, eyes a mixture of fear and fury. In the distance, the chief inspector could hear the sound of a tractor; it seemed strangely incongruous for a scene charged with such emotion.

'I ain't going to let you take me,' said Cranmer.

'We are going to have to,' said the chief inspector, holding out a hand. 'Give me the club. It's over.'

'War ain't never over,' said Cranmer, mud-streaked face twisted with anguish, fighting to keep back the tears, but grasping ever tighter to the weapon until his knuckles glowed white. 'And I ain't going to prison. I'll end it here if I have to.'

'It's already ended,' said Blizzard softly.

'It ain't,' rasped Cranmer.

He turned and ran out of the copse, out across the bare

field, having spotted a gap between the closing uniforms who had run round the far side of the copse.

'Shit,' gasped Blizzard.

'I'll get him,' said Colley and set off in pursuit.

From the edge of the field, over to their right, there appeared a red tractor, driven by Robin Harvey. Spotting the fleeing figure of Tommy Cranmer, he changed direction and drove towards the running man, accelerating all the time, engine roaring. Cranmer turned and gave an alarmed shout and, as the tractor neared at speed, he stumbled and fell. It was enough for David Colley and he hurled himself on to Cranmer and wrenched the club from his hand. Cranmer swung a punch but Colley, releasing the pent-up anger from the blows he had received a few minutes earlier, struck out, his fist catching Cranmer clean on the jaw. Cranmer fell backwards but leapt to his feet and advanced on the sergeant, which was when Blizzard reached the scene. By now, Robin Harvey had jumped out of his tractor and run to Colley's defence. Cranmer looked as if he were about to launch yet another attack when Blizzard intervened.

'If you keep running,' said the chief inspector, harsh edge in his voice. 'That will leave your father to take the rap for this alone. Is that what you want, Tommy, for him to die in a prison cell after all he has done for his country?'

Cranmer stopped and eyed him uncertainly for a moment.

'A cheap shot, Chief Inspector,' he said at length, defeat in his voice, 'but no, that is not what I want.'

'There you are. Besides,' and Blizzard looked at him shrewdly, 'men from the Hafton Regiment don't run out on their comrades. You stand side by side in the face of the enemy, don't you? Wasn't that the regiment's motto: *Stand As One*? Isn't that was this is really all about, Tommy?'

Cranmer looked at him in silence for a moment then hung his head.

'Yeah,' he said in a voice so quiet they struggled to make out the word.

'Give me the club,' said Blizzard, taking a step forward and holding out his hand again.

Cranmer let the weapon drop from his grasp and Colley darted forward to pick it up and produced a set of handcuffs from his pocket, nimbly clipping them around Cranmer's wrists. The big man did not resist; the fight had gone out of him.

'Did you really think you would get away with it?' asked Blizzard, walking up to him.

'A promise is a promise, Mr Blizzard,' said Cranmer, sounding calmer now as he stared at the chief inspector.

'Yes, but it wasn't your promise, was it?' said Blizzard.

'It were my Dad's promise,' said Cranmer sadly. 'And that made it my promise.'

'But did Edward really want—?'

'Edward ain't my dad.'

'What?!' exclaimed Blizzard.

'Na.'

'Then who was?' asked the chief inspector.

'My Dad was Harry Crooks. Edward and his wife adopted me after Dad died,' and Tommy Cranmer looked at them with pain his eyes. 'See, I never met my Dad, Chief Inspector. All I have is an old photo of him and a name. Can you understand what that feels like?'

Blizzard recalled the black-and-white photograph he carried in his wallet and gave an involuntary nod; he could understand it only too well.

'Tell me about him,' he said.

'Private Harry Crooks, Hafton Regiment,' and Tommy sounded proud to say the words, before his expression clouded over. 'Died 1942 when his troop ship went down.'

'The *Clarissa*,' said Blizzard.

'Yeah,' said Tommy with a crooked smile. 'Dad sailed on the *Clarissa* with your uncle. And he died with him.'

'I know,' said Blizzard, tone softening. 'I know, Tommy lad.'

'So you see,' said Cranmer, 'it *was* my promise. They were my Dad's last words, Chief Inspector, and I had to do it for him.'

'There are other ways.'

'No,' and there was hatred spitting through Cranmer's

voice this time. 'No, this was the only way. And you needn't look like that, Mr Blizzard. I did it for Frank just as much as the others. I did it for you.'

'That I doubt,' said Blizzard firmly.

One of the uniformed officers emerged from the copse and walked towards them with heavy steps.

'Did you find Elspeth Roberts?' asked Blizzard, noting the constable's grim expression.

'I am afraid so, guv.'

'Dead, I take it?' asked the chief inspector, his face impassive.

'Yeah. Skull bashed in. It's a real mess,' and he shuddered. 'Blood everywhere.'

Blizzard nodded and turned to Cranmer, noticing the look of savage pleasure on his face.

'No, Tommy,' he said wearily. 'You didn't do it for Frank and you didn't do it for me. Take him away, Sergeant.'

'Yeah,' said Colley then looked surprised as the chief inspector started to walk across the field. 'Hey, where are you going?'

Blizzard made no reply. Staring out over the misty fields, he was transported to a wild place, the man's place, and heard again the roar and clatter, felt the panic as the man fought for his life, heard the death rattle of his final breath. Saw the pain in his face – many faces. Blizzard glanced skywards and noticed that the pale winter sun had vanished behind the clouds. At the going down of the sun, he thought, we will remember them. And in that moment, John Blizzard remembered them. Remembered them all.

And mourned.

·· CHAPTER twenty-five ····

AS THE SS *Clarissa* sailed through the clear Atlantic waters on a night in September 1942, the moonlight creating a golden causeway to mark her way, her passengers were blissfully unaware that they were taking part in her last hours. Most of them were asleep, the only exceptions the bored crew members standing watch. None of them knew that by the first streaking light of dawn, their bodies would be floating still and noiselessly in the tide.

Such a fate did not await Sergeant Edward Cranmer, of the Hafton Regiment, the only man who would survive the sinking of the *Clarissa*. Perhaps his fate was worse than that of those who died that night, because for every day of his remaining life, he would relive those terrible events and hear the screams, his nights tortured by grotesque nightmares of the friends he left behind in the chill waters of the Atlantic. At least they only experienced it once. In his dreams, he would reach out as if he could touch them, but they were long gone and each time he awoke, it was with a sharp stabbing pain in his chest. His doctor blamed angina, Edward Cranmer said nothing but knew it was guilt.

Now, sitting in the interview room at Abbey Road Police Station as dusk fell on another winter's evening outside, Edward Cranmer stared into the middle distance and recounted in quiet words the scenes that his mind had rerun every night for more than fifty years, heard again the explosions and the rending of metal, the screams and the frantic thrashing in the water, the sizzle of the bullets strafing the surface of the water. Then the silence, broken only by the gentle lapping of the ocean as the bodies floated still and life-less around him, their grey eyes appearing to mock the only man left alive in the dead sea. Shoulders bowed, eyes sunken, lips hardly moving, Edward Cranmer told his story in a voice that was hardly audible to the two detectives sitting opposite him.

John Blizzard and David Colley listened without speaking. For Blizzard, this was as much the story of his uncle's last hours and, for the first time, he was able to hear it from someone who was there. And as he listened, Blizzard was transported to a wild place, Frank's place. The chief inspector saw again in his mind's eye the photograph of the baby, precious Charlie, held in Frank's arms as if he were made of cut-glass, and as he listened the chief inspector felt the tears welling up. Colley, also deeply moved by what he was hearing, said nothing but listened in silence to Cranmer's testimony, occasionally glancing at the chief inspector with concern.

The SS *Clarissa* was a 17,300 ton ocean liner, constructed in one of Hafton's bustling shipyards for a passenger line and launched amid much fanfare in 1913, another mighty vessel of which the city was so justly proud. Her picture was used tall and proud on the front page of the evening newspaper, another testament to the skill of the shipyards' craftsmen. Within a year, though, optimism had turned to something darker. Pressed into action as a troop ship during the Great War, *Clarissa* plied her trade between the English east coast and France, taking excited and optimistic soldiers to the trenches and bringing them back, wounded of body and broken of mind. Several times, she came close to being sunk but each time the U-boat torpedoes fizzed harmlessly wide and, somehow, *Clarissa* survived unscathed. Some said she was charmed. Other, more experienced, mariners, said nothing. Perhaps they sensed her time was yet to come. Perhaps they knew that the sea always claims its own.

When peace returned to Europe, *Clarissa* went back to her life as an ocean liner, hosting parties in her dining-room, witnessing cheery deck games, defying mighty storms and huge seas to ensure that her passengers reached their destinations in safety and comfort. And even though other liners sank to the bottom of the sea from time to time, *Clarissa* sailed on. She was, some said, a lucky ship. The mariners still kept quiet.

Then came 1939 and the advance of Hitler's Nazi war machine across Europe. *Clarissa* was once more pressed into service as a troop ship and, in August 1942, she was berthed at her home port of Hafton for several days at the end of which 485 men of the Hafton Regiment trooped aboard, ready for the journey to the desert battlefields of the conflict with Rommel and his Afrika Korps. Slipping noiselessly out of the port on the evening tide, *Clarissa* sailed down the English Channel and headed past France, Spain and Portugal, bound for North Africa, evading all the time the U-boats which criss-crossed the sea in search of prey. Veering slightly more west than her captain would have wished to avoid a ferocious Atlantic storm, *Clarissa* was in the Azores when her time came, as the old mariners knew it must.

Her nemesis was a proud-eyed U-boat captain called Martin Schwere. Unbeknown to *Clarissa*'s crew, she had been tracked for six hours by his vessel which had slipped noiselessly through the dark waters unseen and unheard, its captain eagerly watching *Clarissa*'s every move like a hawk as he ensured he kept well out of detection range. Martin Schwere was a ramrod-straight blond young man with Aryan features and piercing blue eyes that hid a dark secret. Before the war, he had been Martin Hasse, one of the notorious gangster brothers developing their criminal empire in Hamburg. As the police closed in on them in 1939, the outbreak of war came as a golden opportunity for Martin Hasse to disappear so he changed his name and joined the U-boat service. It was not just about evading the police, though, because, unlike his more mercenary brother Franz, Martin was a patriot, a German who believed in Hitler's dream and who was prepared to lay down his life for the fatherland.

The young Schwere, a keen sailor before the war, soon distinguished himself as an able mariner and rapidly worked his way up the ranks, eventually being given his first command of a U-boat in the early months of 1942. His commanders' faith in his abilities was well placed and, that night, as he tracked *Clarissa* across the Atlantic, Schwere should have been a satisfied man. His vessel had already claimed four British vessels under his captaincy, three troop ships and a couple of frigates, sending them to the bottom of the sea with unerring aim. Many hundreds had died, many more were rescued more dead than alive from the cold waters by Allied ships. Schwere had watched the carnage with satisfaction, knowing that he was serving the Führer.

Each kill added to his growing reputation but also to his growing trepidation. Martin Schwere was a worried man. Word had reached him that his exploits had not gone unnoticed by the high command and that a medal ceremony was planned the next time the U-boat docked, his picture due to be widely circulated as part of the Nazi propaganda effort. That was bad news for Schwere, whose dreams of an anonymous war were under serious threat and who feared that the police would arrest him next time he docked. Already that night, as he contemplated his next move against the *Clarissa*, Martin Schwere was thinking further ahead and decided that the time had come for him to disappear again.

But all this was for the future and, as he eyed the ship through his periscope, he knew that the time had come to move in for the kill. On board the *Clarissa*, the troops and the crew were unaware how close the U-boat was. Among them was newly married Frank Robinson, who had joined the army in 1939 and was already a veteran, having been among the men who escaped the killing fields of Dunkirk. The days before he had joined the ship had been among the happiest of his life. Having been transferred to the Hafton Regiment a few weeks earlier, ready to join the North Africa campaign, he was allowed leave to return to his native Lincolnshire to see his family.

Frank spent happy days with his wife and his sister and revelled in the time he spent with his new-born nephew Charlie. Revelling in being Uncle Frank, he had posed in the garden for a picture taken by his brother-in-law, a copy of

which was now safely tucked away in his kitbag. Precious
memories of a precious time but a time which came to an end
all too soon. Tearful goodbyes were mumbled, and, watched by
his sister, Frank walked to the end of the lane with heavy
foot, never looking back, never daring to. He could not have
known that as she watched him disappear from sight through
tear-filled eyes, his sister glanced down at baby Charlie,
peacefully asleep in her arms, and said quietly, 'we'll not see
him again, little one.'

Now, Frank was on board *Clarissa* in his bunk, also asleep,
dreaming of summer fields and village cricket matches. His
was not to be as peaceful a slumber as Charlie's, though,
because shortly before midnight, Schwere gave the order to
move in and the hunter-killer slipped smoothly towards the
vessel, releasing two torpedoes when she was within range.
The first one smashed into the bow, the second struck amid-
ships and *Clarissa* lurched, throwing the sleeping men from
their beds and causing widespread panic throughout the
decks. Although crippled, *Clarissa* was still afloat, listing
badly to one side, and her captain desperately rapped out
orders from the bridge in an attempt to get her moving away
from the U-boat, which had now surfaced. *Clarissa*'s gunners
trained their fire on the German vessel but without effect and
twenty minutes later, Schwere lost patience. Alarmed at
reports that a British warship was in the area and had been
alerted to the incident, he ordered two further torpedoes to be
fired. Fizzing across the still sea, they found their target with
unerring accuracy. Not for nothing had Martin Schwere and
his crew won the respect of the fleet.

One of the torpedoes slammed into the armoury and with
a mighty roar, a great wall of flame lit up the night sky.
Clarissa, scarred and ruined, lurched even further to one side
and started to tip over and her captain ordered his men to
abandon ship. He did so with a heavy heart; it was the second
vessel he had lost to U-boats on this treacherous run to North
Africa. On the first occasion, he had drifted for fifteen hours
before being picked up. Not so this time. Within minutes, he
would be dead. All but one of them would be dead.

Martin Schwere watched with grim satisfaction as the panic-stricken crew and troops rushed for the lifeboats being lowered down the side of their ship. Those unable to scramble aboard hurled themselves into water soon foaming with their frantic thrashing, and the air was filled with the terrible cries of drowning men, many already horribly burned from the explosion. Further blasts rent the night air and the ship groaned and cried out in her pain; with a final sigh, *Clarissa* sank beneath the boiling waters, sucking many men down to their deaths with her. It was then that the U-boat moved in. The survivors watched in horror as, the moonlight glinting off her sides, she moved noiselessly, majestically, grotesquely, towards the bobbing lifeboats. Standing atop the conning tower, Martin Schwere looked down on the sailors' plight, allowed himself the thinnest of smiles – and gave the order.

Cranmer paused.

'What order?' asked Colley, increasingly rapt by the story and desperate to find out how it finished.

Cranmer shook his head. Words were beyond him.

'The order,' said Blizzard quietly, looking at the broken old man sitting before him, hunched over the table. 'To open up with the machine guns.'

'Jesus,' breathed Colley, looking at the chief inspector in horror.

There was silence as Cranmer fought back the sobs now racking his body. After a few moments, he looked up at them with haunted eyes. Ghost eyes. The eyes of a dead man walking.

'Was Frank one of them, Edward?' asked Blizzard softly. 'Was he one of the men who were machine-gunned?'

'I really don't know,' said Cranmer. 'I could not see anything except....'

His voice tailed off.

'Except the U-boat,' said Blizzard, finishing the sentence.

Cranmer nodded dumbly.

'So what happened to you?' asked Colley. 'How come you survived?'

'There were three of us,' said Cranmer, finding fresh

strength. 'Clinging to a piece of wood, not sure what it was, a bit of a lifeboat I think.'

'Who was with you?' asked the sergeant, who had now taken over the questioning as Blizzard sat in silence and composed his thoughts.

'Ronnie Illingworth and Harry Crooks.'

'And Harry was Tommy's father?' asked Colley.

'Yes. We saw the U-boat heading towards us,' and Cranmer shuddered. 'I see it every time I close my eyes, Sergeant. We knew they were our last moments. Schwere had already started strafing the boats. It was only a matter of time before it was our turn. That was when we made the promise.'

'And what exactly was the promise?' asked Blizzard, coming to his senses.

'It was Harry's idea. He said we had to promise that if any of us got out of there alive, we had to find the U-boat captain and kill him.'

'And you agreed?'

'Yes,' and Cranmer shrugged. 'I thought I was about to die. What difference could it make? But Harry was insistent. Wanted to make sure we were genuine, said he wanted to die knowing that there was a chance his child would be avenged for the loss of his father.'

Cranmer shook his head sadly.

'He'd never even seen Tommy,' he said. 'He had only heard that his wife was pregnant the day before we embarked.'

'Then what happened?' asked Blizzard, trying not think of Charlie.

'The U-boat approached,' and Cranmer's eyes assumed a far-off expression as he relived those moments again. 'As it got nearer, we could see Schwere standing on the conning tower. I looked straight into his face and he looked back. But there was nothing, no emotion in his eyes. I swear to this day that he smiled. Then the guns opened up.'

Cranmer started to cry.

'Ronnie went first,' he sobbed, seeing again the foaming waters. 'Gave a cry and disappeared beneath the water. Then Harry. The bullets just ripped him apart.'

'But not you,' said Colley.

'I wish they had,' said Cranmer bitterly.

He paused again to compose his thoughts.

'I was hit twice,' he said, so quietly they struggled to make out the words. 'In the back and shoulder.'

Another pause.

'I went under,' and now the words were coming fast. 'It's true you know, your life does flash before you. Then I was on the surface again and the U-boat was heading away. All around me were bodies, floating on the surface, but there was no sign of the two lads.'

'When were you picked up?' asked Blizzard.

'Five hours later,' and Cranmer's eyes assumed a glassy expression. 'Five hours in a dead sea, Chief Inspector. Do you know what that is like?'

'No,' said Blizzard with a shake of the head. 'I have tried to imagine it many times but I can't.'

'You never can,' said Cranmer. 'Not unless you were there.'

'And Martin Schwere?' asked Blizzard. 'When did you see him again?'

'A couple of years later,' said Cranmer. 'When he was brought into Hafton POW Camp. I couldn't believe it.'

Martin Schwere's journey to the camp had been a circuitous one. Within a week of the sinking of the *Clarissa*, and with his U-boat closing in on port and having briefly surfaced one night, he had disappeared, missing presumed drowned, but having swum ashore and re-invented himself as German soldier Horst Knoefler. Joining an infantry regiment, he hurled himself back into the war as an anonymous infantryman with no past. Eventually, he was injured as the Allies pushed through France in the weeks following D-Day. Ironically, at one point his unit was just a few miles away from the men of the Hafton Regiment, Edward Cranmer among them. When he was captured after a firefight, Knoefler was shipped back to Hafton POW Camp to spend the remainder of the war behind its fences. By that time, he had tired of war, had seen through the Nazi dream and felt sickened by the things he had done. Now, he was happy to serve his time and had already decided that he did not want to go home when peace came to Europe.

'I recognized him straight away,' recalled Cranmer. 'First time I saw him, playing chess with one of the other prisoners.'

'Did he recognize you?'

'No,' and Cranmer shook his head. 'Why should he? I was just another victim.'

'And what about the promise?' asked Colley. 'Did you try to kill him?'

'Thought about it,' and Cranmer gave them a soft smile. 'Felt I owed it to the boys but somehow I never had the opportunity. Not that I was too disappointed, we'd all had enough of killing by then. So, I left the camp and I thought that was that. I tried to put him out of my mind.'

'But you couldn't?' said Colley.

'He was always there,' nodded Cranmer. 'Then four years ago, I saw him in Hafton High Street, coming out of a bank. Recognized him straight away. Couldn't believe it.'

When the detectives sat down later to put all the pieces together, they surmised that after the war, having rebuilt his life, kept his latest assumed name and tried to forget what had happened, Knoefler found all those old memories rushing back when he heard about the plans to build houses on top of the old wartime graves. Appalled at such an indignity for old comrades, Schwere headed for Hafton, hoping to persuade the Ramages to sell him the field in a secret deal. But, as he quickly discovered, there was no reasoning with a man like Henderson Ramage and he was forced to leave, the farmer's racist insults still ringing in his ears. Saddened by what had happened, he nevertheless resolved not to try again; he had tried and he could live with that.

But not for much longer, and it was in Hafton High Street that the chance event that was to cost him his life took place.

'How come you recognized him after all those years?' asked Colley. 'You were both fifty years older.'

'The eyes, Sergeant. Sometimes, they looked straight through you – like you weren't there. They did it that night in the Azores, they did it when he played chess and they did it on that day in Hafton High Street.'

'So, what did you do?' asked Colley.

'Nothing. But when I got home I rang Tommy. Told him everything.'

'Why do that after all those years?'

'I'm not sure,' shrugged Cranmer. 'Suddenly I felt I had carried the burden alone for too long. And I never thought for one moment that Tommy would react the way he did.'

'I take it Tommy knew he was Harry's son?'

'Yes. It became harder to keep it from him when he was a child. We put it off as long as we could and eventually told him when he was fifteen or sixteen, I think it was.'

'How did he take it?' asked Blizzard.

'He said nothing but I could tell he was devastated,' and Cranmer shook his head. 'I talked to someone else who was adopted once and they said that when you find out, it's like the earth on which you stand has been shifted and you don't recognize the new place. I have never forgotten that.'

'Did you tell Tommy about the promise when you told him he was adopted?' asked the chief inspector.

'No, there seemed no reason for him to know. I think it was for the best.'

'Why?' asked Blizzard.

'He changed when he found out he was adopted. Always seemed so angry. It got worse as the years went on. That's what did for his marriage: he hit his wife. After the third time, she took herself and the kids off and he never saw them again. And he lost a couple of jobs after fall-outs with his bosses. Punched one of them. God knows what he would have done if he had known about the promise.'

'But you did finally tell him,' said Blizzard.

'Yes, the day I saw Schwere in the high street.'

'Not a smart move, Edward.'

'I know, but seeing him had shaken me up. I suppose I was not thinking straight, and I guess I felt that so many years had elapsed that Tommy would not do anything about it. I suddenly had this idea that it would help him make his peace with himself if he could meet Martin. See that he was a man who was simply doing his job.'

'But you were wrong,' said the chief inspector.

'I didn't think I was, at first. Tommy said he would like to meet him.'

'So how did you find Schwere?' asked Colley.

'It was easy. I guessed he was over on business so I rang around a few hotels and tracked him down. Wasn't difficult,' and Cranmer allowed himself a dry chuckle. 'They didn't have many Knoeflers in that day.'

Despite the situation, the detectives allowed themselves a smile.

'The rest was easy,' said Cranmer. 'I told Martin I wanted to see him again, maybe have a game of chess for old times' sake. Didn't let on that I knew he was the U-boat captain, of course.'

'Then what happened?' asked Colley.

'We brought him back to my house in the evening, gave him a couple of whiskies and Tommy offered to drive him to the hotel. Martin was already in the car when Tommy came back into the house and said he owed it to his dad to carry out the promise. I was shocked, he'd been as nice as pie all night. I tried to talk him out of it, honestly I did, but he just would not listen.'

'You could have called the police,' observed Blizzard.

'Tommy's my son, Chief Inspector,' and Cranmer gave him a crooked smile. 'Besides, I'd made a promise, hadn't I? And if the truth be told, I didn't try to talk him out of it very hard; part of me wanted the bastard to die. Does that make me an evil man, Chief Inspector?'

Blizzard made no reply.

'So what happened then?' asked Colley.

'Tommy told me they went out towards Hawkwith. Said he stopped in a country lane and hit him with the car-jack. Buried him on the farm with the other prisoners. He reckoned that even if the bodies were dug up, no one would check too carefully if there was an extra body. Everyone knew that was where the influenza victims were.'

'They nearly didn't check,' murmured Blizzard, recalling the scepticism he had encountered when first arguing that something was not right at the grave. 'And I assume Moira Savage had to die because she knew what you had done?'

'She didn't know anything, why should she?' said Cranmer, surprised at the suggestion. 'We hardly went around advertising it. No, her death was nothing to do with us.'

The detectives exchanged glances. 'Henderson,' mouthed Colley.

'But you did kill Elspeth Roberts,' said Blizzard.

'I never wanted her to die,' and Cranmer shook his head sadly. 'But she came to the house this morning, said she had worked out that Horst Knoefler was really Martin Schwere and that she had told you about it. She tried to get me to give myself up. Said the courts would go easy on an old war hero. Tommy turned up at the house, bundled her into the car and you know the rest.'

'Sadly, we do,' nodded Blizzard. 'There is one thing that still puzzles me. You say you only bumped into Martin Schwere again by accident yet our information suggests he was spooked by something years earlier, sold his house, stopped contact with his embassy, that sort of thing. Are you sure you did not plan this thing well in advance?'

'No, we did not but I may be able to shed some light on his behaviour. You see, when he spent the evening round here, Martin said that since the death of his wife, he had decided to go home to Germany. It was time to face up to his past,' he said.

'Which would explain why he sold the house,' said Blizzard, looking at Colley. 'Maybe he rented somewhere and was killed before he had time to inform the embassy of his new address.'

'Did he mention trying to buy the field where the grave is?' asked Colley.

'No,' and the old man looked surprised. 'Why would he want to do that?'

'Said it was wrong to build houses on the grave. He wanted to stop it happening.'

'No,' said the old man with a sad shake of the head, 'he never mentioned it, and even if he had, I don't think it would have made any difference. Tommy's mind was made up.'

'I guess it was,' nodded Blizzard.

'Besides,' said Cranmer, 'Schwere never showed any respect for the men he slaughtered that night, did he?'

'No,' said Blizzard. 'No, he didn't.'

'Chief Inspector,' said Cranmer, turning fearful eyes on him. 'What will happen to Tommy?'

'Not sure. We tried to interview him a couple of hours ago but he wouldn't talk to us. The doctor reckons he may have suffered some form of mental breakdown.'

'No one wins,' said Cranmer softly.

'You're right, Edward,' said Blizzard. 'And for what? You'll be locked up....'

'Yes, but I will be dead in a few months,' smiled the old man sadly and tapped his chest. 'My doctor says it's only a matter of time now.'

'Maybe,' said Blizzard.

'Besides,' and Cranmer allowed himself a smile. 'Like Elspeth said this morning, do you really think they will lock up an old war hero? They'll send me to a home, won't they? Lots of rice pudding and dry toast and fresh bed-linen on a Thursday. Not exactly the worst place to end my days.'

'Probably not,' said Blizzard. 'But Tommy will go to jail.'

'Perhaps he will, but in a way he's free at last, isn't he?' and Cranmer smiled softly as his mind went back to those dark Atlantic waters. 'Don't you see, Chief Inspector? For the first time in fifty years, it really is over for him.'

'But there is still—' began the chief inspector.

'Something you perhaps do not appreciate,' said Cranmer. 'Do you remember Tommy telling you he was in the Haftons? Well, that is true as far as it goes, but he was discharged after basic training because of a persistent knee injury.'

'And how did he take that?' asked Blizzard.

'He was devastated; the sense of failure stuck with him throughout his life. Tommy used to say his dad died a hero but his son achieved nothing. Then suddenly, the man who killed his father walks into the room. What else could Tommy have done? In Tommy's eyes, after all those years, he has proved his worth to his dad. Remember the regimental motto Stand As One? Well, that's what he did.'

And, with a searching expression on his face, Edward Cranmer looked at the chief inspector as if in some way hoping to receive approval, forgiveness, understanding, something, for what had happened. Blizzard made no reply; somehow he could think of nothing to say.

·· CHAPTER twenty-six ····

'HEAR THAT?' ASKED Gerry Hope cheerfully, reaching for the mug of tea on his desk and looking at Blizzard expectantly.

'Hear what?' asked the chief inspector, glancing around the scruffy office in bemusement.

'That sizzling sound.'

'What sizzling sound?'

'It's the sound of gonads being dragged out of the fire!' and Hope burst out into laughter. 'A bit singed round the edges but OK all the same. You see, things here have been moving faster than you could ever have imagined, old son.'

'Oh, I don't know,' murmured Blizzard. 'We've not exactly been snail-mail at our end.'

It was the day after the Cranmers were arrested and the two men were sitting in Hope's office at the ferry terminal shortly after 4.30 p.m., the darkness gathering once more outside the window. The rain had just started to fall, squalling in off the river and flecking insistently at the grubby glass. For all it was not a particularly salubrious office, Blizzard was pleased to be there; the invitation had given him the chance to escape from Abbey Road for an hour or two and the drive across the city had given him much-needed thinking time.

A lot had happened since the events at Green Meadow Farm, not least that both the Cranmers were now in hospital. The day had started early for the chief inspector. Having experienced yet another disturbed night, he had arrived at the police station shortly after seven to marshal his thoughts for what he knew would be difficult decisions to come. His first meeting of the day was shortly after 10 a.m. when he, Ronald, a lawyer from the CPS and a local psychiatrist sat in the superintendent's office to discuss what to do about Tommy Cranmer. In the end, the decisions were more straightforward than anyone might have imagined.

Since his arrest, Tommy had said nothing, his condition steadily deteriorating as he sat in his cell, rocking forwards and backwards, refusing to eat and taking no notice of anyone who spoke to him. It was as if, Blizzard told Colley after another unsuccessful attempt to converse with Tommy, the former soldier had retreated into his own world. Perhaps his adoptive father had been right, mused the chief inspector, perhaps Tommy was finally free after all, perhaps he was somewhere else. Colley's only reply, having looked in on the prisoner, was that, wherever it was, it looked a pretty dismal place.

Despite the initial scepticism of the custody sergeant, Blizzard was convinced that Tommy Cranmer's breakdown was genuine. The chief inspector, who had seen many a villain try to fake mental illness in his time, felt instinctively that this was not one of those moments. Cranmer seemed to be genuinely breaking apart, as if capture had released decades of pent-up tension. It was as if, Blizzard said at the meeting in Ronald's office, they were watching a taut rubber-band snap. Like the custody sergeant, Ronald was sceptical at first, which was when the psychiatrist stepped in to support the chief inspector. Blizzard swallowed his dislike of 'ists' to thank him and nodded approvingly when the CPS lawyer agreed that Tommy was not fit to be charged. After a nod from Ronald, Cranmer was taken under police guard to a nearby mental hospital for assessment. Having seen him in the hours before his departure, Blizzard was pretty sure he would not be coming out for a long time. If ever.

The strain proved too much for Edward Cranmer as well as, having been bailed into the custody of a local retirement home the night before, mentally and physically drained by his confession to the detectives, he collapsed in his room shortly before 10 p.m., complaining of severe chest pains. With a severe angina attack diagnosed, he was now hovering between life and death in the intensive care unit of the general hospital. Blizzard told Ronald that he hoped the old man died, but it was not meant cruelly and the superintendent knew it.

With other strands of the investigation coming together rapidly, and the chief constable taking an increasing interest in events at Abbey Road, the chief inspector had welcomed the phone call from Gerry Hope. Initially, with all the political pressure surrounding the escape of Franz Hasse occupying his mind once more now the Cranmers were locked up, Blizzard suspected the call might herald more bad news but the cheerful note in Hope's voice assuaged his fears. Now the Customs man sat grinning at him.

'If you smile any wider, your face will split open,' said Blizzard. 'And, pray, whose gonads are we talking about?'

'Both of ours, old son,' beamed Hope. 'After all, they've been sweating in the same onion bag on this one, haven't they?'

'Somehow that conjures up so many unpleasant images,' shuddered Blizzard.

'I'll tell you what happened,' said Hope, unable to contain himself any longer. 'Remember I said I had a mate with the police in Hamburg? Arnie, used to be a copper here.'

'Yeah.'

'Well, I got a call from him an hour or so ago. It's all hush-hush over there so I reckon your bosses won't know what I am about to tell you,' and Hope grinned. 'In fact, you may like to be the one who enlightens them.'

'Enlighten them about what, though?' said Blizzard impatiently.

'Well, according to Arnie, Franz Hasse was nicked trying to smuggle himself in to Hamburg last night.'

'What!' exclaimed Blizzard excitedly, sitting forward in his chair.

'Yeah, the local cops got lucky. A traffic officer pulled over a car just outside the city because a tail light was out and guess who they found hidden under blankets in the back seat?'

'The Pope?' asked Blizzard.

'Naw, our friend Franz,' and he beamed. 'What do you think of that?'

'It's not all good news,' grunted Blizzard.

'God, you can be a miserable bastard!' exclaimed Hope. 'Why isn't it good news?'

'I've already had to be nice to a psychiatrist today, now I'm going to have to be more polite to traffic cops,' said Blizzard. 'Including Danny bloody Wheatley.'

'What's it got to do with him?'

'He's in traffic at the moment. Between me and you, I think that's where he'll be staying when this runs its course. You should hear some of the things he's been saying about me behind my back,' and he suddenly roared with laughter.

'Whoops,' chuckled Hope, enjoying the joke immensely. 'That's another Christmas card list you're off.'

'Yeah. Anyway, this is all very good news about Hasse but how does it help us? I mean, we're still suspected of leaking the info about his escape, surely?'

'Not any more, matey,' grinned Hope. 'According to Arnie, Hasse is tired of running and wants to come clean about everything. Arnie knew about our interest in him and persuaded Franz to talk to him before their heavy brigade arrived and whisked him away for questioning.'

'I'm liking this Arnie more and more,' said Blizzard.

'Yeah, and to think he started on traffic,' murmured Hope mischievously.

'Thank you for that,' said Blizzard with a deliberately pained look. 'So what did Arnie get out of friend Franz?'

'For a start, he got him to confirm that he sprung himself by bribing one of the camp guards. Wouldn't name him but the Military Police have narrowed it down to a lad who lives near Nottingham. They are picking him up as we speak.'

'He'll not need to worry about gonads either once the Military Police have done with him,' murmured Blizzard.

'Exactly, but it does mean that we're both in the clear, me-laddo.'

'Indeed it does,' said Blizzard, adding with an ironic smile, 'and I can think of so many people up at our HQ who will be so happy to hear that. Why, I imagine they'll suggest the force has a statue erected in my likeness.'

'Yeah, and I can guess where they'd like to shove it,' cackled Hope.

'Indeed. Did Franz Hasse say why he was in Hafton?'

'Yeah, we were spot on, old son. He saw the stories in the German newspapers and came over to see what happened to his brother. They'd been in constant touch over the years, apparently, but that stopped four years ago, of course, and he had no idea why.'

'Good stuff,' said Blizzard approvingly. 'Tell Arnie, I owe him a pint.'

'He's coming over here for a few days next month so you might have to deliver on that promise.'

'Gladly.'

'What's more,' said Hope but was interrupted by the ringing of the telephone on his desk.

He listened for a moment or two then replaced the receiver.

'I think you owe me a pint as well,' he grinned, pulling on his jacket and heading for the door. 'Oh, by the way, do you do the Pools?'

'No, why?'

'Because,' said Hope, heading out into the corridor, followed by the chief inspector, 'our lads have just nicked Henderson Ramage. This must be your lucky day.'

'You don't know the half of it,' said Blizzard cheerfully. 'You really don't....'

·· CHAPTER twenty-seven ····

IT WAS 8 P.M. and Henderson Ramage glared balefully at Blizzard and Colley as he sat in the interview room at Abbey Road. A lack of cool thinking had been his downfall. Having lain low in Hafton since the incident at the ferry terminal, he had become spooked by a local radio broadcast about raids being planned for the division's housing estates by Blizzard's team. Everyone knew John Blizzard always came knocking eventually and Ramage finally resolved to make a bolt for freedom in Spain, where he had criminal associates. Pushing him into breaking cover was part of the Blizzard plan – the radio broadcast was a deliberate ploy – and it worked to perfection.

Having let his hair grow long and now sporting a beard, Ramage felt confident that no one would recognize him as he made his getaway, but walking through the departure lounge at the ferry terminal, he was spotted by a sharp-eyed Customs man, who moved so rapidly that the startled farmer had no chance to resist arrest.

Now, he sat and glowered at the detectives. His lawyer Edward Elsden sat next to him, a glum expression on his face. Something told him that this was the end of the line for his client. Blizzard agreed.

'The game's up, Henderson,' said the chief inspector coolly.

'You can't prove nothing,' said Ramage bullishly.

'Actually we can,' replied Blizzard. 'You see, since you disappeared, we have been doing some checking and, do you know, it all points to you for the murder of Moira Savage?'

'Na, that weren't me,' said Ramage, but the voice lacked confidence.

'Actually it was you. You see, we went back and searched your house again last night, which is when we found your little hidey-hole in the roof.'

Ramage started.

'It's very ingenious,' said Blizzard. 'In fact, so ingenious they missed it first time around. Anyway, we got it this time and, guess what, we found your notebook as well. You know the one, the one with Moira Savage's address in it.'

'That proves nothing,' said Edward Elsden quickly. 'My client had her address, so what?'

'Indeed,' nodded Blizzard, adding brightly. 'Hey, maybe, they were in the same knitting circle, eh?'

Ramage glowered at him.

'Trouble is,' said Colley, taking up the story. 'You spelled Moira's name wrong in it, Henderson, just like whoever sent her the death threats. At first we thought it might be Eddie Gayle – he can't spell either – but our handwriting expert reckons it's definitely you. We also think you were the one who threatened Elspeth Roberts because you knew she was helping Moira.'

'Yeah, but I didn't kill the Roberts woman,' said Ramage quickly. 'You can't pin that one on me.'

'So are you saying you *did* kill Moira Savage?' asked Blizzard sharply.

'No, I ain't,' and Ramage looked rattled. 'I'm just saying I didn't kill that Elspeth woman.'

'Stop twisting my client's words, Chief Inspector,' cautioned Elsden.

'Besides,' said Blizzard, ignoring the comment. 'We know who killed Elspeth.'

'So perhaps the person who killed her also killed Moira Savage,' suggested the lawyer.

'No,' replied Blizzard flatly. 'That was old MacDonald here.'

'You cannot prove that,' said Elsden, desperately trying to regain control of the situation. 'Even if my client had sent these threats, it does not prove that he killed Moira Savage. Surely, you arrested her husband for that?'

'We did,' nodded Blizzard, 'but we are convinced that Brian

Savage did not mean her to be killed. No, I think that's down to your client.'

'It's all lies!' exclaimed Ramage.

'Shut it!' snarled Blizzard, fleetingly losing his temper, a rare occurrence in interviews. 'I have had just about enough of your shit! This time you are going down and if I have anything to do with it, they'll throw away the key!'

Colley looked at Blizzard in surprise and Ramage looked as if he was about to say something before a stern look from his lawyer silenced him.

'I warn you,' said Elsden icily, 'that unless you intend to charge my client with an offence, we are going to walk out of here.'

'Somehow I don't think so,' said Blizzard thinly, regaining his composure. 'See, I believe your client thought that when the planning inspector ruled in favour of the housing estate, his problems were over, that there was nothing more Moira Savage could do. Then she started talking about making the site a war cemetery and the housebuilder panicked, threatened to pull out—'

'Rubbish!' exclaimed Ramage. 'That's a pack of lies.'

'Well, you had better take that up with him,' said Blizzard, 'because that's what he told my sergeant here an hour ago once he knew you were in custody and couldn't hurt him.'

Ramage blanched.

'And, of course, Mr Elsden,' continued Blizzard, 'your client could not risk losing all that money. How would he pay your extortionate fees to start with?'

Elsden glowered at him.

'So,' said Blizzard, thoroughly enjoying himself. 'I think our Henderson told the housing company he would sort it then he sent the boys round to silence Moira.'

'You can't prove it!' blustered Ramage.

'Oddly enough, we can,' said Blizzard calmly. 'You see, our forensics team found a couple of fingerprints in Moira's house. They belonged to Mr Ramage's old drinking pal Garry Horton, did they not, Sergeant?'

'They did,' beamed Colley.

'Yeah, well, pin this one on him!' shouted Ramage.

'If only we could,' said Blizzard wistfully.

'Yeah,' leered Ramage, 'except, you won't find him. He's long gone, mate. And without him, I'm as free as a bird.'

'Yes, you are probably right. I imagine the plan was that you hook up with him in Spain,' said Blizzard and glanced at Colley. 'Oh, hang on, though, what were you telling me earlier, Sergeant?'

'Ooh, I'm not sure, my memory isn't what it used to be,' said Colley, also faking ignorance then clicking his fingers. 'Ah, I've remembered now, guv.'

'Then would you care to enlighten our Mr Ramage. I am sure he is dying to know.'

'Know what?' asked Ramage anxiously.

'Garry Horton was arrested by the Spanish police last night,' said Colley.

'What?' gasped Ramage weakly.

'Yeah, got into a fight in a bar. One of their detectives rang us up when he discovered that Garry was from Hafton. Wanted to know if he was wanted. And what do you know?' and Colley beamed. 'Turned out he was. Somehow I think we'll be seeing Garry Horton back in this city after all.'

'Wouldn't that be nice?' said Blizzard cheerfully.

'He won't say nowt!' exclaimed Ramage.

'Oddly enough,' smiled Colley thinly. 'When the Spanish police mentioned you, his demeanour changed somewhat.'

'What do you mean?' asked Ramage uncomfortably.

'My client—' began Elsden.

'Your client can bloody well listen to the sergeant,' snapped Blizzard. 'Pray, proceed, David.'

'Why, thank you, guv, you are too kind,' said Colley with mock politeness and staring hard at Ramage. 'Well, as I was saying, Garry told the Spanish police that he was sick of taking the rap for you. I imagine he meant the attack on those German students. You remember them, don't you, Henderson? Poor old Garry took the fall for you, didn't he?'

Ramage said nothing but stared in horror at the sergeant.

'Indeed,' continued Colley. 'Your mate Garry seemed keen

for the Spanish cops to let us know he would co-operate if we mention his change of heart to the judge.'

'Oh, Jesus,' groaned Ramage, burying his head in his hands.

'I don't think my client should say anything else,' said Elsden firmly.

'No need – all he has to do is listen,' said Blizzard, a harsh edge in his voice, 'because we have only just started. You see, we also think he killed his father.'

'You have no evidence of that,' said Ramage furiously, leaping to his feet and wagging a finger at the chief inspector. 'The old bastard died by accident.'

'Sit down!' snarled Blizzard.

Ramage slumped back into his chair and looked helplessly at his lawyer who was about to speak when a stern look from the chief inspector silenced him.

'Actually,' said Blizzard, 'we do have evidence that it was not an accident. See, you did not exactly keep what you did to your dad a secret, did you, Henderson?'

'I never told Garry Horton!' exclaimed Ramage. 'If he tries to say that—'

'Actually, it was Brian Savage. He has had time to think about what happened and he really is very upset about what you did to his wife. He's quite a changed man, actually. When we saw him earlier today, he told us everything. He had already said you promised to sort Moira out but this time, he told Sergeant Tulley that you admitted to him you killed your father because he was standing in the way of the land sale.'

'Jesus,' said Ramage feebly.

'And we know you were the one who had Dennis Hoare done over at the farm as well.'

'I never did!' exclaimed Ramage but the protestations were becoming less convincing.

'Oh, we think you did, Henderson,' said Colley, the constant switching between officers helping to confuse and rattle Ramage. 'You see, Robin Harvey told us how you threatened to harm his children unless he told you what Dennis Hoare had been saying to us.'

'Anyway,' said Blizzard, 'before you had Dennis done over, he told us some very interesting things about you and the rows with your dad. I am sure you will be pleased to know that Dennis is recovering well and is prepared to give evidence in court.'

Ramage said nothing; his pale features said it all.

'I think I need time to talk to my client,' said Elsden feebly.

'I am sure you do,' said Blizzard. 'Oh, while I remember, there is some good news for him.'

'Good news?' asked the solicitor suspiciously.

'Yes, the person who started this all off – our Herr Knoefler – turns out to be the one person your client did not kill,' and Blizzard beamed at him.

'Have you finished?' asked Elsden glumly.

'Yes. Oh, come to think of it, no,' said the chief inspector, enjoying the alarmed expressions on their faces. 'Actually, I was thinking that in this new heart-warming atmosphere of entente cordiale, your client would like to do his bit and drop Eddie Gayle's fat arse in it.'

'Some things,' said Edward Elsden as Ramage looked at Blizzard anxiously, 'are just too dangerous, Chief Inspector.'

'I imagine they are,' nodded Blizzard, then he stood up with the scraping of chair legs and walked out into the corridor, followed by Colley.

'Bloody hell, we got the bastard,' said the sergeant, punching the air as the interview room door closed behind them.

Blizzard leaned against the wall and closed his eyes.

'You look shattered,' said Colley.

'Yeah, I am. In fact—' but his mobile phone rang. 'Now what?'

Fishing it out of his trouser pocket, he listened for a moment. Colley watched his impassive face but could glean nothing about the conversation and Blizzard said little apart from a muttered, 'Sorry, but you know how it goes,' at one point. The conversation finished, the chief inspector put the phone back in his pocket.

'Who was that?' asked Colley.

'Danny Wheatley.'

'What did he want?'

'Wanted me to know that his move to the chief constable's office has been put on hold. Apparently, the chief decided it would be bad PR to promote him. Instead, he's being moved to Multhorpe.'

'I hope he can talk sheep then,' chuckled Colley, 'because the only thing that ever happens up there is the farmers' mart.'

'Indeed,' said Blizzard with the flicker of a smile.

'So how was Danny?' asked the sergeant.

'Not entirely happy.'

'That's another enemy for your list, guv,' and the sergeant winked at him.

'And what difference will one more make exactly?'

'Aye, maybe you're right,' nodded Colley. 'Hey, I've just had a brillo idea, guv. Matty Roberts has just taken over that pub on the corner of Linklater Street, serves that new beer apparently.'

'What new beer?'

'Black Sheep,' cackled Colley.

'You missed your vocation,' said Blizzard affectionately.

'So what do you think?'

'I think,' said Blizzard, 'that sometimes you have some excellent ideas, Sergeant. Put the word round, will you? Let's get the team down there, and I'll give Gerry Hope a ring, I owe him a pint or three. He can bring his gonads.'

'Guv?' asked the bemused sergeant.

'Nothing,' said Blizzard, clapping Colley on the shoulder. 'And you know, if I've got some change left, I might even buy you one as well.'

'Now you're talking,' said Colley as they turned back into the interview room.

· · CHAPTER twenty-eight · · · ·

THE WIND WHIPPED chill and biting off the North Sea as John Blizzard stood and stared out over the vast expanse of dark water. Something had drawn him to the clifftop a few miles from Hafton that bright Saturday morning in May and, as he stood there, he knew it was the only place in the world he wanted to be. Eyes seeking the distant horizon, his mind went back over the events of the past six months, events which had finally reached their conclusion late the previous afternoon.

Along with Colley, the chief inspector had been in Hafton Crown Court shortly after 5 p.m. when Henderson Ramage was jailed for life for the murders of his father and Moira Savage, as well as an extra eight years for the people-trafficking. He had denied all the offences but it took the jury less than five hours to bring in guilty verdicts on all charges. Sitting beside the chief inspector, Colley muttered, 'Yes, job done,' under his breath when the verdicts were announced. Blizzard secretively extended a hand of congratulation then did the same to Gerry Hope, who was sitting on his other side. The chief inspector had then glanced along the seats to Arthur Ronald, who had nodded.

The judge said that, although Henderson Ramage was not there when Moira Savage was killed, he planned the attack with reckless abandon as to whether or not she would die so must carry as much responsibility as her murderers. Ramage stared at the floor in shocked silence. For years, he had thought himself one of the untouchables; now everyone in the city's underworld knew that John Blizzard could touch them all. It was indeed job done.

Next to Ramage in the dock was Garry Horton, also jailed for life for the murder of Moira Savage and given six years for his part in bringing in the illegal Eastern Europeans. He admitted all the offences and, referring to Horton's co-operation with the police, the judge recommended that he be considered for parole after ten years. Also in the dock was another local hoodlum, the other man who carried out the killing of Moira Savage; he tried to claim that Moira's death was accidental and that he only meant to scare her, but the jury rejected the argument, swayed by Horton's admission of guilt. Horton had been as good as his word and taken them all down with him.

Well, not quite all. He had not taken Eddie Gayle down; no, Eddie Gayle remained beyond the law. Having reappeared several weeks after the arrests, he was questioned closely by Blizzard and Colley over several hours but gave nothing away and they had reluctantly let him go. But, thought Blizzard as the judge made his final comments, there would be other days for Eddie, and now the criminal fraternity knew what they had always suspected, that Hafton CID would come for them all, that as dawn broke one morning there would be the feared knock on the door. Oh, yes, there would be other days, thought Blizzard as the judge commended him and his team for what he called a 'difficult and distressing investigation'. He doesn't know the half of it, thought Blizzard.

Later, as he walked down the steps outside the court, leaving Ronald and Hope to deal with the media, the chief inspector caught sight of Eddie Gayle, leering at him as he stood in front of his black Mercedes parked nearby.

'Next time, Eddie,' Blizzard shouted, 'next time.'

When Blizzard returned to Abbey Road, there was a note from the chief constable, congratulating him for his efforts in leading the investigation. Blizzard screwed it up and threw it in the bin.

As for Brian Savage, the CPS deliberated long and hard and eventually decided not to charge him with anything; there was no evidence to suggest that he knew that his wife would be killed, or wanted it to happen. One look at his broken features as he sat in the public gallery as the others were sentenced was enough to convince anyone that it was the right decision. Brian Savage was a man whose life had been taken away from him the afternoon his wife was murdered. Victims, thought Blizzard glancing at him, always victims. He could not have known that within six months, Savage would be dead from a drugs overdose. The coroner later ruled at the inquest that it was impossible to tell if it was a deliberate act or not but Blizzard knew.

As for Tommy Cranmer, he had appeared briefly in court a few weeks before, when the judge was told that he denied murder but admitted manslaughter on the grounds of diminished responsibility. In a five-minute hearing, Tommy was sent to a mental hospital indefinitely. He would never come out, everyone knew that. And Edward Cranmer? He did not survive to see his adopted son sentenced; having survived his initial collapse shortly after his arrest, the old man was charged as an accessory to murder, even though everyone knew he would not live to see the court case. He died in his sleep a month later at the residential home to which he had been bailed. Blizzard had been to see him a few days before his death, and when he returned to the establishment after the old man passed away, one of the care workers commented that in his final days, Edward Cranmer had seemed at peace. Blizzard could not have put it better himself. And he was glad.

Ironically, Moira Savage got her final wish. Alarmed by the negative publicity and the revelations of its links with hardened villainy, the housebuilder withdrew from the scheme at Green Meadow Farm and, a few weeks later, went into liquidation. Prompted by Malcolm Watts, the city council officer who first stumbled across the huts, the authority announced plans to work with English Heritage and preserve the camp as a tourist attraction. Those POWs whose bodies were not returned home to their families in Germany, were reburied in the same grave at Green Meadow Farm and a headstone placed there to mark the spot. Somehow, the realization that the council's decision was at the expense of the Tenby Street railway station project did not seem to matter to Blizzard as he had stood next to Colley, silent and solemn among the group present at the re-interment ceremony. All through the event, Blizzard felt an uncanny sensation that they were being watched and, at one point, even turned towards the copse, half expecting to see Frank's face again. But he didn't.

He was there now, though, as the chief inspector stood and stared out over the choppy sea. Faces and images rushed through John Blizzard's mind but each time he came back to that one face, the face of Frank Robinson smiling out of the black-and-white photograph. With a deep sigh, the chief inspector pulled the picture from his pocket and glanced down at it for a moment.

'Job done, Frank,' murmured Blizzard, feeling his voice starting to crack. 'Rest in peace.'

Frank looked back at him with that knowing smile. Through moist eyes, Blizzard's gaze was drawn to the baby held so delicately in Frank's arms.

'Oh, Charlie,' said the chief inspector quietly. 'Charlie.'

And the tears suddenly came, sharp and stinging as the winds that whipped in off the North Sea. Then they were gone and, as the chief inspector's composure returned, so were the images banished from his mind. For a crazy moment, as he looked out from the clifftop, Blizzard felt an urge to throw the picture into the wind, to let it swoop and swirl until it fell into the sea to drift endlessly in the dark waters, to join Frank Robinson and Harry Crooks and all the others who died the wicked night the *Clarissa* sank.

'No,' said Blizzard with a quick shake of the head, slipping the picture back into his pocket. 'No.'

He turned away from the cliff edge and started to walk back to where Fee had been standing at a respectful distance, watching him in silence.

'OK?' she asked, noticing his red eyes.

'Yeah,' he nodded, slipping his arm into hers. 'Yeah. Edward Cranmer was right, you know. It is over.'

'Good,' said Fee, then grinned at him. 'Hey, I realize it's the dreaded exercise but do you fancy a walk?'

'Do you know,' smiled Blizzard, 'I think I do, young lady.'

'Come on then,' she said, kissing him softly on the cheek, 'old timer.'

And, arm in arm, they set off along the windswept cliffs.